The Adventures of Pebble Beach

Other books by Barbara Berger

The Road to Power
– Fast Food for the Soul

The Road to Power 2
– More Fast Food for the Soul

Gateway to Grace
– Barbara Berger's Guide to User-Friendly Meditation

Mental Technology (The 10 Mental Laws)
– Software for Your Hardware

The Spiritual Pathway
– A Guide to the Joys of Awakening and Soul Evolution

Are You Happy Now?
10 Ways to Live a Happy Life

The Awakening Human Being
– A Guide to the Power of Mind

Sane Self Talk
– Cultivating the Voice of Sanity Within

The Adventures of Pebble Beach

Barbara Berger

Winchester, UK
Washington, USA

First published by Roundfire Books, 2014
Roundfire Books is an imprint of John Hunt Publishing Ltd., Laurel House, Station Approach,
Alresford, Hants, SO24 9JH, UK
office1@jhpbooks.net
www.johnhuntpublishing.com
www.roundfire-books.com

For distributor details and how to order please visit the 'Ordering' section on our website.

Text copyright: Barbara Weitzen Berger 2013

ISBN: 978 1 78099 779 7

A CIP catalogue record for this book is available from the British Library.

Design: Stuart Davies

Printed in the USA by Edwards Brothers Malloy

We operate a distinctive and ethical publishing philosophy in all
areas of our business, from our global network of authors to
production and worldwide distribution.

The Adventures
of Pebble Beach

Chapter 1

The Vice-President of the Republic Group was grinding away, his red hot ramrod stuffed between Pebble Beach's slim thighs. He was panting and puffing, and the sweat poured from his brow. He was an ugly, disgusting toad – the type of man Pebble would never have considered going to bed with. How she ended up here, with him deep inside her, was something she couldn't quite figure out. She didn't want to remember his face with the friendly eyes behind the toad-like grin or the idiotic sexist comments he was always making when he wasn't pinching her ass or grabbing her tits.

How can I do it?

How can I sink so low?

What's got into me anyway?

This isn't like me at all.

Not at all.

Pebble Beach you see was a good, nice, honorable, hardworking woman.

This will surely screw up my career.

Nobody ever goes to bed with their boss and gets away with it, unless their brains are fluff and all they've got going for them is body. Of course this had to happen to Pebble just when everything was going great and she was finally making good money. Just like Pebble Beach.

No sense of proportion, my mother would say.

None whatsoever...

And a razzmatazz to you too!

If Pebble Beach could climax with the Vice-President of the Republic Group, then she could climax with anybody, a dirty dog included. She thought he was making an awful lot of noise for a vicepresident as he grabbed her tits.

Too hard!

Squeezing her nipples till they hurt. Of course that was when her cunt caught fire.

My nipples hurt!

Holy shit!

Suddenly she wanted it, too. Wanted it bad – and wanted him. Wanted him to come and wanted to come with him, no matter how toady-looking he was.

Who cares about his face anyway!

Or toads at this point in the game.

It's his cock I want...

Cock, cock, cock....

Come on man, what d'ya waiting for kiddo!

She forgot the wart on his nose, too, and the fact that his name was Einar Bro. A name she considered quite idiotic, and especially considering the fact that she thought he was the most unattractive man she'd ever met in her life. Of course that was when one other minor detail popped up: Einar was her boss. She worked for the bloody toad. Or up until tonight, she did. You see, he'd invited her out for dinner, which had happened before, only before she'd been able to withstand his advances and talk about business, and stay cool. The Republic Group you understand was a booming Danish advertising agency, skyrocketing right up to the clouds, and Pebble Beach was their star American copywriter. She knew the score and he knew the score and just about everybody else in the business knew it, too.

Einar needed her, he needed her smart, tight English copy to meet the growing demands of European companies scrambling to go international in the global marketplace of the 21st century. And Pebble, darling Pebble, was talented enough to deliver what Einar needed to keep those heavenly cash registers at Republic headquarters humming. And what's more, Pebble mostly enjoyed knowing he knew.

Mostly, that is.

So even if he mostly really wanted to slip his hands under her sweater, he managed to control himself most of the time. She wasn't that young either, but she was pretty. And most of the time, she did her level best to head him off.

At least until tonight.

Tonight, she failed miserably, and there he was grinding away while her cunt turned from lukewarm to red hot. She'd already forgotten the majestic room he took her to at the Hotel D'Angleterre.

How did I end up here?

Did I drink too much?

She couldn't remember how she got from the bar to the room.

My mind's a blank.

Look at that pretty ceiling, will ya?

What am I, some kind of bimbo?

I mean I'm supposed to be a woman with brains!

Brains, ya understand!

Not just some dumb cunt...

Her breathing quickened...

Oh God, dear God, if only his prick was a little longer and a little thicker, you know...wider...more filling that is...a little more like Albert's...just a little more...oh God, you understand what I mean, I mean...if only he wasn't so short and fat...and had a little more muscle on his body...just a little more, it would make all this a lot more, well you know...fun, you know, and less embarrassing when I wake up later, oh God, can't you move me a little closer, you know to the less cash/more dash department and pronto...

The trouble was, Pebble wanted his sweaty little piece of meat and wanted it bad. So bad that suddenly it didn't matter anymore that he didn't have broad shoulders like Albert and firm muscles and all that stuff that usually got her off...old Einar was grinding away...grinding and grinding and grinding. And no matter his title, face or stature, the old boy had finally reached Pebble's sweet spot...

"Please," Pebble was moaning, "please hurry up..." She

almost forgot his name, her love juices gushing now, the tension building, the heat of her body booming.

Suddenly Pebble loved life, liked who she was, and thought Einar Bro, in spite of his face, his millions and his turdy title, had what it took. He had that mysterious piece of meat she loved and dreamed of and, "Oh God, Einar, now," but Einar had broken his rhythm, which was the rhythm of life itself, the rhythm she loved so much, to put his ravenous mouth to one of her taunt nipples...

Which was when or why Pebble Beach woke up, all alone in her bed, bathed in sweat – a dream of an orgasm only an inch away.

God, the sweetness of sex!

And not wasting time to analyze the bed-partner of her dream, Pebble finished off the job herself, groaning loudly in her empty bed.

Hope to God Adam and Jon are sleeping soundly tonight... Adam and Jon were her kids, you see. Pebble being a single parent.

When it was over, she just lay there, stoned on comfort.

Am I ever going to grow up?

You see, Pebble Beach was not newlywed, but newly divorced and not as gorgeous as she used to be. She was also more than a bit over 40, and all alone in her bed in Copenhagen, Denmark, of all places.

Pebble Beach, or Pebble, as they sometimes call her, was, or is, as you may have guessed, the name of your average insecure woman in her 40s. You'll find her living in most big cities around the world today, and since she was born during the 60s, she's probably something like 43 today, or God forbid, 45. She wasn't a knock-out either, not in any language. But somehow, with a little help from Lancôme, a decent haircut, and some color out of a tube, she occasionally got away with being sensational.

Especially if the lighting's right kiddo – or the party's getting on...either age-wise or booze-wise!

Well at least I'm being honest with myself.

4

Pebble was sitting up in her empty bed now, holding her head, looking around her dark, empty bedroom; still hoping that maybe she'd find a man tucked away somewhere.

It sure is awful being lonely.

Why did I have to fall in love with a man who lives so far away? I could've just as well picked the accountant down the street for all the fun I'm having...

But she laughed anyway, having just divorced her husband, and pushed her newly highlighted hair back from her forehead. And being almost brave, she didn't cry. After all, what would have been the point? She'd just given herself one damned good orgasm, considering she was all alone, and she figured, all things being equal, good orgasms never hurt.

* * *

Pebble Beach lived on Gothersgade, right across from the King's Garden in Copenhagen, Denmark, a most fair and cool city where the sun shines brightly, but not often. A short stop on most package tours of Scandinavia, Copenhagen has the distinguished honor of being the charming, old capital of that unusually small country which Danes unabashedly regard as the center of the universe.

But Pebble didn't care. She was shamelessly in love with wonderful Copenhagen.

When people asked her if she was going to move back to America now that she was divorced from her Danish husband, she'd smile and say, "Well maybe I will." But she knew damn well she wouldn't.

I'd have to be a fool to trade this for the crime and violence of America.

Where else in the world can a woman walk the streets all alone at night and feel safe?

Still, it was doubtful if Pebble would ever win the Danish

Good Housekeeping Seal of Approval, she was too laid back and American for that. Always would be. And besides, that stuff was probably not for the single mothers who worked their knuckles to the bone trying to feed their kids on their own.

No more lies, kiddo, not to myself or anyone else for that matter.

That's what divorce is all about, right.

Getting things straight.

Cleaning up your act.

Figuring out what's going on and what's important to you.

For some reason, Pebble was in the mood to say to herself that the idea that having kids was what prevented her from getting divorced ages ago... was really a bullshit idea...

A bullshit idea?

Being scared cause you've got a couple of kids to support and might not know how?

Are you kidding?

Lots of women are afraid of getting divorced because of their kids.

Pebble put her hand under her warm Danish down comforter and touched her wet cunt and smiled. She liked being honest with herself, even if it was a little late in the game.

I was just scared shitless of being on my own!

That's all!

And with that off her chest, Pebble snuggled contently under her warm comforter.

Oh God, where's that one wonderful person who's gonna save me from myself and this awful loneliness?

Is this what all my dreams have come to?

And not wanting to think more about life, Einar Bro, or her lover on the other side of the moon, Pebble Beach fell sound asleep.

* * *

Which was why, she was immensely relieved when she had to

dash around like a maniac the next morning to make her nine o'clock appointment.

What if I'd been condemned to bed all morning?

I'd have been forced to think about my wet dream with Einar.

Fun way to spend a morning, right?

Feeling sorry for myself.

Stuff like that can be real tricky for a newly divorced woman. You know, dangerous.

Potentially suicidal.

But Pebble, our Pebble, was lucky – she had this nine o'clock meeting out there in the real world, waiting for her. And if she was good enough and smart enough, more real work and more real money would be waiting out there, too.

Her morning progressed at gunshot speed so she didn't have time to consider when she'd ever get to touch Albert's marvelous body again. He was so far away.

Not another adventurer, her mother would say.

Pebble, you sure know how to pick 'em.

You think he's having deep-frozen wet dreams about you all the way up there on icy Greenland where he's holed up for the winter?

All Pebble had to do that morning was face her kids. Something only mildly daunting in comparison to all the other existential questions she was facing at the moment. Jon, who was 16, was not only smart and beautiful; he was into "spiritual matters" too. Which meant that besides the fact that Pebble loved him dearly and that Jon's own bedroom was as tidy as a glossy picture in *Better Homes and Gardens*, he rarely, if ever, lifted a finger to wash a dish in their house.

How did I manage to raise my own son to be such a male-chauvinist pig?

Jon's kid brother, Adam, was mad about Coldplay and righteous causes and mad as hell at Jon for never doing the dishes, especially when his instincts told him his mother might be feeling a wee bit lonely. Then Adam couldn't think of any other way of showing his love besides doing the dishes. Which meant poor old Adam was doing an awful lot of dishes lately.

Sometimes that kid really gets to me.

Especially since Adam was a more plodding type than Flash-in-the-Pan Jon, as she sometimes fondly called her firstborn.

"Well," sighed Pebble, watching Adam pack away his second breakfast that morning. He usually got up early and ate his first breakfast before Jon and Pebble even opened their eyes. *He sure does eat like a man.*

14-year-old boys, now you tell me.

When they're not eating and acting like men, they're farting around like they're eight-year-olds or something.

On mornings like these, when everyone was rushing around and the whole house was a mess, Pebble was ready to shed a tear; she loved her kids so much. Now does that make sense?

Pebble Beach's nine o'clock meeting was at Fem-Ads, a brash, new advertising agency specializing in ads for women. The ad house was owned and run by men – which never ceased to amuse Pebble, who wasn't particularly crazy about going to meetings. Everybody at meetings was usually so together, or so it seemed to Pebble. Since her divorce, she'd been forced to face innumerable moments of minor terror in her valiant and determined effort to succeed in the world-at-large. She knew she couldn't possibly expect her blooming career to really take off if she wasn't cool and competent in the de rigueur world of meetings – no matter how together she perceived other people to be.

No big deal, she would say to herself. *Where's all this newfound insecurity coming from anyway? A child of this brave new world for women shouldn't be feeling this way. Remember, kiddo, you're a winner and you've been out there too doing things for the world – so you know a thing or two!* Pebble told herself all kinds of drivel when things were looking bleak like how she was in Auckland when they blew up the Rainbow Warrior in 1985. Not that anybody at Fem-

Ads would appreciate such feats. God forbid they should know! The thought absolutely terrified Pebble. What would happen if any of her newfound business contacts found out she wasn't as straight and innocent as she looked? People might think it was fun to read about women on the barricades, but to actually work with one of them... *All my assignments might just evaporate overnight.* Pebble didn't want anyone to know that underneath her "trying-to-be-a-winner" clothes she was just an insecure 40-something woman of experience getting older every minute...

Why can't I just be a talented copywriter anyway? Why do I have to go through all this show-and-tell business? I've got my idiosyncrasies and I'm proud of them! Why do I have to love meetings and explaining myself and my brilliant copy to every nerd around a fat gleaming, designer table? Any jerk can read what I write! When I'm famous enough, I'm going to email my copy to them, she thought with satisfaction, *and I'll never show my face at one of these hair-raising meeting rituals again!*

Meetings also reminded Pebble of her highly inadequate wardrobe. Obviously she hadn't put in those obligatory years and years of dedicated shopping. And why should she have? It just so happened that Pebble wrote her best copy at home in her sweat pants. She didn't need Armani or Prada outfits to produce brilliant headlines and copy. But to make matters worse, Pebble hadn't learned the fine art of making do with what she had – another invaluable working woman skill. Sigh as she might, she'd never become one of those careful bees who read women's magazines for tips. If Pebble could have worn whatever she wanted, she would have thrown on one of Jon's shirts – the ones he loved so much that he bought at G-Star or Diesel. But she knew his shirts would never work. *A touch too wild for Fem-Ads,* so Pebble settled instead for her black skirt and grey sweater. *At least I've worn this outfit often enough to feel comfortable in it. Comfortable! Great God, that's not how I want to feel. I want to feel Great. Superb. Smashing. Good God, look what age and single parenting has done to me – am I really willing to settle for Comfortable instead of Great?*

Pebble took one last look at the newspapers and dishes spread all over the kitchen table while Jon heard the last few verses of "Angels" by Robbie Williams. No time to clean up now. Adam had already left. "Hurry up, Jon, we'll be late." She came rushing, face aglow. They raced out the door and dashed for the stairs. No more time for Great/Comfortable debates now. Running down the stairs together, Pebble's heart melted looking at her appealing 16-year-old in his worn jacket. Pebble pulled herself together. *No more of this sentimental crap...MOM...who's going to pay for the new jacket Jon needs?* She gulped, gave Jon a peck on the cheek, then turned and ran down the windswept street after a taxi.

Sitting at the meeting, in the red-carpeted, soundproofed conference room, Pebble felt tense. *Well, if this meeting lasts long enough, at least I'll learn how to live with heart palpitations!*

Thinking of her dream of wild lovemaking with Einar Bro at the Hotel D'Angleterre the night before made her smile. *Wipe that grin off your face, sweetheart – it was only a dream!* She tried to look and feel serious, but it was all in vain. The dirty grin stayed on her face – until another weird thought popped up. *I wonder what I would have felt like if I was sitting across the conference table from Einar this morning instead of here!* Pebble sobered up fast. *God, the man really is a "Worm"!* Pebble shivered. Suddenly she understood why people in the business who weren't particularly fond of Einar's strong-arm tactics called him "Worm" behind his back.

Peter Cato, the sandy-haired Fem-Ads' boss, entered the room looking positively sublime in comparison to Einar. Cheri, the receptionist, swept in behind him and closed the door carefully.

Oh no, thought Pebble, *Cheri!* She'd forgotten about Cheri, the former fashion model who was now Fem-Ads' eye-catching receptionist. Every time Pebble saw Cheri, she was reminded of the sorry state of her wardrobe. And the sorry state of her wardrobe forced her to contemplate the sorry state of her single-parent economy. *I'll never be able to compete with the likes of Cheri if I don't improve my wardrobe!* The thought really bugged Pebble because divorce had been more than just emotionally painful for Pebble, it had been financially draining, too. *Don't even look at her clothes. Don't even try to imagine how much she paid for that divine jacket she's wearing.* Cheri's lips might have been a touch too red, but the jacket was great. *Boy I would look fabulous in that!* Pebble was convinced a jacket like Cheri's would take 10 years off her immediately. *Pebble, you've got to pay your bills first. PERIOD! You've got to fill that refrigerator again. PERIOD! Don't even think...for a minute...that...maybe...no...no, no, NO!*

In fact, things were actually looking up for Pebble. Besides the fact that she hated being negative about anything, her cash flow was really improving. Sure she sometimes got depressed, but deep down inside Pebble was as American as apple pie. She had that outlook, that optimism and was a firm believer in programming herself for success. Pebble was sure she'd make it if she only believed in herself a little more.

Peter sat down and straightened his tie. Everyone else (eight people were present, including Pebble) rustled their papers and had those let's-get-down-to-business looks on their faces. *I hope nobody gets carried away!* thought Pebble, suitably impressed by the general mood of determination. *It's only five past nine and this could be a very long meeting.*

Pebble's problem was that it was difficult for her to take the advertising business seriously. How could anybody who had an uncle who had been to the March on Washington in 1963 and heard Martin Luther King say, "I have a dream" get worked up about all this media stuff? No matter how talented people were – it was still only advertising. The thought kept popping up, even though Pebble was giving it her best shot, and even if she actually liked the work. Still she'd hear that voice going – *after all, it's only advertising.* Funny, the voice had the knack of turning up the volume whenever her copy was lousy. Only then another voice usually shot back – *then why are you trying so hard, sweetheart? Why are you so damned nervous?* Well, nervous or not, the good girl in Pebble was used to going that extra mile. *Sometimes I get the feeling that men are the only people around here who take the advertising business seriously. Maybe all the women are just great pretenders; me included.* Pebble stared at her notes, waiting for Peter to speak. *What do I care? Women are such good rip-off artists anyway. Just think of all the practice we've had.* Looking at the faces of the other women at the table changed Pebble's mind fast. *Brother...do they look serious – and competent, too. Maybe I'm the only one here who's a great pretender.* Sara Sorensen was so efficient-looking that Pebble imagined her sailing effortlessly through the workplace slaying dragons as easily as she tied her toddler's shoes. *Dear God, give me some of her sharpness.*

The business world had a way of confusing idealists like Pebble.

Pebble knew, of course, that she wouldn't be the proud owner of a wallet stuffed with shiny credit cards for very long if she didn't play the advertising game according to the rules. So she was motivated. In fact, she was enjoying the luxury of plastic money so much that she was almost too meek. She didn't have enough experience yet to know that real plastic money is actually easier to keep when you dare. But she did know one thing, though. *I want success without guilt!* Pebble was definitely ready for that. You see success without guilt was something no man had allowed her, or rather, something she'd never allowed herself in the presence of any man. Now she was ready for it and wanted it bad. She wanted to sinfully enjoy spending money before she got too old. She heard the clock ticking in the background of her life.

Peter started talking about the WonderLift campaign they were about to launch. *Am I really a part of this idiocy?* The man had an irritating tendency to drone on in the most condescending way. This wasn't the first time Pebble had worked for Peter. Two years earlier, she was a ghostwriter for him while he was creative director at DDB Needham. She actually came up with the concept and a slogan (for the American market) for a campaign Peter was working on for a Danish company called Nordkyst. Nordkyst made marvelously quirky, high-quality Scandinavian cotton clothes for kids – but the company was a newcomer on the American market. Pebble's concept and slogan were wildly successful in the United States, but she never got any credit for it. Nobody ever discovered that Pebble was the creative genius behind the whole show. Peter Cato was lauded to the skies in the press and Nordkyst turned into an overnight success in the United States. As a result of Pebble's concept, Nordkyst found an extremely profitable niche selling their high-quality, organic cotton clothing to urban professionals who were willing to pay top dollar for upmarket quality for their kids. Pebble hit the money by producing a brilliant concept and copy and a quirky slogan which communicated the Nordkyst sense of style and purity with charming directness.

Pebble never really trusted Peter after the Nordkyst bonanza, but she didn't dare go public either – even if Mel, her favorite uncle in New York, urged her to. When Mel heard the story – he was a senior account director at Young & Rubicam – he roared over the phone, "You'll be rich and famous when people find out the truth!" The line positively crackled with his energy. "People will be pounding at your door, begging you to work for them!" But how could she? Her uncle was incensed by the injustice of it (yes he was the one who'd heard Martin Luther King) – he'd seen how successful the campaign had been in the US way before his favorite niece told him that she had created it. But Pebble was newly divorced and too shell-shocked to comprehend her uncle's words. The irony of Pebble's failure to grasp the situation was that Mel happened to play tennis with the guy Nordkyst hired to run their U.S. operations. "I'll get Richard on the phone today."

Pebble was sorry she'd told her uncle. She suffered from tunnel vision and couldn't see that Mel was offering her a shot at the stars. All she could think of was what would happen if Peter Cato denied her story. "Mel, you've got to promise me, on everything's that's sacred to you (Pebble knew that wasn't much) that you'll never, EVER tell anyone!"

Pebble was in tears. When he heard her crying, he calmed down again, "What can happen, sweetheart? What? In the worst case, you'll come to New York and I'll give you a job." But Pebble didn't want Young & Rubicam in New York. The very thought of life on Manhattan, competing with all those bright and beautiful New Yorkers while worrying about her kids growing up in New York sent chills up and down her spine.

Besides Pebble had other plans and she knew she had to have wings before she could fly. *Maybe I was just lucky anyway. Maybe I just hit the right thing by accident. So who cares what Mel thinks? If he wants to be disappointed in me, let him. What does he know about my life anyway, sitting there in his posh office on Madison Avenue and going to the Hamptons on the weekends?* She needed to take charge of her life in her own way. *And besides, I've got kids to think about. Mel might be my favorite uncle, but I'm not a kid anymore. I'm a grown-up woman who's struggling to be whole and independent for the first time in my life.*

Which was why Pebble put her foot down and was proud of herself for doing the right thing.

In spite of what Pebble thought, Mel really did respect the wishes of his favorite niece, so he kept his mouth shut.

Now, two years later, watching Peter Cato drone on, Pebble wasn't so sure she'd done the right thing. *Maybe Mel was right. Maybe I should have blown the whistle on the guy. But who can tell? That was then and this is now. Peter gave me a break when I needed it.* Which was true. Two years ago, when Pebble walked out on her husband Slim, she needed work desperately. At the time, she didn't even think about how little Peter paid her for ghosting for him (it was all under the table anyway), all she knew was he put food on her table when she was struggling to free herself from a lousy marriage. *I was a nobody then.* Before she talked to Mel, it never occurred to her that the man might have misused her. *I mean that was way before Einar got wind of me…way before I did that campaign for the Wiberg Brothers… I was an absolute zero then – a nobody. How can I blame Peter for taking advantage of my talent when I was the one who was begging for work?* The enormous success of the Nordkyst campaign had caught everybody by surprise, including Peter and Pebble.

Peter fidgeted with his pen while he talked. He was still doing it. Even though Pebble hadn't seen Peter for a while, she remembered how Peter always twirled pens between his fingers when he talked. Today it was a Stabilo permanent fine line pen. Peter's trendy Italian jacket was obviously from one of those upscale men's shops located on Strøget, Copenhagen's Walking Street and fashion strip. *At least the Nordkyst success improved the way the man dresses.* Pebble felt a rush of jealous anger. She wanted Jon and Adam to be able to buy clothes like that, too.

"The goal of our campaign is to tell women that WonderLift is going to revolutionize their lives and their ability to stay young," Peter was saying in his most condescending voice. *How the hell would he know what women go through! Sometimes it really is hard not to crack up laughing. The man is simply too much.*

I think I'll go out and buy myself that black-lace bodystocking I've been wanting to buy for years. Meetings are always a good time to make important, life decisions anyway. And buying a black-lace bodystocking definitely was one. You see, Pebble had been waiting for years, for almost a whole lifetime, to buy that bodystocking. She'd been waiting for the right man to come along, but suddenly, listening to Peter Cato, she realized that maybe she'd already missed her chance at the stars and the right man. At least she was sure Albert wasn't the right man. *At the rate I'm going, I'll be too old for that bodystocking anyway if and when he does show up.*

But getting old, and Madison Avenue and following your star were all beside the point just then.

The point, at the moment, was WonderLift – the name of a new product and the reason why this highly select group of well-groomed and well-educated (and mostly young) people were meeting. Listening to Peter, one had to conclude that WonderLift was going to revolutionize the aging balance of every almost-40 or over-40 woman in the world. And Denmark seemed to have the dubious honor of being the launching pad of this eighth wonder of the world. Pebble couldn't help but like the man for talking about the female body and the challenges of aging with such ardor.

Her job was to create an English-language campaign and media kit for WonderLift. Peter was counting on the fact that Pebble would have to come up with a catchy slogan, too, if she was going to be live up to her reputation as the rising star in the Copenhagen ad world. During the preliminary briefing a week ago, Peter had emphasized to the group that Pebble's campaign and media kit were mainly targeted to the American market. (Peter hadn't forgotten Nordkyst either). But to keep things under wraps until they were ready to launch WonderLift in the US, the English material Pebble created would first be translated into other languages. It amused Pebble no end to think that she'd soon be in print describing the latest do-it-yourself Danish facelift in Spanish, French, Italian, Greek, and God knew what other tongues.

Looking at how young everybody else sitting around the shiny conference table was besides Peter and herself, Pebble had the odd thought that maybe Peter didn't hire her just because she was a great copywriter. *Maybe he figured that at my age I've had enough experience in the various challenges facing women to be able to tell other women how to use WonderLift without dying of shame.* Obviously, Shawn O'Brien, the brawny, beer-drinking Irish copywriter who was another hot number in Copenhagen at the moment, wouldn't have qualified for the job! The thought tickled her until she noticed seven pairs of very-qualified eyes focused intently on her.

It was her turn to speak. She was supposed to present a broad outline of her concept for WonderLift. It was a crucial moment for Fem-Ads, because if Pebble came up with a good angle, they might just be able to work all the visuals and the online campaign around her ideas, too. Peter must have had his fingers crossed, hoping this silly goose would lay another golden egg.

Pebble's heart thumped loudly in her breast. Writing was easy; talking about it was the hard part.

"LOOK LIKE YOU FEEL!" Pebble Beach read the phrase from the notes she spread carefully before her on the gleaming table. That was how she wanted to headline WonderLift. No introduction, no mention of WonderLift, no nothing – just flash bam – LOOK LIKE YOU FEEL!

Late at night, working up a storm in her tiny office, she thought she had the makings of a slogan. She remembered how she jumped with joy when "LOOK LIKE YOU FEEL" flashed on her screen for the first time. It was like playing the slot machines and hitting the jackpot. She must have written 50 versions of it before she got it right. Other people, even highly qualified people in the business, didn't really comprehend how hard it was to get it just right. Only another copywriter would appreciate how difficult it is to say something easy.

She continued, throwing out ideas which took hours to produce, "IT'S EASY. AND IT LOOKS SO NATURAL!" "LOOK AS YOUNG AS YOU FEEL!" She knew the phrases were simple, but simplicity can be deceptive.

Maybe I thought they sounded good in the middle of the night, but now I'm not so sure. She thought everything she said, everything she thought was so powerful, sounded strangely flat. Pebble might be a brilliant copywriter, but she certainly wasn't a brilliant speaker.

When she finished, Pebble looked at all faces around the table – Anne, Jakob that wonderful Art Director, Peter, Sara, Cheri and the rest – they were all players on the same team. For a fleeting moment, Pebble was afraid everybody looked bored, until she realized they were all playing with her phrases – turning her words over and over again and wondering if "LOOK LIKE YOU FEEL!" had that special greatness which is the cornerstone of so much good advertising. She was positive Peter continued to fidget with his pen on purpose. He'd never let that poker face of his show anything, especially not when all the Fem-Ads grunts were sitting around the table just waiting for him to give them a sign.

At home, when it was safe to be free and creative, she'd been bold enough to write: ENJOY LIFE AS A WOMAN! Now she threw it out – one last tidbit.

Enjoy life?

Who am I kidding?

Pebble Beach felt much too warm. *Why can't I just email my ideas to meetings like this? Someone else could read them.* Mel, her hotshot uncle in New York, would have laughed at her shyness. What intimidated Pebble most was the silence. She called it "the Scandinavian silence". That was the hardest part of it, even though she'd been living in Copenhagen long enough to know that Scandinavians are a strangely unemotional lot. She should have been prepared for it and actually she thought she was, but it still got to her. No standing ovations this far North! (If you're Swedish, you're getting downright emotional if you go as far as raising an eyebrow.) But it hurt. Being American, silence still meant disapproval in her book. She saw the success she'd been dreaming of and all her shiny credit cards with PEBBLE BEACH engraved upon them fading rapidly into the sunset. *Why aren't they clapping? Why aren't they cheering? Come on fellows, a little applause wouldn't hurt...or at least a smile?* Peter kept quiet. Slowly people began to talk. No wild praise, just talk. People liked her ideas, but she didn't care. *I need strokes.* And even if she knew Peter wasn't going to jump up and offer her a fat job as the new

Fem-Ads Veep, well he could at least have nodded in satis-faction. *Dream on sweetheart, Peter's always been a cold-hearted, manipulating, money-hungry...well okay...so he didn't jump up and cheer... Get a hold on yourself, Pebble!*

Pebble sat back in her chair and sighed while everybody else talked. Peter was writing furiously on his yellow legal pad. She knew that was a good sign. *Well at least I must have inspired him.* Then Anne Lind, the project manager, started using the flip-chart and talked a bloody blue streak about timetables and deadlines and launch dates and simultaneous ad thrusts online, in the newspapers and in international women's magazines around the world – all normal procedure when launching a new product like WonderLift. Peter didn't even look up, but continued to write furiously. Cheri went out to get coffee.

Pebble would have given much to see what Peter was writing. And well, there went another day in the life of Pebble Beach – your newly divorced, 40-something, trying-hard-to-be-successful-fast-tracker woman-of-the-world – well sort of.

Then Peter got up and made a big deal out of announcing the launch date for WonderLift. "If anyone breathes a word of this..." he almost hissed, his voice so coarse that it sent chills running up and down Pebble's spine. *But he's their leader...he's our leader.* Pebble watched those young, glowing faces turn worshipfully towards him. *I guess I'm just too old for this stuff... I guess I'm so old that I'm old enough to know that at my age, my presen-tation would have been a whole lot better if only I had been a whole lot younger...*

Chapter 2

When Pebble Beach got home from Fem-Ads, there was a message on her desk from Adam, complete with doodles and scribbles, telling her to call Einar Bro immediately. Adam had underlined "immediately" about twenty times – something he never did – so it must be important.

What could it be? thought Pebble thinking of her dream. Einar couldn't possibly know what I dreamed last night, now could he? She shook her head at the ridiculous thought. *I really am getting paranoid...*

She picked up the phone and called Einar, trying to muster up her brightest voice. All he wanted (or so he said) was to take her out to dinner that evening. Still, after she hung up, she shivered. It was too much of a coincidence. And when he took her, wrapped in elegant ugliness, to dinner at the Hotel D'Angleterre, Pebble Beach muttered under her breath, *I don't care what he offers me, I'm not going to bed with him!* As if it was some kind of a threat...

It was hot inside the restaurant, and Einar was wearing an almost jazzy shirt under his long black leather coat. He checked both his coat and briefcase in the cloakroom and Pebble surrendered her slightly worn three-quarter jacket, too.

"I just realized," Einar was saying as the maitre d' led them towards an intimate corner table, "that I haven't had a chance to talk to you in several weeks, Pebble, and since my meeting tonight was cancelled..." He was holding her arm tightly. "Well, I'm glad you weren't busy..."

The few times they'd been out before, he talked to her like this, quite stiffly. Pebble smiled her most non-committal smile, hoping there would be no serious changes in this arrangement tonight. *I hope I look as bored as I feel.* But her larger-than-life smile seemed to freeze on her face. *Why does the Vice-President of the Republic*

Group have to be such a God-awful toad? Why couldn't he be somebody luscious and sexy?

Pebble ordered the salmon and left the appetizers and wine to Einar. He seemed to take great pleasure in discussing the wine list with the waiter. Finally they agreed on one of the hotel's exceptional Pouilly Fumes, but Pebble didn't care, as long as the wine didn't make her forget what she was saying or get a headache.

After they ordered, Einar looked at her in an appraising way and said, "So what did you do today?"

"Oh," she replied, trying to think of what happened that day that was worth mentioning to the Vice-President of the Republic Group. "Well, if you really want the truth, I spent most of the day at this boring meeting at Fem-Ads." She was ashamed she didn't have something more exciting to tell him.

"Fem-Ads?" Einar didn't seem at all surprised.

Pebble wondered how well Einar knew the agency, it was so new.

"You know about Fem-Ads, don't you, Einar?"

"Oh yes, I went to school with Peter Cato."

"You did? I didn't know you knew Peter. Besides owning Fem-Ads, Peter is leading the creative team I'm working with."

"What are you doing for Peter, Pebble?"

"Oh nothing as exciting as a Republic Group assignment." She thought that was the diplomatic thing to say. After all, the Republic Group was a booming advertising agency – one of the best in Scandinavia. Einar was known in the ad world for his uncanny ability to land prestigious clients and keep them satisfied. People rarely strayed from the fold once they were in his clutches.

"How's Peter doing?" Einar asked. Pebble thought his eyes were much too bright.

"Well I don't really know much about Fem-Ads. The agency just opened. I mean how long have they been in business now? It can't be more than six or seven months."

There was the appropriate amount of fanfare in the Danish press when Fem-Ads opened their doors for business. Here was a hot new agency, launched by none other than Peter Cato, former creative director at DDB Needham. Peter's track record was formidable. People still remembered his Nordkyst success; and now he was the driving force behind an agency with a new angle: Women! Just like Peter to think of something like this. He said a whole lot of preposterous things to the press the day Fem-Ads went live. Pebble remembered reading the following gobbledygook in the paper that morning, "One day Fem-Ads will be the most powerful female-oriented agency in all of Europe. We'll have offices in every major city on the continent. Why? Because women today have more clout than ever before, and they want to hear the voices of other women." Pebble remembered thinking it all sounded pretty high and mighty at the time. Just like Peter.

"I guess Peter's been in business about six months," Einar said, after thinking about it for a while. Pebble felt vaguely uncomfortable, but she didn't know why. Einar was always so well-informed.

"When did you start working for him?" Einar asked as the appetizers arrived.

"Well, this is actually my first assignment for Fem-Ads," Pebble picked at tiny North Sea shrimps, elegantly served. Maybe it was just the wine, but Pebble seemed to have forgotten her dream about Einar and was beginning to relax.

"You know," Pebble chirped in her wise-cracking American way, "I'm getting more and more popular every day!" She wanted to lighten up the evening. She didn't know why, but she felt a strange gloom clutching at her heart. At the same time she was wondering if Einar knew she had been Peter's ghostwriter on the Nordkyst campaign. The very thought sent chills up and down her spine, but on second thought, why shouldn't the man

know? *He seems to know everything else worth knowing in this town.*
She made a determined effort to push that thought from her
mind. It was imperative to act as natural as possible with Einar.
*He's the source of some of my best assignments. I've got to make it clear
to him I've got other jobs...that my life doesn't depend on him... I'll
never get through this dinner if I keep thinking about all the good
assignments he funnels my way.* Republic Group assignments
represented a sizable share of Pebble's fast-growing income.
Again she saw all her shiny credit cards – the ones with PEBBLE
BEACH engraved so beautifully upon them – slipping away.

Oh well, it's only money. But even if it was only money, Pebble
sure liked having her own. Money had a lot more power than
Pebble cared to admit. *And to think I wandered down all those
garden paths to end up at the D'Angleterre with none other than the
powerful Einar Bro himself.* But even if success was very important
to Pebble, she still felt extremely uncomfortable with Einar. If it
hadn't been a question of money, she would have liked nothing
better than to leave. Or to never have gone out with Einar in the
first place. But she knew that attitude wouldn't do. You'd have to
be crazy to pass up an opportunity like this – dinner at one of
Northern Europe's swankiest hotels with one of the most influ-
ential men in the Copenhagen ad world... Pebble wasn't that
dumb. Still it was awkward. You needed "drop dead" money to
call the shots in these situations. And drop dead money was
something Pebble didn't have. Not yet anyway. *But I'm working
on it.* Besides, being in Copenhagen complicated matters, too. For
a metropolitan city, Copenhagen was basically a small town –
almost provincial. Everybody knew everybody in ad land and a
disapproving nod or two from Einar Bro could stop Pebble dead
in her tracks – especially when she plied a trade with such a
limited focus. How many Danish companies had muscle enough
to even consider the international market – and thus marketing
material in English? Besides, where would Pebble go, if she
walked out on an opportunity like Einar? *You're pushing 45 babe,*

so be realistic. It would be the end no matter where she turned if she didn't graciously accept whatever Einar offered her. There were hungry copywriters all over town who'd give their right arm for 15 minutes of this man's time.

If only I was 25... Pebble sighed. *Remember how I looked back then... The flashing green eyes, the slim body, and not a wrinkle anywhere. If only I was 25 and knew as much as I know now... But it never works like that, does it? To know what you know, you have to age to get there.*

Today was another era, an era with limits. She couldn't go blowing in the wind like she did when she was 25. She had kids to support and besides, the world had changed since then. *Who knows? Maybe I could be a little more of the woman I once was and still be the woman I am today.* Life in the fast lane sometimes confused Pebble. *Why does operating in the world of business mean I can't be me? Why should making money exclude the world I once inhabited? My creativity is the very quality that makes me valuable to people like Einar Bro – and it springs from the fact that I was who I was, that I lived the life I've lived, and that today I am who I am. There are undertones of funkiness about me which I don't want to give up...*

"What are you working on?" Pebble was amazed at Einar's persistence, considering what a boring topic of conversation Fem-Ads was. *He must have other things to talk about...or maybe not... You almost have to feel sorry for the guy. So much power, and still so ugly.* Sometimes she wondered if men like Einar needed power to compensate for not being attractive. How else could they get women?

"I'm working on a campaign and media kit for this new product they're launching."

"Oh really?" Einar wiped his mouth and pushed his empty dish aside. Pebble was sure that the heat in the restaurant had made his nose swell. "Now I wonder...whatever could that be?" His words spilled out teasingly, like he was telling a dumb joke to a bunch of schoolboys.

The waiter appeared with the main course. The salmon was surrounded tastefully by green bouquets of broccoli on a gold-rimmed dish. The startling pinkness of the fish made Pebble smile with pleasure. They ate for a while in silence. Glasses clinked around them and elegantly dressed people spoke in hushed voices.

That was when Einar said, "This WonderLift campaign that Peter is launching…" he let his words sink in slowly. If Pebble thought WonderLift was a secret…well Einar knew all about it. "…when exactly is the launch date, do you know?"

So that was it. Pebble was furious. *How could I be so dumb?* She felt like kicking herself. Here she was worrying about Einar trying to get her to go to bed with him while all he wanted was information about Fem-Ads. Peter had made such a big deal about keeping the launch day secret. She felt like throwing up, or at least throwing her gold-rimmed plate at Einar. It wasn't nice, it wasn't ethical. She wasn't supposed to tell anyone and Einar knew damn well she wasn't. That was part of her job, the pact she made as a freelancer. Freelancers are like doctors, they have to keep the secrets of the people they work for, or else they'd be out of work very fast.

He really is an ugly toad, she thought, disliking him more than ever. *I wonder what else the Worm's got up his sleeve… Probably the Republic Group is going to market something similar and wants to jump the gun on Fem-Ads.*

"How well do you know Peter?" she asked, trying to change the subject tactfully and hide the fact that she was furious at him.

"Well actually, we were best friends at school."

"Oh really," said Pebble, "well, what happened, aren't you friends anymore?" She was thinking that Worm, as she now called him, could have just as well picked up the phone and called Peter himself, if they really were such good friends.

"We had a falling out, some years ago." Einar's voice was flat.

"Oh," said Pebble, sipping her wine and trying not to show

too much interest. Tiny beads of sweat clung to Einar's forehead as he poured more wine into her glass. *Wine, wine, the way to loosen the tongues of women.* She knew that was what he was thinking and hated him for it. It was all so obvious. She promised herself she'd be on guard. *Ugh, I hate being dependent on the goodwill of men like Einar.*

"Peter used to work for me."

That was a bomb. "Oh I didn't know."

"No," replied Einar, "how could you? That was way before you started working for us. Peter's a very intelligent guy – but ruthless."

Pebble made no comment. *Who wasn't in this business?*

"He had an affair with my wife." Another bomb. The Worm looked her straight in the eye.

Dear God, what am I supposed to say? Pebble was still furious. *As if Peter's having an affair with your wife makes everything you're doing alright.* Then she remembered the dream she had the night before and blushed. If Einar only knew.

Maybe he saw her blushing, because he reached across the small table and took her hand. His gesture was so sweet and impulsive, so out of character, that she wasn't prepared for it. There was no time to react, and once his paw covered hers she didn't know how to extricate herself.

"You're so marvelously naive, Pebble," Einar said, and there was real warmth in his voice.

Suddenly she didn't think he was toying with her. For the first time since she'd met him, he seemed genuine. She didn't know exactly why, but she didn't especially like feeling sympathetic towards him.

"I don't think I was a particularly good husband," he continued, "and I guess Birgitte needed a man who was more caring than I was. I was always so ambitious. All I ever wanted to do was be the best and make a lot of money."

Pebble Beach felt sick. *I don't want to know, Einar. Please spare me the details.* Of course he knew that sharing his secrets wouldn't make things any easier for Pebble. Maybe this was just another form of crafty manipulation. *I don't know whether to like him or hate him,* but given the choice, Pebble was the type who preferred when in doubt to like people. In Einar's case it was mighty hard giving him the benefit of the doubt. But she had her career to consider, so she did her level best. How else could a woman like Pebble manage to deal with a situation like this if she couldn't allow herself the luxury of really believing there was a warm, kind person inside this Worm?

The heat of her dream came flooding back.

"Will you pour me some more wine, Einar?" she asked quietly. Lascivious thoughts flashed through her mind. *So I'm lonely... so what? So what if I do go to bed with him?* She ached for male companionship. *What good is Albert anyway? So far away when I need him... The untouchable man on that ice island when the heat of real life is burning me up...here and now?*

"Einar, I'd like a drop more wine," she repeated softly. Apparently he didn't hear her the first time or else he knew he'd have to let go of her hand to pour the wine. *I've got to get out of here. Somehow, tactfully. Before I make a mistake I will live to regret.* When he let go of her hand to pour the wine, she quickly put her hands in her lap. *If I get drunk enough I know I'll either open my mouth or spread my legs...*

Well aware of the shark-filled waters surrounding her, she drank anyway. She drank because it was the only escape from this web of business, intrigue, and sex. *This is all too much for me...* Pebble felt the heat of more liquor hit her. It was hard to focus. Too much. *What do I care about careers anyway? Right now I'm out of my league.* Her head swam.

Einar was watching her.

"Shouldn't we have coffee and brandy in the lounge?" he suggested, his voice too honeyed.

"Yes," she smiled weakly, not able to read his signals right.

Of course he noticed how wobbly she was when she got up.

In the lounge, lingering over a second brandy, Einar suddenly said, "I really think you have potential, Pebble, you know that."

She smiled weakly. *Potential, now there's a word.*

"I keep thinking you'd be a great assistant... I really do need an assistant you know...the way business is picking up... Actually, I'm planning on hiring someone soon." There was a faraway, romantic look in his eyes and Pebble knew he was holding out warm bait. And what bait! A chance to be Einar's assistant... What a job opportunity! Wow! The shock cut sharply through the booze-haze in her brain. She couldn't help but consider all the golden occasions that would be connected to working for Einar. She knew there were hoards of people out there who would happily grovel in the dirt to work for Einar. *And he's talking about me – me becoming his assistant!* Besides the money, there was the prestige. Pebble saw all those tightly shut doors open magically.

Hey, kiddo, wake up in there. She tried to rouse herself from brandy on top of too much wine. *You're a freelancer, kiddo, remember? Freelancers have their own code. Like the Wild West. We're the free people. Remember? We don't like getting tied down.* Pebble had seen a lot in her life, but this was quite unexpected.

And besides, I'm an American. She didn't know why, but sometimes the thought helped.

So what if I never get another gig from the Republic Group? She drank a drop more brandy and coffee. *I'm so drunk another drop won't hurt... There have to be other powerful men out there in little Denmark, besides this ugly toad and his very big company. Worm, I need this, like I need a hole in my head.*

Pebble wished desperately that her brain was clear or that at least one of her really good friends was there. Somebody like Clare, somebody who'd seen her tired, without her make-up. Somebody she could laugh with while trying to sort all this confusion out. But she was all alone in this very tricky situation with Worm Bro in the Hotel D'Angleterre which didn't seem so ritzy anymore, just cold and glitzy and not at all like home.

Outside, Denmark was cold too, she knew, and very Nordic. Pebble found herself longing for the superficial wonderfulness of good fast friends. *Why couldn't I be at a noisy cafe down the street in my faded jeans, laughing and enjoying life? Without giving the idea of scoring a fast buck the slightest thought. Because I'm not. That's why. Because I'm here. That's why. Just goes to show you what happens when you're too ambitious, Pebble. Too smart and too fast. You find yourself all twisted up in knots, and end up seeing a complete stranger in the mirror in the morning.*

That was when she noticed that Einar's hand was resting on her thigh. How he'd managed to get it there was beyond her. She didn't remember a thing. They were sitting on a light blue sofa for two in the hotel lounge, and she realized she was sitting far too close to him. He was babbling on about making her his assistant and she was smiling, only God knows why, her very best little girl smile at him. Make-believe stars shone in her eyes.

Why did I drink so much?

He didn't remove his hand.

She didn't want him to. Pebble actually wanted to go to bed with Einar now – ugliness and all. It seemed like the logical thing to do. What other conclusion could there be to a night like this? With a man who just offered her the stars, in exchange for a little slip of the tongue. There really wasn't any other way out. Not in her present state. *And who cares anyway if I go upstairs with him? To the very room I saw in my dream. It'll be just okay. God knows it might even be fun and I'm horny enough. Besides basically every-thing's okay, right? Everything.*

But Einar didn't want to. Or if he wanted to, he didn't. It was almost funny. He made no attempt whatsoever to seduce her, even though he kept his hand firmly planted on her thigh, and she couldn't get her mind off that patch of highly sensitive skin. It was as if her whole being was concentrated under his sweaty hand. Which of course confused her even more. *So what's with this guy? Maybe, in spite of the booze, he remembers what he really looks like. Or maybe he looks worse with his clothes off!* Or maybe he really did think Pebble was one talented gal who'd make one hell of an assistant, and he didn't want to risk spoiling anything. Or maybe he was just biding his time, not wanting to be too fast or take advantage of Pebble's drunkenness. It could even be that Einar really felt something for Pebble, some real emotion he wasn't yet ready to share. Or maybe, when all was said and done, he was just a mensch. Some men really are.

Pebble never realized how lucky she was that night, but that was true of so many moments in her life. She never noticed the loving hand that protected her.

All she knew when she got home that night was that she had too much to drink, and that she probably said more than she should have. But she also knew she didn't to go bed with Einar or tell him the launch date for WonderLift. The rest probably didn't matter anyway. So what if she'd been a trifle too sentimental and promised the man who might soon be her boss the moon and the stars? She could always change her mind, couldn't she? Laughing too much and sitting too close to the Vice-President of the Republic Group was probably the dream of more than one Danish secretary, even if he did look like a toad. So what if she'd let him keep his pudgy hand on her slim leg? Human contact is nice, right, and it was still her leg, wasn't it?

Chapter 3

Thursday found Pebble Beach lunching with her mother Molly at Victor's, one of those "must" restaurants in downtown Copenhagen. Molly had flown in from New York for a couple of days to see Pebble and her grandsons. Mainly, Molly was concerned about her daughter. A reoccurring problem in Molly's normal American life, Pebble used up a lot of Molly's mental energy. And since Pebble's divorce, Molly had become uncommonly brave. Suddenly she was capable of making transatlantic trips all by herself, as if some of Pebble's newfound independence had rubbed off on her. (Both women were aware of Molly's startling change of behavior, but neither mentioned it.) Molly was also firmly convinced that Pebble needed her as never before.

Since Molly had a habit of talking too much (when she got worked up it didn't matter if it was long distance or not) and since she was not a member of the Skype generation yet, it made more sense to fly to Copenhagen for a couple of days than to talk on the phone. Quite probably she enjoyed getting away from Morris, too. Pebble's father seemed to get more and more demanding as he got older – and obstinate, in his opinions and habits. Molly, of course, would never have admitted to anything of the kind. She was a product of the old school: Women with husbands who are good providers don't complain. Molly preferred to explain her frequent trips to Europe (to both friends and herself) by saying, "My daughter needs me." No woman of the old school could readily admit to needing (let alone enjoying) a little excitement in her well-ordered life.

Sometimes Pebble wondered about Molly. *Am I the only woman in the world with a mother like Molly?* Did other women have mothers who planned and schemed like Molly did? Not that it mattered anymore. Pebble was older now and more or less in charge of her own life (finally). Molly would go on being Molly for the rest of her life, no matter what Pebble did. No force of nature could change that. And the fact that her only daughter, the apple of her eye, had passed 40 hadn't made a bit of difference. (Pebble gave up hoping that age would change her relationship with her parents long ago.)

Pebble could have spared Molly some of the bloodier details of her life – it might have been easier on Molly. But why should she? *What's the use of having a mother if you can't confide in her?* The years of cold war between Pebble and Molly had ended. Both had survived Pebble's turbulent youth, each in her own way. Now, at the beginning of the 21st century, both discovered they were getting older, faster than either liked. Conversation was one of the few amenities they had left. Both understood this, which helped lunch at Victor's considerably.

And being newly divorced and singularly pleased with her singleness, Pebble had no one to be loyal to – except herself. And Molly was an unexpected comfort.

Actually, if Pebble had been more calculating, she probably wouldn't have told Molly about Albert (or Einar Bro for that matter). What good would telling Molly do? The whole idea of her romance with Albert was insane. Maybe Pebble already knew it, but sitting with Molly in the sumptuous Danish restaurant on that cold winter afternoon, she was in no way ready to admit it.

Still, explaining Albert to Molly wasn't going to be easy. The man just happened to be the essence of everything Molly disliked and feared…but after all those years being married to Slim… No, Molly would never understand: Boring marriages were an intricate part of Molly's world.

"Why don't you marry a rich man this time?" Molly asked Pebble for the millionth time.

Molly had lived all her life in one secure marriage. She'd never been fucked, front, back and sideways by a new and exciting man at that fascinating age of a little more than 40. How could she know the thrill? Just when you think the game's over and you find, to your eternal dismay that you were on the losing team all along, you wake up and find yourself moaning and groaning in a wonderful king-size bed getting your brains fucked out by the best lover life ever threw your way. How would Molly ever understand that? Pebble couldn't imagine Molly moaning and groaning in any bed ever. *Did my mother ever do things like that?* Pebble knew her kids had no illusions about her – her apartment was too small for that. (*At least living in Europe was good for something!*) Molly's sex life, however, was a complete mystery to Pebble, who spent her whole childhood sleeping way down the hall from her parents' bedroom in their Manhattan townhouse off Central Park on the Upper East Side.

"There are rich men out there, you know." Sometimes Molly sounded like a broken record. "You know you're no spring chicken anymore, darling."

"I'm glad you care," was all Pebble could muster up. She had somehow hoped that when her mother landed at Copenhagen Airport at 8 a.m. that Thursday morning (after flying all night) she'd show up with a new and soothing voice and the mind of Mother Teresa. Rich men would be a thing of the past. But one look at Molly as she walked through the airport's sliding doors convinced Pebble that if anything, Molly's energy level was at a new all-time high. The Marry-A-Rich-Man Crusade was still in full swing. For a moment, Pebble wished she could discuss serious things like sex and ethics with her mother, but she knew she couldn't – not yet anyway. Molly still needed some breaking in. This burgeoning mother-daughter intimacy required a little more mileage.

Besides talking a blue streak, Molly looked absolutely marvelous. Her facelift continued to fascinate Pebble Beach. *Is this really the same 68-year-old who used to be my mother?* Pebble inspected Molly's face for the thousandth time and came to the exact same conclusion she came to every other time she examined her mother's face – *She might sound the same, but she sure as hell doesn't look the same.* The truth of the matter was – Molly looked marvelous. The facelift had somehow mysteriously changed her personality, too. She even acted more marvelous.

Anyone who saw them walking, arm in arm like close friends, through the airport doors that cold winter morning would have been surprised to know how stormy their relationship once was. Years ago, when Pebble Beach had been quite the rebel, she'd unwittingly almost broken this old woman's heart.

But now that Pebble was almost 20 years older and Molly looked almost 20 years younger, they were able to meet. They could even wear the same outfits since Molly was almost as thin as Pebble. Pebble liked the fact that Molly had surprised everyone and gotten that facelift. It really changed Pebble's opinion of her. Molly called Pebble one day, while Pebble was deep in the divorce gloom and said, "Guess what? I'm getting a facelift Monday." Pebble had nearly dropped the phone. A long silence followed. Pebble knew she had to say the right thing. It was important – significant – that she did. So after thinking that long minute, Pebble shouted, "Marvelous!"

While Molly talked, Pebble Beach wondered if she should tell her that whenever she dreamed about her, she still had her old face. Molly's facelift hadn't been able to penetrate Pebble's dream world.

Pebble toyed with her food which certainly didn't taste as good as it looked. They were lunching at Victor's because Molly understood the importance of being seen in the right places, long before Pebble woke up to the fact. As she continued toying with her food, Pebble wondered if she could tell Molly about her recent evening with Einar Bro. She needed to talk to somebody about Einar, but Molly probably wasn't the right person. Molly had never worked a day in her life, never hustled, never been divorced, never... *God, we live in two different worlds.* Still, Molly was smart. She read stuff; she watched what went on around her.

Maybe she felt sad that she'd never really had any adventures in her whole life. *God,* thought Pebble, wishing she had a suit like the soft tan leather one Molly was wearing, *it probably cost enough to pay all of my bills for the next two months.*

Pebble didn't know how to tell Molly that she'd changed. Matured. (Molly already knew.) Or how to explain that she was trying to earn lots of money (she didn't need to explain, it was obvious), or that somehow she looked at life differently now. Molly knew it all, and even realized that Pebble's rebel days were a thing of the past – still it was a difficult subject to broach. So they didn't.

Instead, Molly was saying, her mouth full of salad, "I only want what's best for you, darling. Now tell me, this Albert, is he the best?"

Pebble knew he wasn't – not in Molly's world. Probably not in hers either.

"What's with him? Am I going to meet him?"

Never I hope, thought Pebble, full of dismay. "He's got a job on Greenland, Mom."

"Greenland?" Molly was so surprised that she almost choked. Maybe Pebble hadn't changed, after all. After gasping for breath, she popped an olive into her mouth, flashing bright red fingernails.

"What will your father say...? What does Albert do for a living? And Greenland... Pebble, have you lost your mind."

"I don't know how to explain it, Mom."

"Easy to see why," Molly replied a bit too fast. Then her voice softened, "Darling, I only want what's best for you...think about your life. I mean you finally got divorced from Slim, and you have two lovely sons, now why can't you do something nice for yourself? For once in your life? Pebble, listen to me. Why don't you find a nice man who can take care of you and the boys?"

"Oh Mom, I wish I could explain it..." Pebble tried hard to look like she was concentrating on the food she'd ordered. How could she tell Molly that she was insulted? Her mother would never understand that she didn't want a man to take care of her. She wanted a companion, a friend, someone to share adventures with and not a man to pay her bills like the boring men in Molly's life.

"Albert's an engineer, Mom. He really does make good money." Pebble knew her reply was too weak. Molly would never accept anything but the best for her daughter and any man, engineer or not, who worked as far away as Greenland, had to be strange in one way or another.

Why don't we ever talk about sex, thought Pebble. *If I could just tell her how he makes me feel, she'd understand.* But she couldn't. She didn't dare, *It's hopeless.* Pebble couldn't imagine her mother understanding anything so elementary as raw naked passion at the age of almost 45. So she sulked, like a teenager, which was how Molly managed to make her feel.

"Now if only you had money..." Molly continued. Then she blurted out, "Why don't you move back to New York?"

"I know, I know," replied Pebble, who had been thinking about it, "but I'm making good money here."

"But you could make good money there too, you know. You're so talented."

How could she tell Molly she wanted to spend more time in bed with Albert first? Or explain that (at that very moment in time) even if being poor and divorced wasn't fun, she just didn't know how to get her act together. Not with the way her sex-crazed body was playing tricks on her. The funny part was that Molly would have understood. She'd had her midlife flirts, too. But Pebble didn't know and couldn't imagine her mother being younger – and feeling all those hot juices flowing. Pebble was too preoccupied with her own problems to notice the look on Molly's face. But if she had noticed, she might have got an inkling of the troubles Molly faced in dealing with a patriarch like Morris. Pebble might have realized that with Molly's mindset, age and lack of skills, there was really no way out of the relationship Molly both loved and hated.

But understanding Molly was beside the point just then. Pebble needed sympathy, not advice or speeches. She needed to talk. She needed a mother, but didn't dare reach out to the one she had, sitting right across the table. Of course, the meager sexual education Pebble received from her mother when she was young didn't make communicating any easier.

Oh God, sex! Pebble was thinking. *Why does it have to hurt so much? Why do I have to need him so bad? Why does he have to be so far away and so delicious, so touchable, so lovable? Albert's all man – all I've ever wanted – and still it's all wrong.*

When Pebble Beach was young, she'd been programmed by everything around her to believe that love was all that mattered. Material possessions and a good education might be nice for a woman, but the most important thing was love. Nothing really mattered except love. Passionate, insane love. Pebble was a wild child, a party girl, but so were millions of other middle-class kids. But the memory was dim and sitting there, drooling over her Mother's new leather suit, Pebble almost found it difficult to understand the passions that drove her during those turbulent times. Looking back was so confusing. *Maybe Molly was right all along. A rich husband and a good education would have made for so much smoother sailing.* What was Pebble now? A divorced woman, struggling to support herself and her two sons? What was so great about that? Suddenly she thought of her dinner with Einar Bro. Would Molly understand how she felt the other night? Could she comprehend the temptation and how disgusted she was with herself at the same time? Her father had always protected Molly. She'd lived her life on a silver pedestal – always taken care of.

"The Vice-President of the Republic Group took me out to dinner the other night."

Molly was all ears.

"The Republic Group?"

"Yeah, probably the most successful advertising agency in Scandinavia. I write copy for them."

"Is he married?"

"Yes."

"Then why did he invite you out for dinner? It wasn't a business meeting, was it?"

"No, Mom, it wasn't."

There was silence at the table as this information sunk in. Molly would just have to learn if she was going to be Pebble's counselor and confidante.

"He is just about the ugliest man I've ever met, Mother, but he's rich and powerful. He can do wonders for my career if he wants to."

"How old is he?"

"About 57, I guess."

"Did he make a pass at you?"

"Mother," there was irritation in Pebble's voice, "why do you think he invited me out?"

Molly's mega energy seemed to fade, as her mind processed her daughter's words.

"He said he was thinking about asking me to be his new assistant. I mean, it's just such a great opportunity, Mom, you have no idea. This man is so powerful in the ad world here. Creative people are drooling all over him, hoping for a chance to work for the Republic Group. And he offered me the job. I mean up until now, I've only worked for Einar and the Republic Group on a freelance basis. But he says he thinks I'm talented – which I am – and with the agency growing so rapidly, he really does need an assistant. God it's difficult to figure out."

"Why is it so difficult?" Molly really didn't understand. "You're smart, you're talented, you're good-looking. Why shouldn't he be attracted to you?"

"But it doesn't work like that, Mom. We're talking about a

good job, about a great opportunity and lots of money – and a man who wants to go to bed with me."

"Don't sleep with him."

"I didn't." Pebble didn't dare tell her how close she'd actually been. There was so much Molly didn't know. And then there was the Fem-Ads thing.

"There's more to it," Pebble continued. "God I wish Mel was here. He'd know what to do."

"Mel?" replied Molly, both puzzled and jealous at the same time.

Pebble's favorite uncle, Mel, the one who worked at Young & Rubicam in New York, was Molly's younger brother.

Then Molly added, trying to hide her annoyance, "Well if you need Mel, call him. You know he always loves to hear from you." Molly was hurt – to think that Pebble would rather talk to her kid brother. Actually Mel (who was 10 years younger than Molly) and Pebble had been extremely close throughout Pebble's childhood. Mel often took Pebble for long walks in Central Park and it was around the time when Mel was 25, Pebble was 10 that he started calling her Pebble Beach. At first it was a tease, but for some reason, the name stuck. Up until then, Morris and Molly's high-spirited daughter had been Marsha to the world, but pretty soon everyone called her Pebble. Nobody ever knew why. But the truth was it all started with Mel, who once fell in love with the small ocean community on the West Coast overlooking the Pacific Ocean called Pebble Beach...

"Einar wanted me to give him some inside information about a competitor I'm doing a campaign for," Pebble continued, realizing she'd offended Molly by mentioning Mel. "It was a totally unethical thing to do. I was shocked, but I can't afford to alienate Einar. He could ruin my career."

Molly listened with satisfaction. Mel might be a bigwig on Madison Avenue, but she was no dope either. The fact that Pebble was telling her all this confirmed it, too. Molly felt it was of the utmost importance to help Pebble deal with this situation – without Mel – or Morris, for that matter. In the old days, in situations like this, it would have been the men of the world, who'd know what to do. But times were changing and Molly felt herself growing with her daughter.

"Would you consider working for Einar?"

"God, Mother, it's such an opportunity. I might never get a chance like this again. But you know when I was out with him, I just hated the man...and he's so ugly." Pebble didn't know how to explain her exasperation.

Molly laughed.

"Why couldn't he just be handsome and single?"

Molly kept on laughing; it relieved some of the tension and brought them closer together.

Pebble reached out and took her mother's hand. Molly's hands were so wrinkled, they could have used a facelift too, but Pebble loved them just the way they were. Even the bright red nails and expensive rings couldn't change her mother's hands.

There was a tender moment between them.

Suddenly Pebble thought, *What will I do when she dies?* Pebble knew the world would look different without Molly. Molly had given her the opposition she needed to define herself. She'd been a mirror for Pebble, showing her, without mercy, the life she could have had and the success she never achieved. Molly represented all the pleasures and comforts Pebble missed along the way while she was out chasing adventure.

The thought of losing Molly terrified Pebble, even if she vividly recalled times when she bitterly disliked her mother. Still Pebble knew that – face-lifted or not – Molly would have to move on just like everybody else. It was hard to accept, now that they were finally finding each other again.

Why am I thinking like this? thought Pebble, not wanting to contemplate life without Molly any further. "You know, Mom, the thing about Einar is...well...he's just so ugly that it's hard to imagine him if you've never seen him."

Molly laughed again and Pebble enjoyed the warmth that radiated across the table. She changed the subject quickly, wanting to preserve the magic harmony which flowed between them. *We've had enough of Einar and Albert! Let's talk about something fun!* Pebble had the perfect topic – the one that was Molly's absolute favorite – the one that was all the way up on the top of her hit list – Pebble's ex-husband! Talking about Slim absolutely fascinated Molly. She could talk about Slim for hours on end and enjoy every minute of it. Pebble's divorce was perfect for another reason, too – no matter what was said both mother and daughter were in total agreement, down to the most insignificant detail. To hear Molly tell it, she'd never been in doubt about Slim – not from the moment she laid eyes on him. Molly claimed he was a male-chauvinist pig, which was a very strong opinion for Molly. She was also convinced (and no ifs, ands or buts about it!) that Slim had taken advantage of Pebble's good-natured naivety right from the start. Now, looking back, Pebble tended to agree. So when Pebble said, "Slim…" the conversation really perked up. Suddenly the possibilities were infinite. Whatever they said, it was bound to be enjoyable. Both mother and daughter sighed with relief. Many moments of unlimited harmony were right down the road! Not only was Slim poor, but believe it or not, Molly never approved of the old-fashioned way he'd treated Pebble Beach.

"He was a true European," was Molly's standard refrain. "He never let you use your talents." No matter how many times she said it, the thought incensed Molly. Having a male-chauvinist pig for a son-in-law infuriated her. It was totally irrelevant that Morris treated Molly in exactly the same way. All Molly could see was that Slim prevented her precious daughter from becoming a success. "Just think of where you'd be today if you'd been using your talents all along," Molly fumed, "instead of waiting on him, hand and foot."

It was funny hearing all that stuff from Molly. Pebble smiled. Suddenly lunch was fun. Albert was forgotten (for the moment) and Einar Bro was put on hold. Molly was a real paradox. An opinionated old woman who'd never once stepped out of her glass cage. She had no idea what it was like to survive out there, no conception of what women faced. Still she was fierce when it came to her daughter. Even Pebble understood that Molly reacted like this because she wanted more for her daughter than she'd had. She wanted Pebble to be a woman in her own right, not the shadow of some incompetent man. Molly simply couldn't imagine Pebble not being a success. The grief of watching Pebble trapped in a long, lousy marriage had been hard to bear. Now at least, Pebble was free, so Molly fought desperately to keep her from getting involved with the wrong man again. Besides, Pebble didn't seem to understand that she didn't have forever. Molly was acutely aware of the fact that time was running out, but she didn't know how to explain it to her daughter. Life looks incredibly short when you're 68, but the message was hard to pass on to a daughter whose juices were flowing. So Molly stuck to their standard routine: Slim, which was quite okay because Slim turned out to be such a good subject. The list of grievances against her daughter's ex-husband had this curious way of growing. Just when they finally thought they'd exhausted the matter, new items popped up. And there was so much room for improvisation! Once they got going even standard items, like what a lousy father Slim had been, could always be expanded upon. So actually, Slim, in spite of all his failings as a husband, turned out to be a divine gift as far as this mother/daughter relationship was concerned! Instead of eating their hearts out talking about the past or worrying about the future, Slim provided these two women not only with a lot of laughs but with ample opportunity for cosmic understanding. So much so, that even the most casual observer could not fail to notice how well this mother and daughter seemed to be getting along.

Chapter 4

Later that afternoon, after Molly had slept off some of her jet lag, she happened to answer the phone for Pebble who was working on a draft for the WonderLift campaign. It was Einar Bro. Molly spoke to him as if he was an old friend. It was an easy thing for her to do, being American (Scandinavians are notably introverted) and quite innocent when it came to the ways of the business world. She ended up inviting Einar to Pebble's apartment that evening for a drink.

"Oh no," groaned Pebble Beach, resting her head in her hands when her mother came into her office and told her the news. "How could you, Mother?" The walls of her tiny office were off-white and a large bulletin board was cluttered with notes and reminders. Pebble couldn't believe her mother had been so dumb. Einar Bro in her apartment? She was aghast at the thought.

"He sounds like a perfectly charming man," replied Molly, not at all moved by her daughter's obvious distress. "I'd love to meet him." She concentrated on her red nails; one was chipped and needed a touchup.

"But, Mother, I work for the man, and he's married and he put his hand on my thigh the other night! Didn't you hear a word of what I told you at lunch?"

When that didn't sink in, Pebble added, "Mother, do you remember that I said he was talking about offering me a job!" Pebble was so angry that the real reason came out, too, "Damn," she pounded her table, "I just don't want that man in my apartment! Can't you understand that? I mean he's so rich, he lives in this gorgeous house up on the coast, north of Copenhagen."

"Oh, Pebble, don't be ridiculous, your apartment is perfectly lovely! You've fixed it up so tastefully, I'm sure he'll love it."

"But, he's not supposed to know how poor I am. It only puts me at a disadvantage," Pebble groaned, thinking her mother had no brains at all. "Weren't you listening when I told you he asked me to give him secret information about a competitor? God, Mother."

Molly wasn't interested. She tossed her head, turned and walked out of Pebble's office and headed towards the kitchen to make coffee. *Maybe Pebble's getting her period*, she thought, not used to seeing her daughter in such a huff. Molly thought inviting Einar Bro was a positively brilliant idea. She wanted to meet the man. Of course, she'd heard every word of Pebble's story about Einar. In fact, Molly had listened very carefully. She thought the man sounded like an appropriate challenge for Pebble. And quite possibly a good match, too. As far as Molly was concerned, there was only one real problem – Einar's wife. But the fact that he'd already shown serious interest in Pebble, was considering hiring her, and was such a rich and powerful person on the Copenhagen advertising scene, intrigued Molly. If there was one thing this mother wanted to do for her daughter, it was to show her, somehow, that she was capable of living the life Molly thought she deserved.

Molly was an absolute miracle that evening when Einar arrived. For a moment, Pebble thought that it was Molly, not herself, who was hunting for a husband. Molly looked younger than her 68 years, her silver gray hair, thick and wavy, and her movements light and airy. Her face-lifted face radiated energy. She positively sparkled in a bright red cashmere dress. Pebble was still wearing jeans and a sweatshirt. She'd worked almost straight through on her WonderLift draft until Einar arrived. She really didn't have an evening to pull out of her calendar, so she felt her work clothes were justified.

Once she calmed down, Molly told Pebble not to worry about the arrangements. Molly prepared dinner and straightened up the apartment for the honored guest. In a few short hours, Molly transformed Pebble's cozy but messy apartment into the attractive, artful place she claimed Pebble was living in. While Pebble worked on (she'd promised Peter Cato a first draft by Monday), Molly had not only cleaned the apartment, she had bought flowers and arranged them tastefully on the coffee table. When Jon and Adam arrived home for their usual late dinner, they were stunned by the change and asked Pebble what was going on.

Both laughed when they heard.

"Why didn't you just tell her you don't want Einar coming here?" demanded Jon. He was into honesty. He was wearing a flowered shirt with the appropriate tears in it and baggy trousers. He looked gorgeous anyway. Sometimes Pebble saw a trace of Slim in his slender face, but it didn't change a thing.

"I did," replied Pebble, hoping her son would understand her predicament, "but Molly had already invited him, without asking me. And he said yes."

"So call him up and tell him you don't want him to come."

"Sure," said Pebble, who went back to her room to finish touching up her make-up. "Teenagers, even gorgeous teenagers, are hopeless," she muttered under her breath and felt like nobody was on her side.

The evening started out beautifully. Molly lit two candles and placed them on the coffee table so their light flickered and made the roses look even redder in Pebble's white living room. When Einar arrived, she served coffee in Pebble's delicate rose-colored cups and talked a blue streak. Sometimes Einar looked at Pebble with special eyes, but Pebble tried not to notice. Molly talked about New York and her brother Mel and Young & Rubicam and how talented Pebble had been as a child.

"Mel always said Pebble would be a great copywriter," Molly said, swelling with pride. "Actually I always thought he was grooming her for Young & Rubicam, until she went off to Europe and never came back. It was such a disappointment for Mel."

Pebble drank her coffee and cognac and listened, wondering if she really was the talented star her mother and Mel thought she was. *Maybe that's why Einar's always hanging around.* Listening to Molly was a real eye-opener. Her mother had an answer for everything. *Sometimes it seems like everybody in the world knows more about what's good for me than I do myself,* she thought. It had been that way with her ex-husband, too. He firmly believed, in spite of the enormous amount of energy Pebble spent trying to convince him otherwise, that all the decisions he made were right for her, which was probably why Pebble fiercely disliked people who proclaimed to know what was good for her. Pebble came close to hating both Molly and Einar that night, too.

"Tell me about the Republic Group," Molly asked.

"Well, besides a few of the bigger American agencies like Young & Rubicam, we're probably one of the top groups in Scandinavia."

Molly was suitably impressed. "My brother probably knows all about the Republic Group. I'll have to ask him about you when I get back to New York." Having a brother like Mel made Molly close to being an expert.

"Well you may have heard of our president, Thomas Nielsen," Einar said quietly.

"Thomas Nielsen?" Molly almost shrieked with joy. "Why, isn't he the one who just spoke at the Guggenheim about European advertising?"

Einar smiled. "That was him. I guess you could call him the grand old man of Scandinavian advertising. He really doesn't have much to do with running the Republic Group on a day-to-day basis, but it's nice having him on our board."

"I see," Molly said with just the right amount of awe, "but I suppose he doesn't have to worry with a vice-president like you, Einar."

Pebble almost cringed. *Mother, please stop!* she shrieked inside. Fortunately Einar changed the subject. "I think your brother

Mel was absolutely right about Pebble. A talented woman like your daughter should go far in this business." Pebble noticed there were no beads of sweat on Einar's forehead as he spoke. She remembered his hand on her thigh that night at the Hotel D'Angleterre. Outside she heard the winter wind howling as the clock ticked on the wall and sounds of TV drifted in from Adam's room.

"What Pebble needs is a mentor," Molly was saying, "that's what my brother's always said. Someone wise enough to channel all her creativity in the right direction."

"Mother, please," Pebble was not only embarrassed, she was quite sure the evening would end in disaster.

"I like strong-headed women like Pebble," Einar replied, sipping his coffee and chuckling, "but Pebble's going to have to be strong-headed, not to mention pig-headed, if she thinks she can keep on working for me and for one of my competitors...at the same time."

"Oh come on, Einar, I'm a freelancer." There was frustration in her voice. She wished she hadn't said it like that. She didn't want Einar to know how ill at ease she was.

The phone rang and Pebble heard Jon answering it down the hall.

"Mom, it's for you. It's Albert."

"Albert?"

Pebble was so surprised that she knocked over her glass of cognac as she stood up.

"I'll take it in my room," she called back to Jon. "Excuse me."

Molly didn't look at all pleased as Pebble dashed off to her room, nor did Einar.

But Pebble didn't care. Calls from Greenland were extremely rare. Albert didn't seem to be a big fan of phone conversations but this time, they managed to talk for 20 minutes, even though Pebble thought the conversation was far too short. She was hoping he'd be more romantic, but he wasn't. There was never enough time when your lover was off somewhere on the other side of the moon. But he wanted her to visit him soon; he was sending her a plane ticket. She was going to go to Greenland, somewhere she'd never been. It was almost too much on top of the cognac and Molly and Einar. But by the time she emerged from her room, her cheeks burning with desire, she'd almost forgotten Einar and her career.

The living room was empty. Einar was gone.

Molly was out in the kitchen putting the coffee cups into the dishwasher and fuming.

"Where's Einar?" asked Pebble innocently.

"You couldn't expect the man to just sit there and wait while you talked for hours with some man on Greenland!"

"I didn't talk for hours, Mother, even if I'd have liked to."

"It was inexcusable, that's what it was. And don't you come crying to me if Einar doesn't offer you that job. How could you be so dumb?"

"I never said I wanted that job, it's you who's trying to organize my life..." Pebble stormed out of the kitchen and slumped into her blue sofa. *Give me a break.* She wanted to be alone and savor the sound of Albert's voice. It wouldn't be long before she'd be on her way. All she had to do was finish her assignment for Fem-Ads, get Molly off to New York, and...

God how could she ever wait? Molly would be insufferable now. Between Einar's visit and Albert's phone call, she'd never hear the end of it.

Chapter 5

It was 29 degrees below zero, or so the captain said, when Pebble Beach landed in Søndre Strømfjord, Greenland. Dreams of romance prevailed. Our heroine had managed to pack Molly off to New York again, finish the first draft of the campaign for Fem-Ads, and send a hefty invoice. Having survived both her mother's visit and Einar Bro, Pebble decided that it was time to pay serious attention to the dictates of her aging body and not worry about her future or her bank account for a while. So in spite of Molly's dire predictions (and they occurred regularly during her five-day stay in Copenhagen), Pebble Beach was now proceeding steadfastly (and innocently) in search of one more thrill.

Molly did not succeed in instilling sufficient fear in Pebble Beach (not a new situation). And it wasn't due to any lack of persistence on Molly's part. Molly tried every trick in the book to persuade her daughter that traipsing off to Greenland was not the thing for an up-and-coming, newly divorced career woman to do. But when it finally dawned on her that her marry-a-rich-man-this-time tactics had failed, she resorted to other, coarser scare tactics like danger, disease and disillusionment.

"What if you end up way out in the wilderness and you don't even like him?" Molly probed. "I get the impression that you hardly know the man." They were drinking coffee together in Pebble's white living room, the afternoon before Molly's departure for New York. Pebble was happy her mother would soon be out of her hair, but hated to see her go. If only Molly would talk about something else.

The problem was Molly was right. Pebble didn't really know Albert, but she didn't want to admit it. If her mother had known the truth – that Pebble had never spent any amount of serious time with Albert – she would have thrown a fit, right there on

Pebble's authentic hand-woven olive-green and black Greek rug.
Which would have made their last afternoon together even more
gloomy. Copenhagen winter afternoons are dark, even at three.
And foreigners, like Molly, always tend to get depressed in the
cold Nordic dark.

"How can you live in such a gloomy place?" Molly asked for
the hundredth time, hoping Pebble would tell her she was
moving back to New York next week.

"I'm used to it," replied Pebble, glad at least that Molly had
changed the subject. The weather was a lot less dangerous than
talking about Albert. Pebble didn't want her mother to know she
was only chasing a dream. She just wasn't ready to admit it yet,
not even to herself. Not so soon after her divorce from Slim. She
needed something to deaden the pain of being on her own while
she struggled to build a successful career.

But how could she explain that to Molly, who'd never spent a
day alone in her entire life? Molly had no way of understanding
the cold-turkey syndrome that newly divorced women go
through. Pebble needed her dream, and Albert was far enough
away to be perfect. He couldn't destroy her illusions. Pebble was
glad Molly didn't ask her how many days she had actually spent
with Albert last summer when he passed through Copenhagen.
Pebble could count the days on one hand.

So what could Pebble, who was determined to go to
Greenland anyway, say?

When Molly got back to New York, she made one last-ditch
attempt to bring Pebble back to sanity – a midnight phone call
right before Pebble's departure.

"Who ever heard of going to Greenland, in the middle of
winter, for a vacation?" Molly croaked over the line. Pebble was
half asleep, her plane scheduled to leave Copenhagen the next
morning at 10 a.m. She thanked her lucky stars that Molly was on
the other side of the Atlantic.

"And what if Einar Bro calls you," Molly tried another angle.

"He might want to get in touch with you to offer you that job he's been talking about." Molly thought she was scoring a major point. Pebble knew her mother was right, but didn't want to give her the satisfaction of agreeing with her.

"I have the right to take a vacation without asking Einar Bro for permission." Einar actually called her that very morning and they had an appointment for lunch in two weeks' time. Neither mentioned Einar's departure or Albert's call the other night. Einar needled Pebble again about the WonderLift campaign, asking her how her assignment was progressing and when it was due. But she just babbled away without revealing anything, Pebble didn't even tell Einar she was going to Greenland. "Mother, I'm going to lunch with Einar when I get back, so don't worry. I'll call you from Greenland. They do have phones up there."

And so Pebble went (not without suffering excruciating last-minute doubts when her flight was delayed at Copenhagen Airport). And finally she landed, somewhat older than when she left, at the Søndre Strømfjord airbase on the West Coast of Greenland in the middle of the night (instead of at two in the afternoon as scheduled) with a planeload of drunken cowboys. The delay was so long (normal procedure on routes to Greenland due to the fierce and unpredictable weather up there) that the planeload of Greenlanders and other assorted mavericks had ample time to get pissed and crazy. (Free food and booze provided at the airport couldn't be turned down, especially when most of these people were going to self-imposed exile on an enormous icecap. Except of course for the native Greenlanders who, like most conquered Indians, just liked to get pissed for the fun of it.) All the drunks on the plane didn't exactly make Pebble feel any better. She'd heard plenty of stories about Greenland from her friends before she left Copenhagen.

Mainly what they said was this, "Most of the men who go to work on Greenland are misfits. (The few women who go are definitely misfits!) They're all wild or crazy or have broken marriages behind them." *Not the kind of men you want to bring home to Daddy. Or Molly.* "They have problems adjusting to life in the real world, so they go up there. Some to hide; some just to get away from the problems they can't handle down here. How else could they stand living up there? It's a hard, lonely life, and they're almost completely cut off from the rest of the world." Or so people said when Pebble told them she was going to Greenland to visit a man. "You've got a boyfriend up there? When did this happen?" None of her friends had met Albert. Even Clare, her closest girlfriend, shook her head in dismay. Pebble's accountant, stable enough to be the kind of man Molly would have loved for a son-in-law, added, "Greenland isn't just cold and far away, Pebble, it's a lonely, primitive place. I'm sure it's beautiful up there, in a cold, harsh way. But I wouldn't want to go there, even to visit. You hear so much about the drinking and the violence. A lot of the people who live up there are alcoholics."

Pebble had tried not to listen.

She really didn't want to know. Why did people always have to justify every little thing they did? Wasn't there any room for experimentation? Why was everybody always warning her? Couldn't she be permitted to chase her dreams in peace? She didn't want to have to explain to her mother or her friends, because she couldn't. And if there was violence and alcoholism on Greenland, Pebble didn't want to know.

But later, sitting on that middle-of-the-night run, Pebble was convinced that everything her friends said was true. They were right; she'd made an insane mistake. What was she doing on a plane full of drunken Greenlanders? Horny men with foul-smelling breaths were pawing all over her. Quite a change from business meetings in soundproofed conference rooms at advertising agencies, or sipping drinks at the Hotel D'Angleterre on Copenhagen's classy Kongens Nytorv. She might have been chasing a dream, but she wished she'd have chosen a more comfortable and safe way to do it. She didn't belong on that plane. How come she hadn't realized it before she'd bought her ticket? Why was she so pig-headed? If Albert loved her so, he could have visited her. Obviously! Why hadn't she thought of that before? What if Albert turned out to be like the rest of the drunks on the plane? She wouldn't know what to do. Fourteen days could be a very long time.

These are the very same guys, thought Pebble Beach, *who would have gone West in America, digging for gold if they could have.* Maybe that was their problem – they should have been born a couple of hundred years earlier. But in a world without frontiers, where could men like this go? *I guess Greenland is one of the few places left,* thought Pebble, wishing she was safe in her snug walkup apartment on Gothersgade across from the King's Park. Soon spring would return and the chestnut trees would bloom. Copenhagen was always glorious in spring. People plastered on park benches everywhere, lapping up the first rays of sun.

Franz, the man on her left, (she'd removed his hand from her thigh numerous times during the five-hour flight), was asking her if next time (NEXT TIME!) she went to Greenland she'd like to fly with him in his little Cessna. Pebble shivered at the thought of flying across this ice continent all alone with a horny guy like Franz. Molly, safe in her New York apartment would have died at the thought.

"Sounds like fun," Pebble smiled, trying to keep a cool distance. He leaned way over towards her and smelled of booze. He wanted woman.

"My plane is parked at Roskilde airport outside Copenhagen."

"Isn't it a long way to fly in such a little plane?" Pebble didn't know what to say.

"Well, you can't do it all in one stretch. We'd have to fly to Norway first and refuel, then to Iceland and refuel, and then

Søndre Strømfjord. It takes a couple of days, but think of all the fun we could have along the way!"

Fun? thought Pebble, looking at his strong arms. Actually he wasn't too bad looking, now that she took the time to study him. He was positively gorgeous compared to Einar Bro. But not compared to Albert.

"I've made the flight lots of times," Franz continued. "It's a beautiful trip. Flying across Greenland is like nothing you've ever seen before."

"I'm sure," replied Pebble, thinking, *Holy Christ, a couple of days alone with this guy, flying over the Arctic wilderness. Sounds like just what I need!*

"That way you really get to see Greenland."

Pebble was sure he was right. He'd already told her about his Eskimo wife. He'd been married to her for 19 years, had a booming fish factory somewhere above the Arctic Circle in a tiny village on the Disko Bay called Jakobshavn or Iluissat in Eskimo language. He was making tons of money, but his wife bored him. So he traveled a lot, selling his fish, and keeping his hands in warm places.

Well, you can't say that men like this don't have a certain charm, thought Pebble, who wondered why she was often tempted to let her cunt make decisions for her instead of her brain. *Am I the only 40ish woman in the world like this?* Pebble had to admit that Albert wasn't a whole lot different from all the other men on this plane. She wasn't sure if this was fun or not. Maybe she really liked spending the five-hour flight pushing warm hands away from her body. But it's not exactly easy to admit things like this.

Is this why I'm mad about Albert? Pebble asked herself. *Do I need adventure this bad? Is my life really that boring? (Yes!) Or am I just horny? (Yes!) Oh why do I want it so bad?* The thought puzzled her. It wasn't like she couldn't get plenty of it in Copenhagen. Einar Bro wasn't the only man she knew who'd like to go to bed with her. *What's so special about Albert?* But it wasn't actually the right moment to analyze her feelings for Albert, now was it? Because Pebble couldn't do a whole lot about it, since they were just about to land at Søndre Strømfjord. It would be hard to just change her mind, call a taxi and go home. But the thought bothered her. *What am I going to do,* she thought, *if I wake up and find that I'm just a sex-crazed woman in her 40s, after all, desperately trying not to grow old?*

Pebble's first glimpse of Søndre Strømfjord from the landing airplane didn't do much to cheer her up. The plane shuddered in the wind as they approached. And peering out the window into the pitch-black night, all Pebble saw was a few lights twinkling from what was once a very forlorn-looking American military base, a tiny airline terminal and a few scattered houses. This tiny spot of humanity had just suddenly appeared, out of nowhere, after flying for a very long time over a giant piece of ice called Greenland. Pebble was lucky she'd been flying across that immense island country at night. If it had been daytime and clear, Pebble would have seen that there was absolutely nothing for almost a thousand miles but snow and ice and mountains. The feelings of loneliness which plagued her so often since her divorce would have probably been even more intense. At least as it was, it was night and she was surrounded by warm-blooded human beings. There was some semblance of belonging to the brotherhood of man, even if it was a very drunk and pitiful brotherhood.

Everyone, even the most loud and obnoxious, got very quiet as the plane circled in to land. Pebble thought it was as if for one solemn moment, everyone realized what they were doing and where they were going.

"Nobody really likes Greenland," said Franz on her left in a very serious voice. She turned and looked at him. His blue eyes were kind in his weather-beaten face, and he wasn't lying. The bravado was gone. He placed his warm hand over hers.

For the first time during the flight, Pebble made no attempt to move it.

God, she thought, *I need a man who is real.*

When the plane landed, everybody cheered. It surprised her. She'd never seen people cheer before, even though she'd landed many times around the world. It only made it more scary.

* * *

The midnight cold of minus 29 hurt Pebble's nose as she stepped off the airplane. Franz and the hundred other men tottered off, too. The few women on board all looked either distraught or disheveled. The light glared and the stewardesses standing by the cold open doorway, smiled as if they had just landed in sunny Spain. The ice of the runway crunched under Pebble's feet as she tried to walk without skidding, sliding or falling on her face. Franz walked besides her, but he made no attempt to be a gentleman or help her.

No friends were there to greet her. But she'd known that in advance. She was on her own here. But it hadn't scared her as much in Copenhagen as it did now.

Since she and everyone else obviously missed their connecting helicopter flights to whatever village they were going to, a lot of people were going to be holed up at Søndre Strømfjord. That was what always happened, or so people had warned her. Søndre Strømfjord was only a transit spot, a link-up point to the rest of Greenland. The crowded Air Greenland planes landed in Søndre Strømfjord because there wasn't anyplace else to land. Then people proceeded by helicopter to whatever tiny outpost of civilization they were bound for. Nobody actually lived in Søndre Strømfjord except the pilots and the people on the airbase. But everyone who ever went to Greenland knew they had more than a good chance of getting stuck in Søndre Strømfjord, and God only knew for how long. Albert had warned her on the phone. Some people got stuck there for days as fierce storms raged and conditions were too dangerous for helicopters to fly. Franz had warned her too, on the plane, when it was obvious they wouldn't make their connecting flights. He told Pebble that she could just as well leave her big city restlessness with the rest of her life back in Denmark. Her city ways wouldn't help her up here.

"Here the elements rule," Franz said to her, more than once, on the flight up. He knew she was worried about missing her flight to Albert's village. "There's nothing you can do about it, Pebble, God and the weather have the final say up here."

"Let me buy you a drink when we get to Søndre Strømfjord," he suggested. "It's not a place for a woman like you to be alone in anyway."

Pebble had smiled at him weakly. She didn't want to even think about being stranded in Søndre Strømfjord for a couple of days.

Franz was basically an easygoing guy. His long years in Greenland had taught him well. He really wanted Pebble to just relax and party a little with him. City girls were just so damn uptight. Franz had seen it before, and liked their energy, for a while anyway. How could he explain to Pebble, all revved up to go somewhere and sleep with some cowboy that there was nothing else to do in such a godforsaken place anyway? Albert wasn't going nowhere no how. If her boyfriend lived up here, he knew the score. Pebble could just as well pass the time pleasantly with Franz.

But Pebble didn't know what she wanted to do. It did occur to her more than once as they approached Søndre Strømfjord (when it finally sunk in that she'd be delayed) that Franz was too masculine and she was too vulnerable. She didn't trust herself. But she didn't want to be alone in Søndre Strømfjord, surrounded by hoards of intoxicated men either. The Arctic night was too cold for that.

"We'll go over to the club for a drink," he said. "I know it's late," (it was 2 a.m.), "but you won't be able to sleep right away anyway."

I wish I knew what life was all about, thought Pebble. Her heart beat with fear as she accepted his invitation. Albert wasn't there to protect her. *Why do I do the things I do?* Travel had a way of waking Pebble up. Adrenalin coursed through her body. Stepping outside her daily routine, away from her kids, the rat race, making money, things looked different. Who was she anyway? She knew she wasn't important. The universe was immense. She was just a tiny spot of lonely woman on a cold night. The air was startlingly clear. Everything felt crazy, new. Why not live? Right now, this moment? What was she running after anyway? Was it just love? Adventure? Money? Mind-boggling orgasm? She wasn't different from anyone else. Being so far away, she could admit it. Thoughts raced through her brain. She might feel scared, but she also felt incredibly alive. And aging fast. 40 had already passed. A blink of the eye. *Why am I so afraid of living?* She took Franz's hand, too far away from the world she knew to care.

How can you be afraid of life and long to live it, both at the same time?

The smoky atmosphere at the club, even at that late hour, helped Pebble relax a little. Franz knew everyone and everyone wanted to know Pebble. In this company, she was more than a star. She was a gorgeous creature from another world. You don't find women like Pebble wandering around on Greenland. They treated her like a queen. Any new woman in town was an event at Søndre Strømfjord, and Pebble radiated big-city energy. Franz and Pebble sat down at an empty table and Franz ordered beers. Jaunty-looking helicopter pilots who'd been sitting at the bar came over and joined them. They were the kind of men who could make Pebble's mouth water. Men who could drink and laugh and make her feel real and alive. Not the two-toned, cautious types Molly swore by. Would Molly ever understand?

Pebble felt a myriad of emotions, colors and temperatures.

Her tiredness disappeared. She was on a roll. This was life, no matter what it looked like in the morning. She drank another beer. It tasted good. Would she sleep with Franz? Everyone expected her to. And what if she did? Who would ever find out, back in wonderful Copenhagen? And what about Albert? Did she owe him her allegiance? Was she supposed to be faithful to a man she hardly knew? Now that she was divorced and finally free? What would Molly think if, God forbid, she ever guessed that she'd mothered a daughter with such lascivious desires as Pebble Beach? Was that why she'd come to Greenland? To be far enough away to take a good look at who she really was? Did she really need all that ice and snow to do it? The streets of Copenhagen offered everything the heart could desire. But that was home. That was where she lived, where she knew people, where people would recognize her, and where people had memories. Here she was scot-free, ageless and unknown. It was like having a second chance. She could try it all out if she wanted, taste it all, who'd ever tell? Even her children would never know.

I must have drunk too much, thought Pebble as she stumbled back towards Franz's trailer. His warm hand now buried deep in her pocket.

* * *

Once inside the door, he smothered her with kisses even before she took her coat off. It was nice. The hot air of the warm trailer helped her thaw. She liked Franz, but didn't want to know him better. As he undressed her with an expert's hand she realized that once he was inside her, he wouldn't even know who she was. The perfectness of that impersonalness was suddenly wrong. She wished she'd been wiser and checked into the transit hotel. By now she'd have been sleeping like a baby, dreaming innocent dreams of Albert in Holsteinsborg. Feeling her warm pussy with her own hand and wanting Albert bad. Instead, another man was touching her. But it was too late to turn herself off, even if she felt like it. She knew enough about men to know that was too dangerous. You never knew what might happen. Women who did things like that in midstream were playing with fire; they might end up getting beaten up. Some men were jerks or psychopaths. It was wiser to investigate things first. But since she'd forgotten to scrutinize matters carefully this time, she let Franz continue.

The next morning, the weather had cleared up. When Pebble woke, with an aching head, the sun was already shining brightly in the trailer's windows. Franz was gone. He'd left a note on the little table by the bed. "Pebble, I have to fly up to Jakobshavn for a meeting. Be back tomorrow night. F."

Pebble was relieved.

Maybe she could even forget their lovemaking the night before. But she doubted it. Franz had left nothing to the imagination.

She wrapped herself in his bathrobe and looked around the trailer, hoping to find a shower. There was none. So she made do with the sink in the bathroom. At least the water was hot, but the pump made an awful racket. She peeped out the window. It was awesome. The entire expanse of Greenland's majesty was out there waiting for her. Snow everywhere. Franz's trailer, parked a short distance from the air terminal, was a tiny spot of warmed-up metal in a vast terrain. The sky was so blue that Pebble couldn't remember ever having seen one like it. She wondered how cold it was outside and if her helicopter would fly to Holsteinsborg today. If Franz had gone to Jakobshavn, she could probably go, too.

She felt cheerful, happy. Like a young girl starting a new life. No reason to dismay or think about who she'd made love with the night before. At least she'd managed to slip a condom on him before he entered her. So what harm could it have done? *This is the very first day of the rest of my life,* Pebble told herself, looking at her somewhat beautiful face in the somewhat foggy bathroom mirror. She liked herself immensely just then, with all her more than 40 years.

Chapter 6

The waiting Sikorsky S-6IN helicopter had Air Greenland painted on the side in white against a red background. The night before, Franz told Pebble that those in the know called Air Greenland "Imara Airways". "Imara," he'd told her, "means *maybe* in Eskimo language." At that time, sitting comfortably on the Boeing 757, Pebble hadn't understood what Franz was talking about. But now, walking through the snow outside the Søndre Strømfjord air terminal towards the helicopter, she did.

Helicopters, Pebble realized, surprised at the thought, *are sensitive birds, they can't fly in just any old weather.* And this bird looked more than sensitive, the sturdy helicopter – the legendary Sikorsky was the model the US used in Vietnam – was positively tiny, dwarfed by the giant snow-covered mountains surrounding the base's single runway. At least today there were no hurricane winds, blizzards, sudden storms, fog or any other whims of nature afoot to delay Pebble. An Eskimo was loading the chopper, while Pebble and the 15 other Eskimos waited. For some reason, they weren't boarding and Pebble wondered why. The cold was intense. Pebble's big city cowboy boots weren't warm enough and she stomped back and forth, cold and impatient.

A grey, battered pick-up truck drove up in a hurry and screeched to a halt. Two Greenlanders jumped out and unloaded a long wooden man-sized box and carried it on board. It wasn't until Pebble climbed into the chopper that she realized it was a coffin. The 15 Eskimos all sat towards the back, as far from the coffin as they could, leaving Pebble alone in the single seat right behind the cockpit and next to the coffin.

I don't belong here, thought Pebble. The coffin spooked her. She realized this was Indian country. The Eskimos of Greenland look just like American Indians. The chopper started to move. *Jon and Adam would love this,* she thought, thinking fondly of the two grown sons she'd somehow spawned in Denmark. Life was absurd. *But Molly and Morris would die.* Sometimes she actually liked being in the middle of her own life adventure, even though her attempts at living usually looked (and sounded) a whole lot more exciting in retrospect – when she'd had time to filter out the anxiety. Sometimes Pebble had good instincts, but not always. Her antenna told her the 15 other people in the chopper were as different from her as day was from night. Their world was populated by people and spirits she'd never met.

The helicopter rose slowly and hovered in midair. When they were about 50 feet off the ground, Pebble, who'd never been in a chopper before, wondered if they were going to crash. She didn't know that choppers just seem to hang in midair as if they were suspended before they really start to fly. And Pebble, whose nerves were already raw, saw her life ending, a red blotch on the white snowdrift below. Then the chopper's nose tilted forward and head down, they flew away.

In less than a minute, Søndre Strømfjord was completely gone. Vanished, without a trace, as if it had never existed. Peering out the window into the glaring sun, Pebble saw only snow. It seemed as if Greenland was one vast emptiness which stretched as far as the eye could see in every direction, and farther still. There wasn't a house, or a tree, or a single sign of life anywhere. All Pebble saw was mountains, immense, twisted, snow-covered movements of earth, running here and there, massive and glittering gold in the morning sunlight. Greenland might be spectacular to look at, but it sure was frightening to contemplate. How could anyone live in such a place? There was nothing to burn or eat for hundreds and hundreds of miles. Still Eskimos had managed to live here for centuries; it was their country, long before Greenland became a Danish colony.

The plain wood coffin bothered her – reminding her guiltily of the carnal passion that drove her so far north. Damn! Just her luck to be sitting next to a stiff when she was flying to meet her lover. *God couldn't have planned it better!* What was He trying to tell her? Pebble sometimes believed in omens, especially when she was living on the edge.

A pamphlet called "Survival in Arctic Regions" was stuck in the plastic pocket on the wall by her seat. She pulled it out, trying to forget her life, the coffin and how badly she wanted Albert. She studied the diagrams of people huddled in thermal suits – the suits were apparently stowed under the very seats they were sitting on – waiting to be rescued. But the pictures did little to comfort her. The extreme vulnerability she felt, amongst natives who called this Arctic wonderland home, didn't go away.

Why doesn't Albert work on a Greek Island? Pebble pouted, feeling the fool, when suddenly a tiny patch of snow-clad humanity appeared in the distance. Pebble Beach looked at her watch – they'd been flying about 45 minutes. Only 5,000 people lived in Sisimiut, as Holsteinsborg is called in Eskimo language, so Pebble wasn't exactly expecting skyscrapers. But the village looked so tiny and forlorn! A blotch of insignificance in a sea of ice. Then as the helicopter hovered over the landing place, ready to descend, Pebble started tingling all over. Albert would be down there waiting for her! She saw him vividly in her mind's eye. Black hair, the French mannerisms, the cigarettes he rolled himself, the masculine cowboy. The dream. In a few minutes, he wouldn't be a dream anymore; he'd be flesh and blood. And she'd be with him, in real life. With all that implied. (He'd be someone she'd have to deal with, too.) Instead of thinking about that, she pictured herself wrapping her arms around him and her mind zoomed in on her sense of touch. Exquisite sensations pulsed through her body. The tingling stopped when she noticed a group of Eskimos comforting a wailing woman as the chopper neared the ground. She remembered her companion on that strange flight – the corpse. Maybe whoever it was wasn't the only person on the chopper who was going to meet their destiny. Then she caught a glimpse of Albert, leaning up against the heliport, hands deep in the pockets of his battered pilot jacket. Her heart thumped as the helicopter thumped down on the pavement.

How can I possibly lift my body out of this seat? thought Pebble, trembling all over. She wanted to remain locked in that moment forever. You see, Pebble was smart enough to know that she'd probably never feel happier in her life than she did just then. No matter what the future would bring, nothing would ever be able to surpass the intensity she was experiencing, sitting as if turned to stone next to her companion the corpse, peering out the window at Albert. He hadn't spotted her yet, but she already knew that neither of them would be able to live up to the expectations that had brought her thousands of miles to this moment.

* * *

Albert, a French cowboy who'd discovered the wild beauty of Greenland years back, was from Chamonix, a small village in the French Alps. Early on he found he was too high-spirited for that strict, little ingrown Catholic community and had sought adventure as a forester in the wilds of Lapland. Now sitting with Pebble Beach in the living room of the tiny red, wooden house he rented on a cliff overlooking Holsteinsborg, he said, "We've got to stretch out this moment, Pebble." He was drinking a beer and enjoying the lust in Pebble's green eyes.

Pebble was so happy that it didn't matter if it was all wrong. She only saw how the muscles of his arms and shoulders moved underneath his faded red flannel shirt. He was so sun-burned, from endless hours on skis exploring the wilderness around Holsteinsborg that he almost looked like an Indian. Her panties were wet, and she hoped he wouldn't know how badly she wanted him. But considering how far she'd come to be with him, it couldn't be that much of a secret. She inched closer to him on the couch, wanting to feel the warmth he radiated. She gently moved a lock of hair away from his forehead, even though a moment earlier she'd vowed not to touch him first. He smiled as she studied his profile. The glass in his hand – she hadn't counted how many he'd drunk – was empty.

It made no difference that once his hair had been jet black, Pebble didn't notice the grey creeping into his thick head of hair anyway. All she felt was the tingling that rushed through her loins every time she was with him. On some primitive level, her cells wanted his cells; that was how she explained it to herself. The few times she'd been with Albert, she felt trapped inside a magnetic field of enormous intensity. Energies and feelings circumvented her brain. She was all body. Pebble had never had a relationship like this before.

"Darling," he turned towards her, the energy full-blast now, kissing her lips. It was as if he was initiating some ancient ritual, the moment was that solemn. His hands sought her breasts. Pebble Beach felt herself be drawn into the circle of his power until an odd, uncomfortable thought set off warning bells in her mind. *What if our lovemaking doesn't live up to my expectations?* She awoke momentarily from her trance as her mind screamed, *What if our lovemaking doesn't live up to his?* And for a short moment, Pebble's brain worked perfectly – just as it did when she was writing advertising copy – and she remembered all the palpitating pleasures she'd imagined, alone in her bed in Copenhagen. In her sizzling dream world, she'd been young as pliant springtime. And Albert was a master of carnal arts who was able to stretch time until she was begging for the ultimate pleasure. He'd lead her down pathways to a world of sensations she'd never experienced before. But now that he was actually going to touch her, her brain was sending off desperate signals she didn't want to hear. She knew dreams had a way of evaporating, but she didn't care. She ignored the warning bells (what could she have done anyway – ask Albert to undergo a personality check?) and slid comfortably back into the ancient ritual they were enacting.

Maybe our heroine needed dreams more than reality anyway.

What, in fact, was so great about the real life she lived before? Her marriage to Slim and all that? Was that great? The yearning of her cells drowned out the murmurings of her brain as she leaned tenderly into his body, letting herself go, flowing into his presence. So what if he was just a man? So what if she'd invented him? At least she could feel him now, touch him, enjoy her own invention. And what if this was the end of the garden path? She was ready to run the risk, accept the challenge – even if most of what she knew about Albert was a product of her own imagination. Did it really matter? Where did physical attraction like this come from anyway – if not from her mind? Was there anything in this entire universe powerful enough to set compasses spinning before the mind even knew the name, except the mind itself?

If Pebble knew surprisingly little about the man who was now leading her to his bedroom, it was probably best that way. The taste of happiness is extremely hard to describe and Pebble Beach, after much failure in life (though well-camouflaged), couldn't help but enjoy it, even if it was a pleasure she'd manufactured herself. And even if things were bound to change.

* * *

Choppy water always follows a calm golden sea. Pebble Beach learned that Albert was stubborn and hard as a rock, and drank more than he should. He took her skiing in the snow-covered mountains beyond Holsteinsborg. And the landscape was as empty and cold as the moon. There was nothing out there.

"The Arctic dream, Pebble, this is the Arctic dream," Albert shouted into the icy wind, a mad glint in his eyes. But Pebble didn't see any dreams. All she saw was an environment so harsh and hostile that few human beings could survive there for long. She ached for the warmth of city lights and people and cafes. If there'd been a bus stop on the corner, Pebble would have hopped on the first bus and gone anywhere. That was how out of place she felt – trapped by Greenland's enormous emptiness. She didn't understand how Albert could stand it. Everywhere there was cold aching nothingness. It scared her.

But who could she tell? Not Albert. He'd never understand. He'd climbed Mont Blanc when he was 17 and roamed the wilds for years, thriving on the wilderness. He was a loner. Pebble might not have wanted to admit it – but the barrenness of Greenland forced her to – Pebble and Albert had very little in common. When he talked, recounting his mad adventures, she couldn't do much but listen. What could she tell him? About the thrill of having a brand new computer in her home office? About the glorious chaos of doing business with the best advertising agencies in Copenhagen? About WonderLift and the female revolution, or about Peter Cato? No, Pebble's life had so little relevance up here it hardly made sense to her anymore. How would Albert understand?

Albert was an engineer. He made his money building electrical plants at different locations around Greenland for Greenland's Technical Organization. At the moment, due to a lull in plant construction, he was teaching engineering to a select group of Eskimos at the small technical school in Holsteinsborg. Pebble didn't think his life was exactly exciting either (what did the man really have besides the great outdoors?).

Once the sumptuousness of that ancient ritual began to wear off a little, Pebble noticed how much he drank. She didn't want to make this discovery, but the slur in his voice made it hard to ignore. That was when she'd panic and think, *Here I am, thousands of miles away from home, stuck in some tiny outpost of civilization, getting my brains fucked out by an alcoholic I hardly know.* It was enough to frighten the shit out of her. The same thing had happened every night since she arrived. She'd be curled up against him, trying to listen to whatever he was telling her, when it would hit her – goose bumps and all, and panic right in the pit of her stomach. Her insides would say, *What am I doing here?* And the wave of fear would follow. *How did I get myself into this? Why can't I go home? ... I want to go home! I really do! Right now!!* The more she thought about it the worse it got. But Pebble knew she couldn't go home. The helicopters that Air Greenland sent out to these small Eskimo villages only picked up people from Holsteinsborg when the weather was good. At the moment, fierce storms raged all along the West Coast of Greenland. There hadn't been a single helicopter since the day Pebble arrived. Nobody could leave. Not even Queen Margrethe herself could have gotten out. If you were going to take your leave from the planet earth, well you'd just have to do it in Holsteinsborg. There was just no way you could get on a train or plane and say Goodbye Charlie.

* * *

Two nights later, Pebble and Albert were invited to a little party at the home of one of Albert's friends. Pebble decided she wasn't going to worry or let any of her silly panicky feelings stand in the way of her and fun. After all, that was what she'd come for. Right? Fun – yeah, plain simple fun, and now she was there, right? Right in the middle of all this real-life fun, right? Well, maybe she was feeling anxious and maybe she was really stuck, but if she was, she figured she might as well enjoy it. What else was there to do? What else could anybody in their right mind hope for in a situation like this one – besides fun? If she was lucky, she'd be out of there in a week's time anyway. (Besides, the thought of this romantic adventure dragging on for more than another week was probably more than anyone could bear – Albert and Pebble included.)

In her attempt to be positive, Pebble finally discovered one good thing about Albert's drinking (there's got to be a payoff somewhere, right?). And Pebble finally found it. It was obvious.

It had been there all along, right under her nose. Yes folks, Pebble's dreamboat became positively sociable when he drank. That was it; the unexpected highlight of Albert's boozing was his conversation. Albert actually talked. And once he got started, he sure did talk a lot. Ten or twelve Tuborgs transformed our hero into a real conversationalist. It was almost impossible to shut him up. The change was that astonishing. Sometimes when Albert got going like that, Pebble wondered if she really was with the same man. Instead of Clint Eastwood in a bad mood, our hero became quite the guy. His eyes sparkled and that strange hunted look disappeared.

Pebble found out another thing, too. She could drink with the rest of them. She marveled at her newfound capacity for booze. She thought it was some undiscovered talent since she'd rarely touched the stuff before her trip to sunny Greenland. Now, she was positively guzzling it down on a daily basis. If she didn't go home soon, she'd end up an alcoholic like the rest of the motley crew Albert hung out with. But Pebble wasn't in the mood for passing judgments mainly because she couldn't see what else there was to do on an icecap but enjoy a couple of nightcaps (or ten)? As far as Pebble could see (and that wasn't very far in this blizzard), freezing to death was no viable alternative to having fun. For all she knew, it might go on snowing forever and she might be stranded there forever – wherever it was she was. So having guzzled a beer or two before leaving Albert's house for the party, Pebble concluded with all the wisdom of a girl from New York – you just had to make do.

Pebble was full of compassion for all the drunken souls she'd seen stumbling around on the frozen streets of Holsteinsborg, swaying in the gale force winds. It wasn't hard to understand anymore (what was incomprehensible in Copenhagen made perfect sense up here)...how else could you handle this? Pebble was convinced that Greenland had to be the most boring place on earth. (You could just see so many Die Hard movies. Wherever they went, people were glued to their TV screens and Bruce Willis, apparently the Eskimo hero of the moment, was on.) It surprised Pebble that there weren't more suicides, but she supposed the Eskimos still had traditions, somewhere, to comfort them. Pebble was disappointed she saw so little of those traditions in Holsteinsborg. *Probably,* she thought, *because advertising has done such a good job selling the white man's lifestyle to these people.* It might have been real Indian country once, it might have been one of the world's last untouched wildernesses, but the Eskimos sure did seem gung-ho in their pursuit of the life they glimpsed on TV. Pebble, who expected to see igloos and Eskimos running around in knee-high furs hauling reindeer and seals, didn't get to see that either. Besides satellite TV, everybody had hot water, electric stoves, cars and computers. Even the grinning Eskimo clerk at the Air Greenland ticket office seemed to be a computer whiz. So no, Pebble had yet to meet an Eskimo who showed the slightest sign of wanting to stop the approaching tide of the white man's civilization (she'd heard there were some – but obviously they were dying out fast). Everyone Pebble saw (when she and Albert found time to emerge from drinking and lovemaking) seemed to enjoy zooming around the tiny village (population 5,000 with a whooping total of five paved roads) in brand-new cars. Pebble couldn't fathom it. The town's five roads went nowhere. But it didn't seem to bother anyone. Pebble got the impression that the entire population of Holsteinsborg was out there celebrating the fun of technology. Besides the one-mile trip from one end of the town to the prefabricated apartment buildings at the other end, you couldn't leave the village by road to go anywhere – you'd only end up in a snow bank. No roads connected the isolated villages spread along the West Coast of Greenland. Distances were too great and the climate too harsh for roads. Helicopter or boat was the only means of transportation.

Occasionally Pebble did see a dog sled, but they were few and far between. Greenland wasn't half as primitive as Pebble expected it to be. Even the Eskimos hanging out inside (it was too cold to hang out outside) the town's few shops, were all wearing blue jeans and street wear, just like the kids back home.

As they entered Martin's house, the flush of warm air was a welcome relief from the blasting, bitter cold outside. The wind had been blowing so hard that Pebble had difficulty walking. She'd spent most of the five-minute walk from Albert's house to Martin's, clutching Albert's arm. Greenland might look modern, Pebble thought as she stomped the snow off her not-at-all-warm city-cowboy boots, but it was only a facade: No amount of modern living was going to drown out the cold vastness of Greenland.

Inside she heard the sound of laughter and clinching glasses. As could be expected at a Greenlandish party, people were already well into the food and booze. If Pebble was hoping for less liquor, she was in for a disappointment. Oh well, at least Albert would talk. But it certainly wasn't going to improve her looks. You see Pebble discovered, much to her dismay, that drinking Greenland style did have a downside, too. She looked like the Black Death the next morning. It never failed. She'd wake up all innocent and groggy and suddenly she'd find herself in Albert's bathroom mirror looking like an old hag. The rude shock of looking at herself startled her awake, as if she'd thrown cold water on her face. She hated the sight of her rubbery face. It was enough to ruin her whole day. She felt like pounding the face in the mirror. God must have made a mistake, she was sure. *Anyone who's newly divorced and stuck on an almost-deserted island with a drunk in the middle of a snowstorm that doesn't show any signs of stopping shouldn't have to go through things like this! It's just not fair.* The worst part was those hideous bags she had under her eyes. They aged her instantly about 95 years. No amount of chamomile tea or ice would make bags like those disappear. *No man will ever mistake me for 25 again!* (A very grave thought indeed, so early in the morning.) Which was why Pebble decided, after a couple of mornings of pure gloom, that a facelift was the only way to deal with this new and discomforting fact of life. She'd have to have one as soon as she returned to Copenhagen (that was if she ever returned and could afford it). *Damn, life after 40 sure does get complicated.*

* * *

Martin, his fat, muscular shoulders heaving slightly as he talked, and Albert, the slur in his voice already noticeable enough, were having one of those "profound" conversations, the kind only men can have when they drink too much. They'd look each other deep in the eyes and speak pure gibberish. It was enough to make you laugh (or cry, depending on how your hormones were doing at the moment). It was as if the rubbish they were spouting was some kind of profound truth. Pebble couldn't bear to listen to them. And Martin's ungainly wife, Kirstin, seemed greatly annoyed, too, though she never said a word. There were other guests at the party and Kirstin knew if Martin didn't watch out, things might get out of hand – the way things get out of hand at Greenlandish parties. But whenever Kirstin tried to get Martin's attention, he motioned her away. The look on her large, plain face invited sympathy, but Pebble didn't feel sympathetic. Kirstin wasn't one of those fun Copenhagen people Pebble was used to dealing with. She wasn't fast or flashy, just plain and ordinary. Pebble should have liked her, it would have been the proper thing to do, the civil thing, but she didn't, even though she wanted to and tried hard to. Kirstin was just so boring, and Pebble didn't have much experience dealing with people like her. It only took Pebble about three minutes to give Kirstin the lowdown on her children, the weather and her job, so when five whole minutes had passed it seemed as if their conversation was in serious danger of grinding to a halt.

Besides the only thing they both passionately agreed on, that "men are hopeless", was off limits. They just couldn't talk about it. It wouldn't have been right. Not with Kirstin's husband and Pebble's boyfriend sitting within earshot. But Kirstin's sighs were plainer than words, at least to Pebble. It was as if she'd shouted to everyone in the room, "Look at those imbeciles." Pebble couldn't have agreed more. She just wished they could have talked about it, wished she could have talked to someone, anyone, about her romance. How could she have fallen in love with a man who drank like a fish?

Pebble Beach was so desperate at that moment, she would have confessed everything to Molly – if she'd been around – but to Kirstin, no. How could she? She didn't even know Kirstin, who was a bore anyway. And besides, Pebble was too proud. After all, she was the one who'd come all the way to Greenland like a bitch in heat to bed Albert. It was downright embarrassing. So Pebble just stood there, smiling like a jerk, telling herself it would be disloyal to even mention how drunk their men were. Which was hard to do since all Pebble wanted was to come out and say, *God I'm so unhappy. Why do the men we love have to act like this? Why can't they just grow up and stop drinking so much? It's so disgusting...* Inside, Pebble felt a kind of anger she couldn't explain. Like when you buy a piece of goods and it turns out to be rubbish. *Disgusting and embarrassing and sad...* Because that's what Pebble would have said, if she could have – if she'd had the courage – right then and there. But she didn't, even if deep down inside she knew that Kirstin probably would have agreed with every word she wanted to say – still it didn't help. *Life with a drunk is like that,* both women thought.

Instead of truth (Pebble knew she'd blown it one more time. *Is this why you keep on being reborn? You get to do this over and over again until you dare go for the truth?*), Pebble and Kirstin talked about all the things that didn't matter while worrying about how they were going to handle their drunken men that night. Because you see women do worry about things like that, even if they never tell each other. How could they not? We've all heard too many stories about women who've been abused or molested or beaten or all three. Pebble and Kirstin, whose husband was bad tired of her plain face, were no exceptions. What law said it couldn't happen to them? Who could promise that tonight wouldn't be the first time Albert or Martin crossed that very thin line. Because you know, it does happen.

Thoughts like that spooked Pebble and made it difficult for her to understand why she was behaving so loyally towards Albert. Why didn't she just get her purse and go? (Where would she have gone? But that was another story...) The awesome question was how she could still love him so. She was all confused. Mixed up. Drinking too much. Damn – she'd come so far to be with him – why did he have to drink like that and ruin everything? Sometimes he could be so wonderful, so gentle, so loving. *I'm just so damn stupid!* Pebble didn't know where to turn. The man was absolutely infuriating, sitting there without a care in the world. Come tomorrow he wouldn't remember a word he'd said tonight. Oh men!

Kirstin's husband, Martin was no better. One of a handful of Danes who'd found their place among that elite group of Danish colonists who governed Greenland until very recently, Kirstin and Martin had lived there for years, just like Albert. Kirstin had seen her life go by in one small village after the next and had grown fat there, too, teaching Danish to the native children and raising her own three children.

In a brave show of sisterly kindness, Kirstin decided to forget Martin and show Pebble some pictures of herself when she'd first moved to Greenland. (Did she sense Pebble's dismay?) She'd been a slim reed of a woman then and Pebble marveled at the pictures. To think this was the same person.

"When was this one taken?" Pebble had asked politely about a particularly beautiful picture of Kirstin with her eyes shining brightly against a very blue sky.

"Oh, that was about 25 years ago, just before I got pregnant with Justin." Pebble took out her glasses; she wanted a closer look at Kirstin's face. Had the cold and loneliness driven Kirstin straight to the refrigerator? Or was it Martin's drinking? Pebble's experienced eye told her Kirstin wasn't a day older than she was.

"Where are your children now?" Pebble asked, starting to like Kirstin despite her ordinary face.

"All three go to school in Copenhagen. My daughter is studying to be a nurse and both my sons go to engineering school."

"Isn't it hard being so far from them?" Pebble wondered how Kirstin did it.

"Well, Martin would never move back to Denmark, and the children couldn't continue their education here. There are no opportunities…" Suddenly there was emotion in her thin voice and tears welled up in her faded eyes. "What kind of a life could they have up here anyway?"

"Come over here." It was Martin. Pebble and Kirstin hadn't noticed that he'd walked over to where they stood talking. He took hold of Pebble's arm and pulled her across the room towards the couch where he'd been sitting with Albert. "Don't go boring our guests with your tiresome life, Kirstin…" He didn't even look at his wife.

Pebble winced; he must have overheard their conversation. She disliked Martin intensely. Steen Moeller, another fellow Pebble suspected she might like about as much as she liked Martin, moved up on the other side of Pebble as they made their way towards the couch where Albert still sat.

"Didn't we meet at the Officer's Club in Søndre Strømfjord last week?"

Pebble didn't remember his face, but knew this meant trouble. Had he seen her leave the club with Franz?

Pebble stared into his drunken face, "You're probably

thinking of someone else..." she lied. She was sure Albert was listening. She caught sight of him out of the corner of her eye, pouring more beer into his half-empty glass. Annika, a young Eskimo woman, slid down into the sofa next to Albert. Maybe she sensed trouble. Annika was Steen Moeller's wife, but Pebble knew by the way she cozied up to Albert, that marriage meant nothing at the moment. Albert had told Pebble about the wild partying that went on all over Greenland – Eskimo women drank as much as the men, and went to bed with whoever they wanted – whenever they felt like it – whether they were married or not.

Pebble moved past Steen and sat down on the other side of Albert. It was a large couch, big enough for all kinds of tribal combinations.

"Do you know him?" Albert's voice might be slurred, but he still could hold her with his eyes. Pebble realized Albert was holding Annika's hand. She felt hot all over.

"I'm not sure," Pebble replied, her voice flat with danger.

Annika chimed in, "Steen told me as soon as you walked in tonight that he'd seen you in Søndre Strømfjord with Franz Helgegaard."

"You were with Franz?" There was surprise in Albert's slow question. He'd almost thought for a moment, but no.

"Yeah, I sat next to him on the plane from Copenhagen. We were delayed you know."

"Why didn't you tell me?" Albert was still holding Annika's hand. Annika, her work done, leaned back in the worn comfortable couch. She was young and beautiful with long black hair. Handmade bone earrings hung from her delicate ears. She was absolutely ravishing; wild, sexy, everything Pebble had always wanted to be but never would become.

Pebble didn't want to stare at Annika, but felt herself drawn, against her will, into those jet-black eyes. Annika radiated an intense animal-like energy that Pebble had never encountered before. Pebble was quite sure Annika could dominate any man, or situation for that matter, with that energy. Pebble still felt much too warm. Primitive spirits danced around her.

You can do whatever you want with me, Pebble thought. *I am captive on your wild island – you make the rules.*

Pebble drank deeply from her beer mug. She really didn't care. She'd come too far to love a man she didn't know how to love and now he was going to find out she'd been sleeping with somebody else on the way up. He'd never understand. Steen pushed his way towards them.

"Why are you holding hands with my wife," his voice cut through their conversation. Albert, who was deep in thought, contemplating Pebble and Franz, looked up in surprise. Pebble was glad Steen was there. Maybe the primitive spirits dancing all around her would go away. If not she'd fall into the well and die happily.

Martin, who felt the spirit dance, too, moved forward, "Albert's an old friend of Annika's, you know that, Steen." Obviously Martin wasn't as drunk as he appeared. Pebble marveled at his control. He reached out and without stumbling, took Annika's other hand. Oh how womanly and slim that hand was. Then he continued, "And she's a damn good friend of mine, too. Now why don't we all drink to that?"

The tension hung in the air a moment longer and then vanished. Albert, who seemed to have forgotten Franz, was positively jolly. Without standing up (Pebble wondered if he could) and without letting go of Annika's hand, he called the men standing across the room, "Hey, Bear, Carsten, Vic, come over here and bring your women, too. Martin's going to drink to Annika." The motley crew of friends didn't care if Albert's voice was slurred or not, but Pebble did.

They crowded around and Pebble had the feeling that every man in the room (including Albert) knew Annika, and knew her well. They were like one big family (these crazy white men and their wild Eskimo women), and for one very short moment, Pebble, who knew she didn't belong, envied them.

Chapter 7

Later that night, it must have been almost 4 a.m., Pebble lost control. Every once in a while, when Albert seemed to snap out of his drunkenness (amazing how drunks can do that, seeming to surface for air for a moment before they sink back into oblivion again) he would hint at the Franz thing, but that wasn't what triggered Pebble's outburst. Pebble was quite sure that no matter how much Albert hinted nor how many insinuations Annika made – and the woman certainly did try hard to make trouble – that the Franz thing would just have to wait until they were alone. Albert might be drunk, but he wasn't dumb. Still, Annika's behavior made Pebble wonder if Annika had a thing for Albert. It wasn't difficult to imagine them together, bodies passionately entwined. Pebble envied Annika's supple youth. She could picture Annika, her slender body flung against Albert's muscular ruggedness, her black Eskimo hair surrounding them both. Picturing Annika with Albert didn't do much to improve Pebble's state of mind. Nor did worrying about Albert's reaction when he found out about Franz (really found out that is) – and he was bound to – sooner or later.

No, none of that triggered Pebble's outburst. When it finally happened, it was because Albert was acting like a jerk. Throughout the course of the night, Pebble found his drunkenness increasingly irritating, but she did her best to tolerate it. She knew she'd lost contact with him completely – she might as well not have known the man at all. Still she managed to keep a tight lid on the cauldron of feelings boiling inside her, not an easy thing for Pebble to do. She just wasn't one of those real controlled people. (She might look good at business meetings, but this was something else!) All night long she kept telling herself to just go with it. The whole thing would soon be over. The party, her trip to Greenland, everything. Even the fantastic lovemaking would soon vanish down that insatiable tunnel called Time. As long as her head was in this "philosophical" mode, it wasn't that hard to keep her mouth shut and just let it all pass. But there was another, a not-so-philosophical part of her that also struggled to be heard. It was the part of her that wanted a decent life *now* – that part of her that felt she had a right to be treated with respect *now*. Which was why the tiniest dent in her very fragile armor probably allowed this long-suppressed craving to come gushing forth – even if she was trapped in a snowstorm at the end of the world. Respect – yes that's what she wanted! And no man had ever given her that. She was always the subordinate; that was the story of her life, her career, even in these heady times of equal opportunities for women. It just hadn't seemed to have filtered down to "her" house or "her" husband or "her" sons. She'd always been the "caretaker" – the one who'd put her needs, her desires aside, for the common good. Obviously it was time for Pebble to graduate, even if she didn't know she was fast approaching graduation.

Any fool could see there had to be grief down the road, even if Pebble, ever the optimist, tried hard not to look. And there was another thing which added to this oppressive atmosphere: It's not much fun sitting around almost sober with a bunch of drunks on an icecap when you're all alone and definitely past your 40th birthday.

It made Pebble feel like an outsider. An outsider to her life, to the world, to everything. It was scary. All these people drinking themselves to oblivion as fast and furiously as they could; and she couldn't join. She was incapable of letting go that much. So instead she started feeling panicky again. It just kind of crept up on her while she was sitting there saying something completely senseless to someone who was too drunk to understand anyway. That was when her heart started missing a beat or two. She tried not to notice, but it happened again and again, even if she changed partners or topics. Pebble started to sweat anxiously.

She became strangely aware of herself and her body. Her breathing was shallow and irregular. *God I'm so nervous I could die. I wish I could get out of here.* It was almost impossible to feel calm and accept that there was no way out. *Why can't I just drink myself to oblivion like everyone else? Why do I have to be the only one who's concerned about the fate of the world just now? Why can't I be off-duty, too, just for a little while?* It would have made Pebble's life so much easier if she could have. But she couldn't. The woman wasn't put together like that, she was too New York and too smart for that. She knew she'd made a wrong turn. That was the problem. And high-achievers have a hard time forgiving themselves. It feels like the end of the world. *Look at me! Look at my life! What have I done?* Especially when you make a serious wrong turn and it takes you all the way to the North Pole. Pebble wanted out. Being stuck in Holsteinsborg was no fun. Pebble was having a full-blown anxiety attack. *I might get hysterical.* Pebble didn't like herself. *I might lose control!* Pebble asked for a refill. *Why do I have to feel like this?* Anxiety attacks are no fun. *Why can't someone help me?* She hated Albert for being so occupied with himself. *God, men are such shits.* Pebble wanted a man who'd take care of her. That's what she'd wanted from the very beginning. He should respect her and take care of her. That was it. Pebble was no different from any other woman. But no such man seemed to exist. All the men Pebble knew had a hard enough time taking care of themselves. It was a stupid dream anyway. *Damn!*

The memory of that incredible tingling sensation that swept through her body when her helicopter first landed in Holsteinsborg a week earlier was long gone. All her nervous energy was focused on feeling bad. Pebble hated everything about Albert and Greenland. She was tense as a zombie.

"Albert," Pebble turned towards Albert and said in her sweetest voice, "let's go." She wanted desperately to make her problems known.

They were sitting on the couch. The ashtrays on the stained

mahogany table were piled high with cigarette butts. Empty and half-full glasses were scattered everywhere. Most of the people had already left. At least Steen and Annika had, much to Pebble's great relief. Pebble was sure Annika had taken the spirit dancers with her.

When Pebble asked Albert to leave, he looked up in surprise, as if Pebble had rudely interrupted his conversation. He'd forgotten all about her and the time and was in the middle of another immensely profound discussion with Martin. Obviously Pebble Beach, nice as she was in bed and nice as she was to have around, had no sense of timing. Anybody in their right mind could see that Albert wasn't ready to leave.

Kirstin and Pebble exchanged looks. Kirstin wanted them to clear out, too, but she didn't dare say anything. She'd been walking around on eggshells for the last couple of hours, trying to avoid Martin's drunken wrath.

"Albert," Pebble's voice was calm, "would you please give me the keys to your house so I can go home. I'm really tired." If respect wasn't forthcoming, Pebble decided to give herself some. It finally dawned on her that she was a grown-up woman and she could go home by herself if she wanted to.

It was no big deal – until Albert refused to give Pebble the keys to his house.

"How will I get in, if you have the keys?" he replied with all the logic of a drunk. What was the woman thinking?

Pebble was so surprised she didn't know what to make of it. How could he refuse to give her the keys? It wasn't like she was asking him to do her a big favor. No sacrifice whatsoever was involved and besides, Albert was supposed to be her great love. As far as she'd gotten in the scenario anyway. What was going on?

"You inconsiderate bastard..." The words just flew out. She knew she wasn't supposed to say that, but she didn't care. She'd crossed over a bridge. Martin and Kirstin watched Pebble and

Albert with ghoulish curiosity. These two, the supposed-to-be-madly-in-love lovers, were the talk of the town. Pebble had flown all the way from Copenhagen to be with this hunk. The looks on their faces said it all. Pebble registered every nuance and wondered why Martin and Kirstin were suspended in mid-air with their mouths wide open. She wasn't sure if it was shock or satisfaction she read on their faces.

"I came all the way to Greenland to be with you…" Albert sat as if turned to stone. "You useless bum!"

It was as if she'd slapped him.

The look on his face stunned her. It said, "I really do love you, in my own way." She didn't want to hurt him, even if he'd hurt her. *Men are strange,* she thought, knowing that she'd never forget him even if they had no future.

He tried desperately to regroup, but the liquor slowed him down. It was pitiful to watch. Pebble knew he didn't want his friends to see him like that. "You'll have to go to the Seaman's Home," he said finally, groping after his dignity. It appeared to demand an enormous effort to press the words out of his mouth. His life had changed. It was almost as if he'd said, "Where's my Pebble Beach?" But he of course he didn't.

Pebble tried not to notice his loss. She focused on the slur in his voice. It was worse than ever. *How can two people like us possibly love each other?* But she knew she loved him, hopelessly, desperately. The Seaman's Home was the only place in Holsteinsborg that was almost a hotel.

Pebble wanted to scream, cry, pull her hair, let all her fear and disappointment come out – for once in her life. She wanted to mourn for everything that she'd never have. But she couldn't. People don't do things like that in public. Instead, one large tear popped out of the corner of her left eye. It was for "impossible love". For Pebble and Albert's. But Albert was too drunk to notice.

She wanted to kneel down besides him and touch his face

tenderly and make all the bad things go away, but instead she stomped out of the room.

She found herself sitting on top of Kirstin's washing machine which was stuffed into the long entrance foyer of the house. Coats lined the walls, and ski jackets, skis, hats, gloves and boots. It was a cluttered, gloomy, drafty place. Pebble sat on top of the washing machine and cried. Not a lot, but some. Because not being a stranger to life, she basically knew that this was the way things were. It is hard to get what you want for more than a minute or two anyway. If you did, you were very lucky indeed. And as she figured it, she'd somehow gotten her share. So she swung her legs back and forth to keep herself warm. Surprisingly enough she felt quite content, her anxiety had passed now that the dream was over. Once or twice, her foot hit the door of the washing machine, by mistake, and when it did, she muttered, almost happily, "Damn," to nobody in particular.

Pebble was still cold so she put on her thermal overalls. She considered leaving and probably would have if it hadn't been 30 degrees below zero outside. She'd really had enough. And it was comforting to know she'd passed her limit. She felt comfortable with that. But she couldn't just go. You just don't go wandering around Greenland in the middle of the night in the dead of winter. There weren't any cafes down the street where you could drink black coffee and nurse your wounds. And besides, Greenland wasn't exactly a hot spot for your average big city woman. So Pebble just sat and let Time pass, which was really quite okay.

All her madness fizzled out. She felt quiet inside. She knew if Albert had had any idea of how bad she was feeling in there he probably would have said to her, "What's the big deal, sweetheart? You've been alone all your life anyway." But he didn't – and that was the rotten part – he didn't know how bad she felt because he was just too damn drunk to notice.

Love is just too depressing, Pebble was dissecting something that was over. Done. That was when Albert turned up in the entrée turned laundry room looking absolutely divine.

Why does he have to look so good? Pebble thought he could have been in a Calvin Klein ad for "Obsession" – that was how good he looked to her. So you see it was difficult and complicated, too. Because Pebble had passed that dangerous age of 40 or so, which didn't make it any easier. And Albert, besides being an alcoholic, was really a kind man. And he loved Pebble, too, in his own way, behind all the he-man bravado. And Pebble was more than just single; she was "newly divorced". She wasn't used to being on her own and she didn't like it. Her heart ached for a man – a real man, to touch and love and care for. Her body cried out in the cruelest most pitiful way. *Oh Lord, please give me someone to love – someone kind, someone gorgeous, someone rich and considerate – someone wonderful and handsome and thoughtful.* And you see it was so bad, this yearning, this aching that Pebble couldn't help feeling, well, if he (that thoughtful, kind, loving man) wasn't around, well at least Albert was. Albert was real love, of a sort. And he had this smile, this devilish, macho, he-man smile that women couldn't resist. Pebble had no illusions anymore; she knew she wasn't the only woman who'd fallen hard for him. He had this wonderful, slightly used body, that was hard and muscular and which worked wonders on her aching loneliness, even if his voice was slurred and he treated her badly. Somehow, the lack of respect changed nothing. Maybe it was because she was that needy. Or maybe it was his lovemaking. Because no matter how drunk he was, Albert could make love. It was like the wind on a day so hot and stagnant that you were begging for mercy. He revived her, made her come alive, why else would she have flown halfway across the world to be in the arms of a man she hardly knew. So you see it wasn't easy to be mad. Because in fact, she'd asked for it. Albert hadn't sold her a bill of goods. She was the one who'd just shed a tear or two for impossible love. She was the one who was stuck as close to the North Pole as any reasonable human being could possibly want to be – without any chance of a dashing captain from Air Greenland knocking on the door and asking her if she'd like to leave immediately – yes *immediately* – yes right this very minute for Copenhagen... Which was why, dear reader, it wasn't long before Pebble found herself out on the icy street, laughing with Albert.

"Ma chérie." He had a way with those French words and the cold air seemed to revive him. He was able to focus his full power on her, in spite of the liquor. She was amazed. He said things she'd never thought she'd hear him say.

"Since you came into my life," she felt his muscular arm right through his pilot jacket, "how can I tell you... I feel like I got a second chance..."

Pebble looked into the sadness of his very brown eyes.

"If it's true about Franz," he almost stumbled under the weight of his words, "I know I will never love another woman again." He paused dramatically, a true Frenchman, arms outstretched in middle of the snow-covered street. "You will be the last woman I ever love."

Bullshit, she thought as she drowned in his eyes. She'd already forgotten that she'd just called him an inconsiderate bastard. *Can you imagine Albert never touching another woman?* Pebble knew it would never happen. He was too...well...too sensual, even if he was a loner. But it was nice to toy with the idea for a moment, even if his body, the pain in his eyes, cried out for a woman. Pebble knew Albert would always need somebody to take care of him and there were plenty of suckers around. She knew she'd been had and loved every minute of it.

"Albert," she pressed her slim body towards his and put one gloved hand against his chest as they walked into the wind, "there will never be anybody but you...you must know that..."

What the fuck, she thought, *if he can tell me a pack of lies, so can I.*

It was only later, when she'd shut the bathroom door back at Albert's house that she had time to review the whole sordid evening. The motley crew of people, the booze. She was thankful none of her friends knew what she'd done. She would give them some bullshit story about what a great guy Albert was and how wonderful it had all been. *God it's crazy to be a woman in her 40s trying to grow up and stay young at the same time.*

She removed as much of her mascara as she could and splashed cold water quickly on her face. She was in a hurry. Albert was waiting for her in the bedroom. He continued to say delicious, wonderful things to her all the freezing way home. Nothing made any sense. She knew she hated him for humiliating her with all his ignorant, inconsiderate boozing and that she loved him for making her feel alive again... But who can find happiness with an alcoholic no matter how alive he makes you feel? *I'm too tired to sort it all out, too tired, too drunk, too confused, too horny.* What she really wanted was to have Albert fuck her brains out. He could do it, she knew. He'd done it before. Brought her as close to heaven as she'd ever been... He could do it again, just one more time, she was sure, even if things had changed, even if real life had entered the picture... *We've crossed a bridge...I know...and we'll never be able to go back.* The spirits hadn't left her after all.

She flushed the toilet and ran naked across the hall to the bedroom where she found him, stretched out on the bed, fully clothed and sound asleep.

* * *

Did anything else happen during Pebble Beach's stay in Greenland? Well, nothing much except on the way back to Copenhagen, on the airplane, Pebble Beach happened to sit next to this gorgeous 24-year-old and she immediately decided that she was going to have an affair with him.

He was, after all, young. And she was, after all, certainly not getting any younger.

Chapter 8

Pebble paced the blue-carpeted floor of Peter Cato's black and grey high-tech office. His clean, minimalist furniture glowed sinisterly in the dim Copenhagen afternoon sunlight. Pebble couldn't believe what was happening.

While she'd been gone, Einar Bro's people had launched YourLift, a product almost identical to WonderLift, precisely thirteen days before Fem-Ads' scheduled launch. It was a catastrophic blow to Fem-Ads. YourLift was selling phenomenally well. The new product had effectively wiped WonderLift right off the map. They wouldn't get a second chance. God only knew the consequences for Fem-Ads, maybe they would fold. All their resources had gone into launching WonderLift.

"Jennifer saw you at the Hotel D'Angleterre with Einar right after our WonderLift strategy meeting, Pebble."

Pebble was in shock, trying to regroup.

"She says…you were so intoxicated you didn't even notice her when she passed your table. She said you were holding Einar's hand."

Jennifer was Peter's secretary.

"I know what you're thinking, Peter – but it wasn't me. I didn't tell him about WonderLift. You've got to believe me."

"Why should I, Pebble?" Peter Cato, the very cool Dane, was livid. Danes seldom lose control, but Peter was very close. Pebble knew he'd staked his private fortune on Fem-Ads. "You turned in your fabulous campaign only a week later. God, Pebble…you're so talented…how could you?"

"It's not true…" her voice sounded lame. She was stunned. She hadn't noticed the YourLift ads everywhere, she'd just returned from Greenland late the previous night. All she did was hop into a cab at the airport and go straight home and to bed. She'd been delayed five awful days because of the storms that raged along the West Coast of Greenland.

"I bet he offered you a job, didn't he?" Pebble wondered how Peter knew. "A position as his own private assistant… "

Pebble didn't reply. She couldn't lie.

"Pebble, you're dead in this town. Dead!" The Dane weighed his words carefully. "Nobody's going to touch you with a ten-foot pole."

"But, Peter, I swear to you it wasn't me. Honest." More than anything else, Pebble wanted to cry. No sooner had she extradited herself from one mess, than she found herself in another. But she couldn't cry. First of all it wouldn't help, and second of all she was a business woman. Business women in Pebble's world wore tailored men's jackets and didn't cry. "He offered me a job and asked me, I admit it, he did, Peter…" Pebble's voice sounded shaky, but she forced herself to continue. "…and I was shocked when he did – shocked – it was so…unethical…but I swear to God, I didn't tell him."

"Am I really supposed to believe that?" Peter slung the words at her. "You were drunk. You're nothing but a dumb broad, like all the rest of them. Maybe you write like a whiz-kid, but Pebble you're as dumb as the rest of them." He didn't know how to insult her. "Maybe you don't even want to believe you told him…or can't remember. God, how should I know? You just said he offered you a job…" Peter's voice trailed off. Pebble was quite sure that if this had been a marital dispute, he would have hit her. He walked over to the window and stood gazing out at the dark lake below. A cold February wind rattled the windows ever so slightly as it blew over Copenhagen.

Pebble gazed at his back. Nobody would ever believe her – that much was obvious. It would be her word against Peter's. She could just as well kiss her career goodbye. Peter was a well-respected member of the Danish ad world; Pebble was a new kid on the block. A woman. A foreigner. A whippersnapper. She carried no weight. She was finished.

Pebble could tell from watching Peter's back that he'd regained control.

"Get out of my office, Pebble, right now." He said it very slowly, without even turning around.

* * *

Maybe I really did tell him. Pebble was walking from Peter's office overlooking one of the Copenhagen lakes towards her apartment on Gothersgade. She moved her body jerkily, as if she was wounded. The grey February day chilled her to the bone. Suddenly Pebble wasn't so sure of herself. *Maybe I really did.* It was a shocking thought, but not impossible. She'd seen Albert drink himself to the point where the next day he couldn't remember a thing he'd said or done. She reminded herself that she had wanted to get that drunk that night at the Hotel D'Angleterre. Maybe she did. She reviewed the scene at the hotel again and remembered how much she hated everything about that night. *Einar, you slimy bastard, I'd like to wring your neck.* Pebble had a tendency to become surprisingly uncooperative (for such a nice person) when people put pressure on her to do things she considered unethical. She wasn't a product of her time for nothing. *Albert always seems perfectly wide awake and sane when he drinks. He can walk and talk and make love and do just about every-thing else – he's just drunk. Maybe I'm as bad as he is and just don't know it. Maybe I told Einar everything he wanted to know and can't remember a thing I said or did.*

It just didn't hold water. *I'm not like Albert.* But it was hard to throw off the thought. It would explain everything. Why else would Peter accuse her? *Whenever I ask Albert about something he said or did when he was drunk, he can't remember the next day. It's a total blank. The man doesn't remember a thing.* The wind whipped through Pebble's hair as she followed Vester Søgade along the lake towards H.C.Andersens Boulevard. *I ought to take a cab and go home*. But she didn't. She kept walking into the freezing wind. February's not your best month in Copenhagen. It's dark and rainy and if you're depressed, it will help you stay that way. *Maybe I'm not any better than Albert. Maybe I told Einar and now I'm just blotting it out. That's what Peter implied, but damn – I just don't remember! God, if only I knew for sure!* The uncertainty tore at Pebble's insides. Just the thought revolted her. *No it wasn't me. I'd never do anything that insane. I'm sure I didn't do it. I'm sure it wasn't me...* But Pebble wasn't sure. How could she be? Especially after what she'd just went through with Albert. The past 18 days with Albert had been a real eye-opener. They put things in another perspective. It was frightening.

Pebble didn't realize people got like that. It's hard to believe if you haven't experienced it yourself. And although Albert was a person she thought she loved – a person who loved her – still she couldn't trust him when he drank. He might betray her, do something awful, and then not remember a thing. *If he could go around and do something and not be accountable for it, why couldn't I? God, booze should be outlawed. Done away with... I had no idea booze could do that to you...* Pebble's recent encounters had unnerved her. No one out there was protecting her anymore. *If I didn't tell Einar, who did?* The uncertainty of her situation struck her like a blow in the stomach. Up until now being newly divorced was a challenge. Fun. But if nobody in town would give her work what would she do? Copenhagen was a very small town. Very tight. Once people bad-mouthed you, you were finished. You couldn't just pull up stakes and move because there was nowhere to move to. The country was too small. *Denmark, the fairy tale country!*

Pebble felt lost. *What am I doing here anyway? With two kids? I'll never really belong!* Pebble wished she wasn't alone. Men are awful nice to have around when the shit hits the fan. *I'm old enough to know better. I should have watched out. I should have guessed. Why am I so naive? I might not be the only person in the world that Einar knows – but I was perfect for this...* But even as Pebble talked to herself, trying desperately to pull herself out of the black hole she'd fallen into, she knew nobody would offer her a job again. Come tomorrow, the word would be out. Peter Cato was a heavyweight, no doubt about it. He had a track record. Pebble didn't. Why should anybody believe Pebble? *Now I'll have to take the job Einar offered me. How else will I feed my kids? Einar will even be able to get me cheap.* Pebble laughed heartily at the thought. *Bastard.* But then another, far more chilling thought followed. *That is if Einar still wants me. Maybe he only offered me that job to get me to talk. Maybe...* The whole sordid mess – the way he tried to manipulate her and play upon her vulnerabilities, weighed heavily on her soul. *My phone will never ring again. I'll be poorer than a church mouse.*

Peter paid me $50,000 for the WonderLift campaign – but how long will that last? After taxes I've only got about half left anyway. Denmark isn't the greatest place in the world to make money. After taxes, most people can go home and lick their wounds. Pebble, who'd been doing nicely, paid almost half of her income in tax. She calculated her expenses. The money wouldn't last long. Chills ran up and down Pebble's spine. She saw herself on welfare, shabby and ragged, ashamed to face her friends. Jon and Adam would never buy clothes at G-Star again. It would be just as Slim had predicted – she'd pay for having the gall to leave him.

When Pebble finally reached her apartment, it was raining miserably. A cold, bone-chilling fog was rolling in over the damp, sleepy winter city. Her light, airy walkup – the one Molly had called "a treasure" on her last visit – was dark and empty. The light of her life (both of them) was gone. She wandered disconcertedly around her empty nest and ended up throwing herself carelessly into a chair in her tiny office. Her desk was still piled high with the messages that had accumulated while she was away. Now they seemed futile. None of the people who called would want her tomorrow. *If only I had known, I could have thrown myself into a snowdrift.*

She arrived home from Greenland so late the night before – in a state of almost manic elation (*I survived! I escaped!*) – that after talking with Jon and Adam for a long time, she went straight to bed. She hadn't even looked at her desk. Adam and Jon had told her that Peter Cato had called "dozens of times" but it didn't register. Both boys kept saying she had to get in touch with him immediately. And Pebble kept replying, "Okay, okay, alright already! I can't call the man in the middle of the night, can I?" The urgency of the matter didn't register. It didn't sink in. She didn't realize they were telling her something "important." That this was hot news. She should have noticed, picked up something, especially since they kept insisting. Usually Jon and Adam weren't that good at delivering messages. But it all passed over her head. She was too elated to notice. She was home! Invincible! Back! That was all she could see. She was back with her kids. Back to her nest. She sensed no danger.

Next morning she called Peter early, but only spoke to Jennifer who gave no clues. So Pebble's antennas weren't out when she walked into the den of the lion. She was as unprepared as a lamb on her way to slaughter. There was even a smile on her face. Pebble rehashed the scene in Peter's office. *Not that being prepared would have helped.* How could she have defended herself? Somehow Einar had gotten the word. Jennifer had seen her at the Hotel D'Angleterre holding hands with Einar right after the WonderLift meeting. The evidence, though circumstantial, was damning.

Pebble reached for the phone. *That bastard Einar!* She was going to give him a piece of her mind. She started dialing his number, but slammed down the receiver halfway through. *Damn! I'm going to need that job.* She felt the angry sweat clinging to her body. Pebble had forgotten to take off her coat. She didn't remove it, but toyed with her keys in the gloom instead. She still hadn't turned on the light.

The phone rang and startled her.

"Hello." She picked it up automatically.

"Hi Pebble," she recognized his voice immediately.

"Hi," she was stunned. *This is all I need.*

"You don't sound too great," he knew her that well.

"Well maybe I'm not."

Damn, she thought, *I don't owe him any explanations.* They were divorced now.

There was an awkward silence. She didn't ask him how he was. *Fuck him.*

"Aren't you going to ask me when I got back in town?" He sounded cheerful. She hadn't seen or heard from him in months. Jon and Adam got letters from him, so she knew he was working somewhere in northern Norway.

"When did you get back?" she didn't sound convincing. She kept thinking, *This is all I need. Why did he have to come back now? He'll love it when he hears what's happened.*

"I'd like to come over and see the boys."

"Well," she hesitated; she didn't want to see him, "why don't you arrange something with them. They're not home right now."

"Really? Where are they?"

She didn't know and didn't like the way he asked. He'd been out of their life for months, what right did he have? *God I hate him.* Memories of their marriage came flooding back. He was a jerk. Pebble remembered the euphoria she felt when the divorce came through. Later she discovered that ex-husbands just don't disappear, they hang around to haunt you. *No matter what I do, it'll never be good enough.*

"Look, Slim, I'll have them call you when they get home."

When they'd hung up, she felt even worse. *Albert's an alcoholic, my career's over, and Slim's back. So what else can go wrong?*

* * *

Pebble woke up the next morning (it was Saturday) with the worst cold she'd had in years. *It must be psychosomatic.* She could hardly open her eyes. Her nose had turned bright red from blowing it all night and her head weighed a ton. *Retribution,* she thought. *I guess I was just having too much fun.* Up until her recent setbacks, Pebble had felt this wonderful sense of elation, like a runaway slave who'd just crossed the Mason-Dixon Line. She'd been on a high, discovering herself, experiencing one long burst of creative energy. She was even making money! But now that the roof had fallen in, Pebble was all snot.

She dragged herself out of bed and looked at herself in the hallway mirror. *This is worse than a hangover.* She couldn't believe she was looking at the woman she thought she liked.

Jon and Adam comforted her with more news.

"Dad's coming over." They'd talked to him after Pebble had gone to bed early. It was only seven when she went to bed, but Jon and Adam knew their mom was like that at times. "Strange" was how they would have put it. They figured she was just tired from her great adventure to the icecap. She hadn't told them much about it yet – but she'd hinted at it with remarks about helicopters and skiing and dog sleds. Just enough to get their imaginations working. (She had to keep up her image.) She hadn't told them about Fem-Ads either. She'd just packed up her gear and gone off to her room. She'd left them a big note on the kitchen table: "JON & ADAM, I LOVE YOU. AM DEAD TIRED. SEE YOU IN THE MORNING. THEN WE'LL TALK. MOM."

When they saw her standing in the hallway in her long flannel nightgown looking at herself in the mirror they guided her carefully back to bed. Sometimes sons are that nice.

"We've made breakfast, Mom. Go back to bed and we'll bring it to you." Adam opened her curtains a little. The sun shone weakly in through her window. It was still foggy. The huge plant by the window, the one she loved, kept growing. Pebble always marveled when she watched this wonderful piece of tropical greenery in her bedroom. *How can it survive?* Pebble was convinced this plant was a special miracle, growing solely to give her courage, that's how little light there is in Copenhagen during the winter.

Her kids brought in a tray with toast and a hard-boiled egg and wonderful coffee. She was moved to tears.

They didn't understand.

"How sweet," was all she could mutter between sobs.

"Aren't you hungry, Mom?" Adam was always practical. He didn't like wearing your emotions on your sleeve.

"We talked to Dad last night, Mom, after you went to bed."

"I know," Pebble dried her eyes, "he called while you guys were out."

"We invited him over." Often, Jon didn't think about consequences, but his heart was good. Looking at his mom, he realized it might be awkward.

"I didn't know you had a cold, I figured you'd be out somewhere."

Adam looked at Pebble, "You don't want to see him, do you?"

"Not especially," she replied.

"We can call him and meet him somewhere."

It was hard for the boys to accept that their father and mother weren't friends.

It was hard for Pebble to accept, too.

"Why can't everybody just be friends?" Jon always echoed Pebble's thoughts. He was thin and sensitive. Already girls (women) flocked to him, ready to lay down their lives (and bodies) to be near him.

"Oh my head," Pebble moaned. She decided to tell them about Fem-Ads. "I've got something to tell you."

She sounded so serious, she caught their attention. Usually their mother was pretty happy-go-lucky. "Do you remember the WonderLift campaign I was working on before I went to Greenland?"

"How could we forget – you were working on it day and night." Adam always remembered situations with a cool, clinical accuracy. He was 14 and deep. Pebble sometimes wondered where he got it from. He picked his friends carefully.

"Well, while I was away, the biggest advertising agency in Copenhagen – the Republic Group – you know Einar Bro – well he's the vice-president… Well, they launched another product – one that's very similar to WonderLift called YourLift – 13 days before we were scheduled to launch WonderLift." Suddenly she started crying again.

"What is it, Mom?"

They both felt the seriousness of her tears.

"Peter Cato, he's the director of Fem-Ads, thinks I told Einar the WonderLift launch date. It was top secret."

Jon took her hand.

"Peter says I'll never work again in this town."

"What makes him think you did it?" Adam asked.

"His secretary, Jennifer saw me holding hands with Einar at the Hotel D'Angleterre the night after the Fem-Ads meeting. I was pretty drunk, too."

"You were holding hands with that creep?" Adam was revolted. Adam had met Einar the night he visited when Molly was there.

"Well, he took my hand and I didn't know what to do."

"Oh come on, Mom, you could have pulled your hand away."

"Yes," Pebble replied carefully, "I could have, but it wasn't quite that easy. You see Einar has just offered me this great job."

"You're not supposed to hold hands with the men you work for," Adam shot back.

"But the worst part of it is – he really did ask when the WonderLift launch date was. But I didn't tell him, I swear I didn't." Pebble started sobbing hysterically and blowing her fiery red nose. "Peter swears he's going to tell everyone and I'll never get another job after this – not in advertising anyway."

"Oh come on, Mom, it can't be that bad." Jon patted her on the back. He always took the philosophical view.

"What are we going to do? And Slim's coming this afternoon." Pebble kept on sobbing.

"I'll go and call him." Adam left the room.

"I wish I could just disappear," Pebble said when she stopped sobbing.

Adam returned, "Sorry Mom, all I got was his voice mail." That meant he would turn up all too soon. Pebble turned over in bed and moaned. All she wanted to do was hide under her warm down comforter.

"I think you ought to meet him when he comes," Adam said as if reading her thoughts. "He is our father." Pebble could see it was important to Adam.

"Okay, I'll try." She'd do anything for her kids. "Just let me sleep for a while."

* * *

After her boys left her room, taking the breakfast crumbs with them, Pebble's mind went wild. She imagined her body working feverishly to get her out of this unpleasant fix. Pebble hated confrontations and remembered all the unpleasant scenes she'd had with Slim before their divorce. He'd holler and she'd tremble. It was enough to make her temperature rise, even now. *Maybe my temperature will rise and I'll get delirious...maybe I'll have more and more difficulty breathing...maybe I'll feel so weak and dizzy that I can't navigate my way to the bathroom.* She pictured herself getting out of bed in her feverish state, and stumbling towards the bathroom. *I'll be so groggy that I can't see straight. The walls will wobble and everything will look strange. I'll feel so dizzy that I'll stumble and walk right into the bathroom door by mistake and knock myself out. Jon and Adam will hear this awful bang and come running down the hall and find me unconscious on the floor. They'll be desperately afraid and call an ambulance and rush me to the hospital immediately. After conferring in hushed voices, the doctors will put me in the intensive care unit and insist that I remain there in absolute quiet for at least two to three weeks.* It was a wonderful thought.

Pebble almost smiled. *No angry ex-husbands, no accusing ex-employers, nor any semi-sober boyfriends would be allowed in to disturb me.* Whoever wanted to pour venom on Pebble's head would have to wait. She could just see Peter, Albert and Slim pacing furiously up and down the hospital hallway. The doctors wouldn't tolerate their agitation. *Ms Beach is in critical condition, gentlemen, so we must ask you to leave at once…at once!* She'd have time to recuperate, rest, get her act back together. And by the time she was as fresh as a daisy, they'd all be gone, especially Slim. He'd be "very gone". Of all the people she knew, Slim was the one with the least patience. He'd never wait two weeks to see her. (She remembered how he'd blow his top if a kid needed a diaper change when everyone was finally dressed for their Sunday walk.) Waiting for two weeks for Pebble to get out of intensive care – no way! The man would be so fed up that he'd stomp out of the hospital and take off on another escapade and not return for at least another 10 to 15 years. The thought was positively invigorating.

Adam knocked on her door.

"Yes, dear?"

He opened it just a crack. "Don't you want to get up and take a shower before Dad comes?" He didn't want Slim to see Pebble looking so wretched.

"You're right. Did you try to call him again?" She clung to false hope.

"Yeah, but he didn't answer. He's supposed to be here at two."

Five minutes before Slim's expected arrival, they were all sitting in the living room, waiting. Pebble had done her best to fix herself up. Behind her make-up, she was miserable. Jon, seeing Pebble's desperate plight suggested she go for a walk.

"You can always come back after he's been here a few minutes."

But Adam objected adamantly. "It wouldn't be right and besides, you'll look like a coward." Adam had a ninth grader's clear-cut ideas of right and wrong.

Pebble, who remained rooted to the couch, suddenly had a brilliant idea. *I'll write a book and call it "Ten Easy Ways to Meet Your Ex and Survive!"* The idea exploded in Pebble's head. It had to be a bestseller; the idea was so hot, Pebble forgot she was feverish and that her make-up just barely covered her red nose. *Just think of the market. I'll be writing for half the adult population of the Western world.* The thought was overwhelming. Pebble had never written a book in her life. She was a copywriter, period. She might write brilliantly, but she wrote what other people told her to write. They set the tone; she just filled in the blanks. It was easy. Writing a book, writing a real book was something else. A whole other ball game. Pebble couldn't see herself being an author. The creator of something original. But the thought intrigued her. *My life sure is due for an overhaul.* Turning author fit perfectly with her up-and-coming out-of-work status. *I'm going to be a hopeless bum on welfare anyway. I could just as well use my time to write a book. Wonder why I thought of this now?* The fear of meeting Slim again seemed to stimulate her creativity. The idea was real, intriguing and Pebble liked it. She saw herself in a whole new light and it scared her. She saw herself powerful, in control. Now that she was nearing rock bottom it was just what the doctor ordered. She might be sitting warm and tight in her apartment with her sons, but the safety of her surroundings was deceptive. She had no one to rely on but herself. *I guess that's how life is.* Having to face Slim again – and face what she'd done with her life – was forcing her to grow, even if she didn't feel like growing. *Maybe something good will come out of this divorce in the end.* She liked the idea of making millions writing about divorce survival. For the moment, it didn't occur to her that the process might enrich her life, too. She only thought of the money. *Making a million would get to Slim.* And Pebble was mad enough at herself to like the thought. If there was one thing Slim couldn't tolerate, it was Pebble's success.

Fueled by the fear of meeting Slim again, Pebble's mind raced on. She discovered dark shadows she didn't want to look at. Pebble was not ready to admit that Slim still had power over her.

"I wonder where he is." Adam broke the silence.

Pebble was covered with a cold, sickly sweat. It was not at all warm in the room. Jon fiddled with a soccer ball he found under the sofa. He'd bounce it and toss it and stop. Then he'd start all over again. Pebble felt like shouting "stop it" but didn't. *The boys are nearly as nervous as I am.* She wanted to comfort them and make things right, but it was too late for making things right again. Divorce might not be death, but it's very final. *Slim is their father. God I wonder how it must feel to be them?*

Her mind went back to her book. *Probably some American psychologist somewhere has already written it. But if it's out there, I haven't seen it yet.* Her mind was calculating the number of couples who had or would encounter precisely this traumatic moment on the way from marital bliss to divorced bliss. Almost everybody gets divorced. At least almost everyone Pebble knew did or would. And they'd all have to pass this milestone in personal development. Pebble smiled. *A book about divorce survival has got to be a bestseller.* Especially if the book wasn't already written. *The market has to be immense. Is there really anybody out there who isn't either thinking about getting divorced, looking forward to getting divorced, dreading getting divorced, actually getting divorced, recovering from getting divorced, or just plain divorced?*

The doorbell rang.

Adam leaped into the air.

The door seemed to open, inch by terrible inch.

"Hi Dad," both boys were there. Pebble thought Adam looked strangely grownup. Behind his chubby 14-year-old features, there lurked the makings of a real mensch.

Slim look chagrined, confused. Hardly the monster Pebble remembered. She softened.

Slim hugged his sons, one in each arm. He wasn't a big man, but thin and tense. She couldn't remember being married to him, ever. He was a complete stranger.

"Hi," she strode purposefully towards them, her hand outstretched. She didn't want to kiss him. The boys would have to accept some limits.

He shook her hand, impressed by her newfound authority. He surveyed the apartment, "her" apartment.

After saying hello, Pebble backed off. Jon and Adam took Slim's leather jacket and bubbled around him, jabbering nervously.

"When did you get back?" Adam wanted to know.

"Just yesterday," replied Slim, brushing his dirty blond hair back from his forehead. "Do you think I'd be here without calling you guys?"

Adam was embarrassed by his question, but wanted to know for sure. The boys ushered Slim towards the sofa. It was an awkward moment.

"Why don't I go and make some tea?" Pebble asked. She wanted to leave her sons alone with their love for their father.

On the way down the hall towards the kitchen, Pebble felt like laughing and singing. *He doesn't have a hold on me anymore.* But she knew it wasn't quite true. Not yet. She was almost free, but not quite. Divorce is only paperwork. Real divorce is something else. It's a process; it takes time, something Pebble wasn't ready to admit. In her feverish mind she enacted weird scenarios, danced dances of liberation. *Maybe I shouldn't have taken that shower and just met Slim in my sweaty nightgown – without brushing my teeth or anything.* She giggled at the thought. *But no – beauty is power. He's always had power over me. My good looks are a part of my power over him.* She couldn't imagine presenting herself to any man, unbrushed and unwashed, body odors hanging out. It didn't work like that. You kept on plugging until the day you died. Maybe the day you stopped plugging was the day you died.

Pebble wished she understood things better. *Life keeps folding in on itself. I'm going to go to therapy.* She was surprised that she was making a commitment to herself, but she was. *I'm going to do something for me.* She put water up to boil and got the jar of Earl Grey tea down from the white kitchen shelf. *It's time to grow up and take charge.* She shook tea leaves into her white and blue Royal Copenhagen teapot. Then she took out the pastry the boys had bought at Van Hauen on the Walking Street and arranged it carefully on a white and blue dish. *I always wanted to understand why. Always. But I never dared. If I wait any longer, I'll be dead before I dare.* It was a solemn promise. Before, there was always someone to ask. Someone to explain things to. Now there was no one.

When she rejoined father and sons, they'd settled down into a normal where-have-you-been-what-have-you-been-doing conversation. Safe and easy. Pebble could handle it. She chimed in from time to time without getting involved. It suited her fine. She didn't want a hassle – didn't want the anxiety. Pebble didn't realize how beautiful she looked sitting there, all calm and quiet, but her sons did. Occasionally she blew her nose. Slim said, "You look run down, Pebble." Adam and Jon shut up tight as clams, the minute the words left Slim's mouth. There was fire in their eyes. Slim might be their father but if Pebble looked run down, it was none of his business. They were with Pebble, if sides were to be taken. Slim got the message. He wasn't supposed to make unkind comments to anyone, he wasn't the boss anymore. The boys might forget to wash dishes and clean up, but when it came to Pebble, they were overly protective. They knew who their guardian angel was. The look on their faces confirmed it. It said: "You guys are divorced now. So if you have anything to say to Pebble, Dad, it better be nice." Pebble almost felt sorry for Slim when Jon and Adam turned on him like that, but not quite. He had caused her enough pain. Being a jerk was no excuse. *Why should I forget?* She was ready to forgive, but not forget.

There was something sad about him, though, behind his forced gaiety. He talked incessantly about his job teaching Laplander kids in the northern part of Norway. Slim started life as an idealist. He believed he could change the world, that people would listen to him. When they didn't, he turned bitter. Somehow it was all Pebble's fault.

Memories came flooding back as Slim talked. It was just like old times, no one dared interrupt him. Slim couldn't tolerate being crossed, something Adam and Jon knew as well as Pebble. So they listened to his description of Laplander life in northern Norway politely. *Doesn't the man ever wonder if we're interested?* He still jabbed the air with his finger as he talked – a habit Pebble found very distasteful. *It's right and good we're divorced, even if the boys don't quite understand.* She saw they almost did. But understanding hurt. Pebble couldn't change that for her sons. At least she didn't have to answer to Slim anymore. *Idealists can be such tyrants.*

When it was all over, the four of them – the unit that once was family – stood at the door of Pebble's apartment and tried to behave civilly. Pebble smiled because saying goodbye can be tough, even though it wasn't a real serious, awful goodbye, an I'm-going-away-for-a-long-time or maybe-forever goodbye still it was a goodbye for now and today. Goodbyes are emotional for broken families. Slim said he wasn't going back to Norway right away.

When the moment could be prolonged no longer, Slim leaned forward to kiss Pebble's check. In that split second, she couldn't determine if he'd been thinking about kissing her for a long time, or if he'd just plain forgotten what he was doing. Either was possible, he was that inconsistent. Pebble accepted his kiss, not wanting to make a scene. Accepted his peck on the cheek, graciously, as if he was the Fuller Brush man himself and she'd just bought herself a complete new set of brushes, making this an event to remember. Pebble with a brush for every occasion. But no. The Fuller Brush man was only an aberrant memory from Pebble's American childhood which placed her at some strange junction of time and space and gave her a name, values and a place in history. But she didn't start the fire and the Fuller Brush man was just an indication of how idiotic she felt at that moment, receiving an awkward, lukewarm kiss from a man she'd slept with hundreds (thousands?) of times and now never wanted to sleep with or see again. *Maybe this is how survivors feel. They don't know if the whole ordeal is a joke or not. The funny part is they'll probably never know. I never would have done this if it wasn't for my kids.*

Watching her kids and Slim hug, Pebble realized that this was not only not a major goodbye, but Slim was going to be around. She'd have to get used to having to face him. It would happen more than once. *Why do I keep trying to make final goodbyes?* Final goodbyes are rare among divorced people with children.

"What about going to the movies tomorrow?" Slim wanted to be with his sons badly.

"Sure, Dad," they replied, "sure." The boys still weren't sure they'd get to see him again, Pebble could tell. She also knew both would have to rearrange busy schedules to go out with him the next day, but she kept her mouth shut. *Glad it's not my headache. I've done my bit. Almost to the finish line now.*

Pebble left them discussing the next day, a smile on her face. She was proud that her nose hadn't gotten too red and that none of her weirder scenarios had materialized. *I did it, I really did! I took a shower, didn't smell, brushed my teeth, combed my hair, wasn't drunk, acted like a lady, didn't commit any serious crimes, didn't throw any wild karate chops, and am not in the intensive care ward at the local hospital.* It was quite an accomplishment. *So I guess I'll just have to make do.* Which is exactly what Pebble did.

But she couldn't shake off the feeling she had when Slim left. It lingered and lingered. It was as if she'd discovered this great tuna fish sandwich hidden away in the back of her refrigerator. The sandwich was one of those really wonderful sandwiches she sometimes made when she was homesick for things American. Then she would use the best tasty white tuna she could find in Copenhagen and lots of mayonnaise, mustard, finely chopped fresh onions, dill pickles and celery. She'd place her masterpiece tastefully on a slice of ultra thin bread (the bread though Danish was almost as good as real toasted Jewish rye from New York) and top it with a nice layer of freshly washed crisp lettuce before adding the final slice of bread. Almost a sacrilege in Denmark because traditionally Danes only ate open-faced sandwiches, but Pebble didn't care. It was one of her best New York-style deli sandwiches, the kind she loved to eat during a lunch break when looking at her computer for five more minutes was more than she could bear, regardless of which side of the ocean she was on.

There was only one problem. She'd made this sandwich a long time ago. She'd put it in the fridge and forgotten it. She might have put lots of love and energy into the sandwich, but it didn't help much because after she made it, she hid it in the back of the refrigerator behind the milk cartons and forgot it. Since she was planning to eat it later and didn't want her ravenous sons to find it and devour it before she did, she'd wedged it in between the orange juice, the jam jars and the salad bowl and went back to work. That was when disaster struck. She forgot her sandwich. Why or when she couldn't recollect, all she knew was she lost track of it. And now it was too late to figure out God's plan for this sandwich. Since it was forgotten long ago, nobody would ever know. At the time, it all seemed so logical. Especially since the sandwich was so tempting. A one-of-a-kind-sandwich. That was until she went and she forgot it. And now that she'd found it again, the sandwich was no longer a miracle. It was just plain old. Its time had come and gone and now the bread was moldy and the tuna fish smelled strange.

So the fact that tuna fish was Pebble Beach's absolute favorite sandwich in the whole wide world didn't help much – because this particular tuna fish sandwich made her feel like puking.

Which was exactly how Pebble felt after meeting Slim again.

She wanted to cry, because it was such a waste and she always loved a great sandwich. But it was obvious, even to Pebble, that no matter how great this sandwich once was, nothing, absolutely nothing was going to save it now.

Chapter 9

Talking to Einar made Pebble definitely decide to go to therapy, right away. The man was quite simply the straw that broke the camel's back. And the funny part was, even though Pebble felt like ranting and raving at him, she honestly didn't know if the man was a friend or foe. The only thing she knew for sure was he had balls.

I've got to do something for me – God damn it! – was a strange reaction for Pebble Beach. More in character was not slamming down the receiver even though she wanted to.

But she knew she'd be broke soon.

Pebble had been home for five days when Einar called and just as Peter Cato predicted, her phone hadn't rung once during the five days. It just sat on her desk, like a wounded animal. The power of speech – that sparkling absurdity which also meant money, friends, food, fun – never touched it. When it finally did ring, Pebble knew who it was before she answered.

"So how was your trip?" He had the driest voice in Denmark.

"It was okay." She didn't know how to feel.

"Are you still so in love?" Einar asked innocently. Pebble had never once mentioned Albert, so how did Einar know? But Einar knew everything.

"What do you mean?" Pebble fumbled with her feelings. She sensed herself in bed with Einar.

"Oh come on, Pebble, why would a woman like you go all the way to Greenland…if it wasn't to visit a man?" Pebble realized Einar was right; it wasn't a particularly brilliant deduction. Anybody could have figured it out.

"Well, it was okay." Every time Pebble thought about Albert since her return, it was like falling down a dark tunnel. God he was wonderful, more wonderful than any man she'd known, but he drank and she had more pressing problems at the moment.

"You don't sound like a woman who's madly in love." He wouldn't let it go.

"I need time to think," Pebble said lamely, knowing that all the thinking in the world wouldn't help.

"Women who are madly in love don't need time to think," Einar shot back.

Pebble knew he was right.

The whole time Einar talked Pebble's mind was racing... *I ought to give the fucker a piece of my mind...but I need work, I really do. The first of the month's coming up and then who am I going to turn to?*

"Did you think about my job offer, Pebble?" He was asking her straight.

It was now or never. Yes or no.

"Well I have..."

"And...?" he wasn't going to make it easy for her. He was a power person.

"Well, I'd like to know a little more about the job." She'd go on welfare before she'd go down on her hands and knees and beg.

"Sure, sure." He had to admit she was cool, he liked her for that. "Why don't you come by my office when I get back from France next week and we can talk about it?" *Damn, he's going to let me wait.*

"Okay," she said, "when will you be back?" Her money wouldn't last forever.

"Let me see." She heard him flipping through the pages in his calendar. "Why don't we meet for lunch on Wednesday, then we can talk the whole thing through."

"Okay," Pebble replied, "Wednesday it is."

"Shall we meet at Copenhagen Corner? That would be easier for me as I'll be coming from a meeting upstairs at the House of Industry."

After a conversation like that, it was easy enough to decide to go to therapy. Therapy, after all, was a vague concept for Pebble anyway, a kind of catchall meaning "help". And whatever "help" was, Pebble sure needed it and needed it bad. She might have been promising herself help for years, but now was different. Before, help would have seemed almost extravagant, but this time Pebble was really in over her head. And there was something else, too. Until very recently, actually until the moment in her conversation with Einar when she definitely decided to go to therapy, Pebble wasn't exactly the kind of woman who did things for herself. Now that might sound strange, but it was true. Doing things for herself was, well, too out-of-character for Pebble, at least up until Einar called.

But, after Einar the Worm, and Peter, and Fem-Ads and WonderLift, and Albert and Slim, she figured why not. She figured, *If not now, then when?* It was all too crazy. Soon she either wouldn't be able to afford it or (if she worked for the Worm) she'd be too busy to go. And besides, Copenhagen in mid-winter was a crazy place no matter what you did. Half the population suffered from SAD (seasonal affective disorder) and was on the verge of suicide anyway, so why should an American like Pebble be an exception to the notable Nordic blues? No one gets through darkness easily.

Once Pebble decided to go to somebody, she was surprised at how hard it was to figure out "who" and "what" she needed when basically all she needed was help. (Help being in Pebble's book something like a loving man and money in the bank.) It was hopelessly confusing, and between friends, rumors, gossip, and the Internet, Pebble realized she was floundering in a sea of hope and promises sometimes called psychological counseling, psychotherapy, cognitive behavioral therapy, rebirthing, Rolfing, gestalt therapy, healing, aura balancing, crystal healing, encounter groups, sister-bonding, family therapy, co-dependency support groups, behavioral therapy, psychoanalysis, NLP, transactional analysis, bioenergetics, creative visualization, alcoholics anonymous and more. Pebble suspected she needed all of it even if it often sounded like a lot of mumbo-jumbo to her. She was, however, quite sure she didn't need Michel Lang. He was the latest hot "healer" in Copenhagen – the rage in circles who dabbled in past lives, astrological dating and aura balancing. Pebble found it hard to believe that a 30-year-old man (he called himself a male therapist) who'd studied with some guru with an unpronounceable Indian name in southern France and attended two Sufi meditation camps in Switzerland could help any woman over 25. *Even if he's the hottest hotshot guru in the world, how can he understand me? First of all he's a man, and second of all he's younger than me, and third of all he's never been married and has no kids. How could he possibly know what the world looks to me when I get up in the morning and see my empty bed and my over-40 face in the mirror?* Any woman who supports two teenage boys on her own wants comfort and Pebble Beach, making her own decisions for the first time in her life, was no exception. She wanted someone who'd understand. If Pebble was going to have a therapist, she'd have to be a woman.

Besides, the man might be a quack, even though he was adored by hoards of lonely Danish blonds. Just the thought of divulging secrets to a man she didn't know upset Pebble. A male therapist might have greasy hair and want to massage her body. Pebble had heard that therapists did things like that in order to "heal" and "relax tensions". And if somebody like Michel Lang massaged Pebble, he might actually touch her. *What if he touched my genitals?* The thought sent chills up and down Pebble's spine. She had all kinds of wild (and erotic) notions about therapy. *You never know these days.* Pebble was more than skeptical, she was downright afraid. She did believe one thing, however – a woman who was a therapist couldn't be a quack. And a woman wouldn't change Pebble's life unless Pebble wanted it changed. That was important, too. A man might.

So what am I going to do? Worry? My phone's stopped ringing anyway. Pebble finally settled on Irene Dorfson because her friend Clare declared in no uncertain terms that Irene was the best therapist in town. Pebble had no idea how Irene actually helped Clare because Clare seemed just as confused as she'd always been, but Clare adamantly insisted that she was happier, even if her life was still a mess. Knowing Clare well, Pebble figured that must count for something.

Irene Dorfson poetically called her approach to therapy a "cocktail" treatment. Pebble thought it sounded dangerous like crack cocaine or something which fried your brain, but Irene's brochure said soothingly "A unique combination of psychotherapy, gestalt therapy, and intuitive massage."

And Clare had sighed profoundly while Pebble fingered Irene's shiny brochure and said, "Irene's so perceptive." Which did it. Pebble had always been a sucker for Clare and her scatter-brained ways.

So Pebble went. *Perceptive or not, the woman's major expensive. I'll have to work for Einar just to be able to pay for this.* Besides the cost, there was another surprise, too. Irene might be a woman, but she filled the space a man would fill. *Why didn't Clare tell me she looked like a man?* Their first encounter was unpleasant. Pebble had been expecting…well she didn't know quite what…but she definitely wasn't expecting Irene. Irene was so big. Her weight, height, appearance, she was positively unsettling. But the worst part of it was that Irene seemed so serenely satisfied. Pebble had never met anyone as serene as Irene.

Is this what satisfaction looks like? Pebble felt intimidated by the woman and guilty for thinking she could just as well have gone to a man. *Am I so afraid of therapy or what? Why can't I even give the woman a chance?* She knew she would if Irene had been a business colleague.

They sat down in two very comfortable chairs in Irene's roomy office which was located in a renovated 17th-century brick building by Christianshavn's Canal in the old harbor section of Copenhagen. It was a fashionable address, and an expensive one, too. Architects and psychiatrists flocked there in droves to live in expensive, renovated designer-condos along the waterfront. And when the sun reappeared each spring, people gathered along the canal to eat lunch and drink beer. But on this mid-winter day, the benches along the canal were deserted.

"Pebble," Irene was saying as Pebble gazed out the window, "the only way I'm going to get to know you, is to give you some homework." She sat very comfortably in her armchair. Pebble didn't like looking at her. "I always do this little assignment with my new clients to get the ball rolling. You see, I don't really know you and you probably don't really know what you want to tell me."

Pebble felt all choked up in Irene's presence. She had planned to say so much, but ended up saying nothing. It was hard enough to smile sweetly. *Why can't I tell this woman that my career is in shambles and Albert is an alcoholic and Slim's back in town?* Before she arrived, she'd thought it would be easy to explain. She'd been planning a quick expedition. In and out fast. No need to drag things out, even if this was therapy.

"What I want you to do is to write down every situation you can think of – in your whole life – when you wanted to say no, but didn't."

Pebble thought that this was about the oddest assignment she'd ever heard of. *What does this have to do with anything?*

"I don't care how stupid the situation was," Irene continued, "just write it down. It could be that you didn't say no because you were afraid to, or it could be that you would have felt guilty if you'd said no. I don't care what the reason was. Just write it down."

"Okay," said Pebble, but she didn't know why. *And I'm paying for this?*

"After you make your list," Irene continued serenely, "and I want you to do this tonight and come back tomorrow so we can get started – I want you to write next to every situation *why* you didn't or couldn't say no. I don't care how stupid it sounds, write it down. Don't censor yourself, Pebble, please. Be honest."

Honest? Pebble wished she could at least look Irene straight in the eye, but she couldn't. She kept gazing out the window while Irene droned on about honesty. "Honesty," her voice seemed to grow even larger, "is the key to successful therapy. I won't be able to help you if you're not honest with me."

Pebble didn't realize therapy was like going to school.

* * *

That night Pebble paced up and down in her tiny office, struggling with Irene. *The woman's dumb. Insane. What does this crazy assignment have to do with anything?* Pebble would have preferred work, anything was better than this. *What if I really do become as well-adjusted as Irene? Will I end up being as fat and unattractive as she is, too? God, what a mean and vicious thing to think. What's wrong with me? What did the woman do to make me react like this? I'm the one who called her for help.* It was crazy. Pebble simply couldn't bring herself to look at the task Irene asked her to do. She was too confused. Life was too difficult, and the list Irene wanted her to make was totally unrelated to anything that was happening in Pebble's life right then and there. *And I'm paying her for this. I guess I really do need help.* Pebble was tempted to call Clare, but Clare would have some idiotic explanation and Pebble didn't want to admit to Clare that she didn't understand what was going on. *I won't do it. That's all. Nobody can force me to.* It was a comforting thought until she realized that she might as well not go back to Irene in the morning if she didn't do the assignment. *Am I going to give up therapy this easy? Well, maybe Irene isn't the right therapist for me. But how will I know if I don't give her a chance?* Pebble wanted to escape from her life, but since she couldn't, she went into the living room to talk to her kids. They were eating popcorn and watching a movie on TV. The last thing they wanted was to talk to Pebble. She wandered back to her office and tried calling Molly in New York, she could always kill a good half hour talking to her mother, but Molly wasn't home. In despair, she sat down and read Vogue magazine.

A chilling thought struck her somewhere between the Hermes scarves and the new Estee Lauder Advanced Time Zone something ad – *That honesty bit Irene talked about. Ruthless honesty she'd said. I have to be ruthlessly honest with her if I'm going to get anywhere. But what good will that do me in the real world? I'll never make a living being ruthlessly honest. All that would happen is that Adam and Jon would starve.*

Once Pebble started writing her list, it turned into a deluge. All kinds of awkward situations popped into her mind. At first she hesitated to write them down. It was embarrassing. Things like not wanting sex, or not wanting to have sex a certain way... God, it got worse and worse. But then she said to herself, *Ruthless honesty's getting easier.* (It was almost 2 a.m. and she had a nine-thirty appointment with Irene).

She wrote and she wrote. *Oh well, I'm the one who's paying for all this.* And she wrote more, which was almost more than she could cope with. *Am I really afraid to say no so often?* It was a real eye-opener. It boiled down to Pebble saying yes an awful lot of times in her life because basically she couldn't handle the consequences of saying no. It also dawned on her that maybe she'd been blaming Slim for things when in fact it was her own fault. She could have just said no. Why blame him because she didn't have the guts to stand up for herself. That wasn't his fault. It was embarrassing because it turned out she was the one who was bankrupt. She was the one who failed to be true to herself. *Maybe this Irene is really onto something...*

By 4 a.m. Pebble was too tired to go on. *I guess I wasn't brought up to say no.* She was so drained that she fell asleep with her clothes on thinking, *Nice girls don't make waves, only loud mouths do.*

* * *

The next morning, Irene insisted that Pebble read her list aloud. Pebble thought it was a pretty stupid idea until she found herself sobbing hysterically while trying to read what she'd written.

If Pebble expected mercy from Irene, she should have gone to someone cheaper. Irene was not only expensive, she was tough. Good and tough. She kept her mouth shut.

"It's funny how one thought leads to another when you start writing it down," said Pebble between sobs, hoping for a respite.

"What's so upsetting about all those situations?" Irene asked. She sounded almost bored. She still filled the space a man would fill.

"Well, if I'd said no, it would have had consequences."

Outside a cold rain mixed with ice and snow battered against Irene's windows. Christianshavn's Canal looked forlorn in the pale February light.

"What kind of consequences?"

"Well, saying no might have caused an upheaval, you know."

"An upheaval? No, I don't know."

"Well, it was especially with Slim."

"Why especially him?"

"He was so bossy," Pebble started crying again.

"Lots of men are." Pebble hadn't noticed how soothing Irene's voice was before. It brought on a deluge of tears. "You said, if you'd said no to Slim, it might have caused an upheaval," Irene continued. "What kind of an upheaval?"

"Well, we might have had a fight."

"And?"

"I mean, he might have gotten furious…" Pebble kept right on crying.

"So?"

"Well, I wasn't sure I could survive without him." The words just flew out of Pebble's mouth. It was a revelation.

"I see." Irene was right there.

Pebble knew her make-up was smeared all over her face, but she didn't hate Irene anymore.

"Pebble, I want you to move over to that chair over there." Irene pointed to a chair on the other side of the room. Pebble couldn't see what was wrong with the chair she was sitting on, but she was too upset to protest. She got up and walked over to the chair by the window. "Here?" She was at a loss. What did moving to another chair have to do with survival?

"Yes there. Now please sit down."

Pebble sat.

"Now I want you to look at the woman who was sitting in the chair you just left. I want you to look at yourself sitting right here besides me, where you were just sitting, okay?"

Pebble looked at the empty chair and tried to imagine herself sitting there. It seemed pretty dumb, but she was putty in Irene's hands anyway.

"Look at yourself very carefully and see yourself just as you were a minute ago, sitting there reading your list and crying."

Pebble understood.

"Now, what would you like to say to that woman sitting in this chair in my office, reading her list and crying?"

Pebble Beach knew right away what she wanted to say – she didn't even have to think about it. Her reaction came so fast it shocked her. Her heart pounded furiously in her chest. She didn't dare say what came to mind.

"Come on now," Irene prodded ever so gently, "what would you like to say to her?" Irene knew that Pebble knew but didn't dare. "Be honest now, ruthlessly honest. Remember what I said."

Still Pebble sat motionless, as if turned to stone.

"I'm never going to tell anyone, Pebble. I promise."

The magical kindness in Irene's voice seemed to set Pebble's inner torment free. "I'd like to say to her... God, it's so difficult..." Pebble put her head in her hands and wept. Irene waited and her silence was kind. When Pebble was done she looked up and wiped her nose with her sleeve, liking Irene more than she'd liked anyone in her whole life. "I'd like to say…" The room was still completely quiet and for no reason Pebble could understand, she noticed the silence and herself and giggled ever so slightly. Irene was present and serene as a Buddha. She didn't rush Pebble, she'd seen this happen before.

"I'd like to say…"

One more false start was one too many. Irene changed tracks unexpectedly from soothing Buddha to competent midwife. It was time to help the birthing, "Well then, say it, girl." Her voice was firm.

It was as if she'd slapped Pebble, but she got at Pebble's words, clung to them and forced them out into the world.

"I'd like to say to myself," Pebble swelled at the insult, the effort, at life. "I'd like to say – *get your fucking act together, woman!*" When they finally emerged, the words were almost a scream. "I'd like to say to myself you don't have to sit there and cry like a nitwit, you jerk. What's the matter with you? What's the matter with me? Why am I acting so dumb?"

Irene sighed as the dam broke. Pebble took a deep breath and rushed on, "Just look at you. You're acting like you completely dissolved – sitting there with your stupid list and crying like a baby. Why are you so worried about everybody else? What are you so afraid of? What can happen? It's idiotic. You weren't put into this world to take care of everybody else. Who's taking care of you? You're a doormat. It's crazy. You don't have to let other people wipe their feet on you. Nobody says you have to jump up and down for anyone. You didn't have to do it before and you don't have to do it now! Not for Slim or for Albert or for Einar or for anyone. You really don't. You don't have to answer to anybody about anything. It's not required. There's no law anywhere that says you have to explain. You just happen to be you, kiddo…" And then Pebble laughed, and it was one of the most invigorating peals of laughter she'd experienced in years. "...and that's quite okay. And if other people don't like you or the decisions you make, or how you act, or what you do...if they don't like the clothes you wear or the way you eat or how you set your hair, well then they can...just go jump in the nearest lake."

Chapter 10

Wednesday found Pebble sitting with Einar Bro at an elegantly set table in Restaurant Copenhagen Corner, which is strategically located across from Rådhuspladsen, the sprawling town hall square, and close to Tivoli Gardens. The restaurant's glass-enclosed terrace faces the statue of Hans Christian Andersen across the boulevard and provides an excellent place to meet for lunch or business.

Pebble dressed carefully for the occasion, she even wore her best black kid gloves with her Armani blazer. But who was she kidding? She was almost out of work, and Einar, of course, would know.

He must think I look smashing. The thought obsessed her. Without good looks, Pebble thought she was dead. She hated Einar for making her feel that way. But Einar was power.

He talked excitedly about the account which had taken him to Paris. A well-known Danish furrier was going to stage a major fashion show in Paris and the Republic Group had won the account. That meant management of the whole event. It was tremendous PR for the agency, too. Whatever else you had to say about Einar, he managed to stay in the limelight. Pebble might not love the man, but she loved the excitement that surrounded him. *And he's so ugly. The man's a frog with power.* It was fascinating. Once again Pebble wondered if men as ugly as Einar used power to compensate for their lack of physical prowess when it came to women. Einar had been in Paris checking out the locations his advance troops had picked as tentative candidates for the show. When they'd done the footwork, Einar flew down to take a look at their results. Apparently he wasn't ready to make a choice yet.

"Why don't we order wine, Pebble. I told Marianne to keep the afternoon open today. I really need to unwind a little." He'd returned from Paris early and had spent the morning in a high-powered meeting at the Industrial Council upstairs.

He motioned to the waiter and asked for the wine list. In spite of the elegant tan Italian suit he was wearing, Pebble still thought he looked like a frog.

"And how have you been doing, my dear?"

"I started going to this wonderful therapist last week," she replied, trying to head off any talk about business. She'd decided upon the tactic before leaving her apartment. She went over their coming conversation a thousand times and every time it ended in disaster. She didn't want Einar to know she was in trouble. If he knew she had no work, he'd have a tremendous advantage. And she'd be forced to ask him about WonderLift. She had vowed to herself not to talk about WonderLift until she was sure of the truth. The problem was, she wasn't sure. Maybe she really did tell him the launch date of WonderLift. She just didn't know anymore. When Peter Cato first accused her she denied his accusation fiercely. At that time, she was certain she remembered what happened at the Hotel D'Angleterre perfectly, but on closer inspection, she wasn't sure. She couldn't remember everything she said. Parts of their conversation seemed faded and blurred. Memory is a tricky thing anyway. She remembered Einar's hands and face – they were vivid enough, but not their words. She remembered getting very drunk, too – for her. If she hadn't just spent almost three weeks snowbound with an alcoholic, she might have felt differently. But being with Albert changed her idea of what alcohol can do to people. Her absolute certainty about her own behavior had evaporated. She desperately wanted to discuss it with Irene. Not that she thought Irene could help her locate the truth, but she needed to get it off her chest.

"You just have to go to Paris and see this show." Apparently Einar wasn't listening when Pebble said she was going to a therapist. He'd been studying the Corner's excellent wine list. Having made his choice, he looked at Pebble, "It's going to be fabulous, just fabulous. The furs John is going to show are simply out of this world." After a week without work, Pebble felt very shaky indeed. *I wonder if he knows how I'm feeling.* She felt Einar was her only option. *God I hope he doesn't know how badly off I am.* It was enough to make her perspire under her best business disguise – an expensive knitted outfit from BKR, a favorite among Danish working women. *If I don't go to work for Einar, what will I do?* Pebble trembled at the thought of going out on the job market again. *Copenhagen's too small for that.* There's not much room for an English copywriter in a place like Scandinavia. *What chances do I have if I want to keep working here?* Writing was Pebble's first love. Anything else would be an anticlimax. Einar looked different in that light. *Maybe he's not such a jerk...if he gives me the chance to write... I wonder what Irene would do if she was me? She's always so serene about life.* Pebble was sure Einar was her best shot. As for the WonderLift thing and him being a jerk, and unethical, well she would just have to find out what actually happened before she could even begin to think about how to deal with it and him.

An immaculately clad waiter took their orders. Einar ordered an expensive Chablis for their lunch.

"Tell me about the man you visited on Greenland," Einar asked, his voice warm and sincere, as if he was a kind, wise uncle.

Pebble smelled danger. Einar was so experienced in the ways of the world. Pebble was a novice by comparison.

"I don't know what to tell you, Einar." It was true; his question caught her by surprise. This was supposed to be a business lunch.

"Well, tell me if you're in love with him, for starters."

"He's an alcoholic." Pebble was stunned by her admission. *Why did I tell him that?* Einar was an expert at surprising people into honesty.

"An alcoholic?"

"Yes. I didn't know before I went there."

"I see," his voice was even kinder. She knew he was

processing this information and that he'd find a way to exploit it. "Is that why you're going to therapy all of a sudden?" So he had heard.

"Well…" It was another good question. "Well, yes and no. Of course I was shocked when I found out."

"I don't blame you." He reached across the table and took her hand just as he'd done that night at the Hotel D'Angleterre, only this time Pebble wasn't drunk. "Pebble, I want you to come work for me. You won't regret it."

He had a way of changing the subject, so he was always in charge. She didn't want him to hold her hand, but didn't know how to free herself from his grip. Being firm with a man wasn't as easy as her son Adam thought. She felt uncomfortable and warm.

"What do you want me to do for you?"

"I want you to be my assistant."

"You said that before, Einar, but what does it involve? You know I'm a copywriter."

"Well, it will be an opportunity for you to broaden your scope, Pebble. You'll still be writing copy for me, but you'll also be in on the decision-making process. I'll want you to help me develop my marketing plans. The job will involve some travel. But if you can leave your boys alone to go to Greenland, I'm sure you can leave them for business trips, too."

The job sounded wonderful. Pebble wanted desperately to be a part of the excitement that surrounded Einar. *I know people who would die for a chance like this.* She just wondered how high the price was going to be. *If I say yes, will he think I'm willing to go to bed with him?* She knew Einar played his cards very close to the chest. *I'll have to be on guard day and night.* Still, she wanted to send him a warning.

"Einar, you know how independent I am."

"I know," he still had her hand, "that's why I want you."

She wondered what the "why I want you" referred to. *Does he want me for the job or for himself?*

"What are you thinking about paying me, Einar?"

"I thought I'd start you off at $125,000 this year and if things go well, we'll talk about $150,000 next year."

Molly will die when she hears I'm making $125,000 a year. Pebble smiled inside. "When do you want me to start?" she said.

Einar let go of Pebble's hand as the waiter approached with the wine. She sighed with relief. *What if one of my kids walked by and saw me holding hands with Einar again?* The waiter opened the Chablis and Einar tasted it carefully. He seemed pleased. When the waiter had poured the wine and left them alone, Einar said, "Shall we drink to your success?"

Einar's question left Pebble stunned. In that split second, she realized she was standing at a crossroads. Strange emotions held her tightly in their grip. She searched the bright, busy restaurant frantically for a familiar face, but there was none. Something was very wrong. If she really was on her way to becoming a first-class businesswoman, why did she still love Albert and the simple life he represented? (Up until that moment, she'd convinced herself that she didn't love him. In fact, since she returned from Greenland, she'd thought very little about Albert.) She knew the man was a hopeless alcoholic – what kind of a life would she have with a man like that? It would never work. It was an impossible dream. She found all that out when she visited him. So why did his eyes grab at her heart now? *Living with Albert's a dream. Alcoholics don't ever change.* She wished the bond between them was broken. Sitting with Einar made her realize it wasn't. *Damn. I don't want to think about Albert – ever again. He can't help me. Nobody can. I'm on my own.*

In that instant, before she accepted the job Einar was offering her, Pebble understood that she still had a long way to go before she grew up. *At the rate I'm going I'll probably be dead before I do.* It was not a comforting thought. She also realized that everyone who heard of the WonderLift scandal would interpret her going to work for Einar as an admission of guilt.

Einar repeated his question, "Shall we drink to your success, Pebble?"

"Yes, Einar, I'd like that," she replied in a weak voice.

Einar raised his glass in triumph, "To Pebble Beach, my new assistant." His voice was lusty.

Chapter 11

I never made love to a guy who's nearly 20 years younger than I am, thought Pebble Beach on her way to her first rendezvous with Per, the gorgeous 24-year-old who sat next to her on the plane on the way home from Greenland.

She knew she was going to make love to Per from the moment he sat down next to her. It was just a matter of getting around to it. Since returning from her fling with Albert, Pebble had been busy putting her life back together. It was early May and many weeks had passed without Pebble even thinking about the sorry state of her sex life. Spring had arrived in this northerly region of the world, and people were beginning to hope again. The days were distinctly and definitely longer as the sun began to spread its gentle warmth over the cold, wintry city. The chestnut trees in the King's Garden across the street from Pebble's apartment were in full bloom. Suddenly, everyone and their grandmother were outdoors, looking hopefully skyward. With the return of the sun, Copenhagen joyfully enacted its yearly spring rites and became a city instantly reborn and inhabited by smiling, friendly people. Pebble spent this happy time settling firmly into her role as Einar's assistant.

Working for Einar was like staking out your turf. He would put a hand here and Pebble would gently but firmly remove it. He would come too close and Pebble would move. Whenever he had an opportunity, he tried. If they worked late, he tried. If they went to lunch, he tried. If they were alone in his office, he tried. He was as persistent as a waterfall, wearing away at Pebble's stony strength. In fact, he was so persistent she hardly noticed his slow progress. But they were getting more familiar, and friendlier. She found new qualities in the man, found herself liking him.

The thing about Einar was that once you got past the

unbecoming exterior and the manipulative manner, you found a sensitive, intelligent man with a deep insight into people and business. Pebble was fascinated by his descriptions of meetings she attended with him. The scenes he described were often a far cry from the meeting she thought she'd been to. Pebble tuned into who said what, period, while Einar was able to provide an in-depth analysis of the "who said what and why". He knew what motivated people. He could explain them and make their behavior plausible. Sometimes Pebble was floored by his insights. How did he know? Of course he'd had a long business career and knew many of these people intimately, but that didn't explain everything. Nor did the fact that he had negotiated with them before and knew their weaknesses. She came to the conclusion that behind the frog face, there lurked a man of considerable talent. When he explained the inner workings of an event to her, she realized there was a world of complex motives, passions and ambitions warring right below the smooth, shiny surface when well-dressed people met in richly carpeted conference rooms. He helped her understand more completely why some decisions were made and others were not. Up until then, she'd been nothing more than a talented copywriter. Now, as Einar's assistant, she was thrown into the heat of battle, naive and green as she was. She didn't know how to read signals – but she was learning fast. *Einar's the best mentor I ever had. It's like going to business school and getting paid, too.* She had to admit, she loved every minute of it. *Einar's done more for me than any other man I know.* Which made it hard to put him down when he got too close. Besides, his brilliance fascinated her. The other men in her life, the handsome ones – like Slim and Albert – what had they done for her? Einar at least shared a wealth of experience with her and taught her invaluable lessons at the same time. It was great fun, being exposed to the world like that.

It did a lot for her self-confidence, too, especially after the WonderLift debacle. Fortunately for Pebble, she didn't know people were still talking behind her back – saying things like "Einar bought her". She thought WonderLift was forgotten, but she was wrong. In her heady excitement, she didn't notice how people stopped talking when she and Einar walked into a meeting, but they did. Danes have long memories.

She was strangely lighthearted and unaware of what was going on around her. So lighthearted in fact (and lightheaded) that she willingly let spring and the thrill of entering a whole new world dazzle her. Everything (except Irene) went on the back burner – WonderLift, Albert, Slim, Peter Cato, even her sex life. Work provided her with a blissful means of escape. Pebble had even forgotten Per, the gorgeous hunk who sat next to her on the plane home from Greenland, until he called her one luminous May evening, out of the blue.

It wasn't until she hung up that she realized how much courage it must have taken for him to call her. *God, I promised to call him and never did. There was so much to deal with when I got home, I just plain forgot.*

And now she was on her way to meet him at Cafe Sommersko in downtown Copenhagen, a playful smile on her lips. Actually, achieving that right, playful state of mind hadn't been all that easy. Pebble, in fact, had to work hard to get there. Most people have no idea of how hard it is for a 40-something woman to dress for a date with a 24-year-old. She was not trained for an occasion like this. *How are you supposed to look when going out with a kid?* It was hard to figure out. First of all, Pebble didn't know if Per had any idea how old she was. They didn't talk about age on the five-hour flight back from Søndre Strømfjord, they just laughed a lot and stared deeply into each other's eyes. She couldn't just sit there and blurt out her age. It wouldn't have been right. Nor could she bring herself to say, *Hey sweetheart, you know I'm old enough to be your mother…*

So she'd spent a long time before their rendezvous in front of her mirror, changing clothes. *Now how 'bout my looking young outfit?* Which translated into something like huge rhinestone earrings, black high heels, and tight-fitting jeans over a very tight bodystocking. *It might scare the shit out of him.* An outfit like that worked wonders when you went to a party and everybody else was over 50. Then Pebble looked great. And somebody like Fast Eddie, her 55-year-old copywriter friend with the thick glasses would say, "God, do you look sexy!" But that outfit with Per? With his 20-20 vision, it wouldn't work. It would be like saying, *Hey, kiddo, I'm still in pretty good shape…you know, no false teeth or anything yet…* She threw the tight jeans onto the growing pile of clothes on her bed.

With Per it would have to be something else. Something timeless. *God, I hope I'm timeless, too.* Young and sexy clothes on a 40-year-old body just wouldn't work with a 24-year-old. *I've got to position myself outside of that game with him.* Still nothing she tried on seemed right. She cringed at the thought of him thinking *Just get a load of this old broad. Who does she think she's fooling?* Looking back at their first meeting, Pebble remembered in dismay that the light on the airplane had been dim and they'd both drunk a lot. Per was ecstatic because he was going back to Denmark (he'd been up there for three months working as an electrician and hated every minute of it) and she was ecstatic, too. There wasn't much that could bring them down. They were like escaped convicts who had slipped out of a maximum security prison. Reality couldn't touch them. *Age? What you talkin' about, sister? Real life? That's news to me.* They were high on the impossible and only cared about the direction of the plane (homeward-bound) and each other. The free-flowing cognac, courtesy of Air Greenland, helped them stay airborne.

Now was different. Pebble was actually going to meet the kid at Cafe Sommersko. This was no longer an accidental event, but a planned occasion involving suddenly more than just the gods of chance. Cafe Sommersko, a Parisian-style cafe which seemed to have been transplanted whole from the Left Bank to the heart of Copenhagen in the 70s used to be one of those places people went – to hang out and be seen. Pebble remembered how when she first came to Copenhagen the place was packed with hopeful musicians, intense university students, and political activists, artists and intellectuals – all hobnobbing with gorgeous-looking creatures of both sexes in the dim, crowded rooms facing Kronprinsensgade. Today the place was more ordinary, just like any old cafe, so Pebble figured it would be okay for Per to meet her there, but now she wasn't so sure. *He'll probably be scared to death.*

She surveyed the pile of clothes on her bed in disgust. Nothing worked. She had tried every thinkable combination from hooker to nice mom, without success. None of them felt right. *Who am I anyway?* If she wanted to get to Sommersko before Per, this was no time for deep questions. A glance at her watch told her she was running late. *Oh my God, I forgot the time. Now I'll never make it.* Suddenly in a hurry, she pulled on her old faithful stonewashed Levis, her white Marc O'Polo sweatshirt (the one she always felt good in), her wonderful, battered leather jacket and her most expensive Italian boots. *The whole point of this exercise is to get undressed anyway!* She looked at herself in the mirror and smiled. Being so clear about her motives (for once in her life) made her feel good. *It's all this ruthless honesty stuff I hear from Irene. Maybe it's beginning to sink in.* Pebble was still going to Irene once a week. It was like a new religion or something, just more expensive. The grin on her face grew, *I guess it doesn't matter how you wrap the package, does it? It's what's inside that counts!* She flicked out the light and ran lightly out of her apartment.

Pebble arrived at Cafe Sommersko early because she was sure Per would turn and run if he got there first. It was that kind of place. You had to be cosmopolitan enough to know how to hang out Danish style to feel relaxed at Sommersko on a Friday night when the place was jammed. Pebble surveyed the throngs of veteran cafe-goers navigating nonchalantly through people deep in conversation over beers and cappuccinos. Per would be too young for this kind of serious cafe know-how. And besides, he was an electrician, and electricians from suburbs like Taastrup don't hang out in places like Cafe Sommersko.

Waiting by the crowded bar, a glass of wine in hand, Pebble was having serious doubts about meeting such a kid. *But who'll ever know?* She told herself it was an experiment. *I mean – who cares anyway? I'm entitled to a little fun, aren't I?* She knew Irene would approve of that attitude, but besides Irene, there was this little voice inside saying, *Shame on you, Pebble, you're nothing but a cradle robber!* Pebble was just about to get depressed (*What would my mother say if she knew?*) when she saw Per come walking through the cafe door. The sight of that man-sized bundle of vitality put a quick stop to the chatter going on inside her head. *If only Clare could see him, she'd die.* Pebble didn't move from the bar. Instead, she allowed herself that wonderful luxury of enjoying the moment of expectation to its fullest. She took in the whole scene – and saw herself standing by the bar in her trusty leather jacket, surrounded by the usual crowd as Per plunged in, as unsullied and innocent as newly fallen snow. Suddenly she realized being over 40 was great. *You have to be, to be able to enjoy moments like this.* She sighed with appreciation. *I'm glad I gave myself the time.* This was a moment, she took for herself. Then, watching Per search the crowded cafe for her face, she thought of Clare. *Clare's such a sucker for bodies, she'd love Per.* Clare had been telling Pebble for ages that she owed it to herself to have a little fun after all those years of marriage and kids.

"Ah, come on, Pebble," Clare muttered on the phone when Pebble told her about meeting Per on the plane home. "Go out and try it – you deserve it!" She sounded just like Irene.

Per's face lit up like a Christmas tree when he spotted Pebble by the bar. He seemed so young and awkward as he approached that she hugged him as soon as he got near her.

"Oh Per, it's so good to see you." Besides wanting to ease his shyness, she meant it. Every ear at the bar was listening, checking them out. People knew Pebble, even the cafe regulars who didn't know her, knew her. Since her divorce, she'd become a familiar face on the Copenhagen cafe scene. Freelancers generally hung out in cafes anyway, sharing gossip and business tips here and there. But Per – nobody had seen him before. Pebble noticed more than one woman sizing him up.

"Pebble," he hugged her in his strong arms then turned tongue-tied.

"What have you been doing with yourself?" She waved to the girl behind the bar to bring Per a beer. She wanted to help Per slide into casual conversation, but he couldn't. Instead he peered in every direction, stunned by the diversity of the crowd. It was as if every lost soul within a 500-mile radius was suddenly gathered in Sommersko to say hi to some cousin who had just turned up out of nowhere. Pebble took his hand and turned the full blast of her warmest, most womanly smile on him, "You look terrific, Per, you really do."

In a flash, his eyes were riveted on Pebble, the crowded cafe forgotten. "Oh yeah... I'm okay... I guess." He thought she looked terrific, too, but he was too shy to tell her.

"Wasn't it great to come home again?" She nudged him playfully. "Do you remember how we hated Greenland?"

That brought a smile to his lips. "Yeah." But he still wasn't ready to talk. On the plane he'd talked a blue streak, but Sommersko wasn't an airplane and they weren't high on freedom anymore. When the girl behind the bar with the punk-like, black spiked hair brought Per his beer, he guzzled it like Pebble imagined an electrician should. Then he took a deep breath, straightened his collar and turned towards Pebble. "Let's get out of here," he said forcefully.

"Don't you like it here?" she asked quietly.

"It's not that, but I want to be alone with you. How can we talk here?" He motioned towards the crowded cafe. "There's such a racket in this place."

"Okay, let's go." She put her arm in his and led him to the door. He looked younger and more inexperienced than she remembered.

Per drove straight to the suburban high rise where he lived. It was quiet there, Danish suburbs always were. What little night life there was, you'd find in downtown Copenhagen. The rest of Denmark was nice, clean, safe and boring. Pebble knew she shouldn't be so critical, but she was a big city girl. She grew up in New York and thrived on excitement. The red-brick Taastrup apartment complex where Per lived was made up of high rises interspersed with neat rows of two-family bungalows. It was only ten o'clock in the evening, but the streets were deserted. Pebble knew that this bland lifestyle called Danish quality living by social democrats around the world was an unreachable dream for most of the world's population. Still, the neighborhood Per lived in looked incredibly boring.

His apartment was boring, too. It looked (and felt) like it was plucked ready-made out of a furniture catalogue for young adults who'd just moved away from home. Maybe it was.

"My girlfriend Louisa moved out last week," he tried to explain the bareness. "She took a lot of stuff with her."

Pebble remembered the girlfriend story from the airplane. When she talked about seeing each other again, Per had clammed up. Pebble (she told Per all about Albert) suggested they have dinner together sometime. It seemed like a good idea, considering how attracted they were to each other. Per's first reaction was, "Oh great!" Then he shut up for the first time since they sat down next to each other on the plane and started talking. It took Pebble a while to find out that Per was afraid of having dinner with her because he had a girlfriend. The girlfriend didn't bother Pebble at all. She wasn't planning on marrying Per anyway, so what difference did a girlfriend or two make? *He's got more than enough body to go around.* As far as

Pebble was concerned, he could keep his soul and his girlfriend, too. She said she'd call him.

"So you broke up?" That was news.

"Yeah," Per took Pebble's leather jacket and hung it on the coat rack. "I told you things weren't going that well, don't you remember?"

Pebble was walking around the room, touching things, surveying the turf. It was different being with a younger man. She felt different.

She turned and walked back towards him and threw her arms around his neck. "I didn't think we were going to let Louisa keep us from going out to dinner anyway..." He wasn't old enough to grasp her concept. She didn't care.

"Can I get you something to drink." He couldn't hold her yet, it was too soon.

"Sure." She sat down on the couch thinking, *What in the world are we going to talk about?*

Per returned from the kitchen with a couple of beers.

Why am I doing this? Pebble wasn't sure if Per was worth the effort. If this had been Hollywood, he would have been a mature and sensitive conversationalist, even though he was only 24. But this was Taastrup, and Pebble felt out of place. *Why can't I just go on one of those larks like the women you read about in bestsellers or see in the movies do? All I ever do is work and schlepp groceries for my kids.*

"Louisa was just too bourgeois for me," Per was explaining. "She wanted to have kids and everything, right away. I just wasn't ready."

Pebble was hardly listening. The debate between her brain and body continued to distress her. *Why do I always have to worry? Why can't I just turn it off?* She snuggled up next to Per, determined to listen to every word he said. *You've got to lighten up a bit and live in the present! That's what everybody says. And stop wasting all your energy worrying...* Pebble found reading self-help books (she had an impressive stack by her bedside) was much easier than actually following the advice in them.

"Do you know why I called you? I mean I knew you wouldn't call me… I just couldn't forget you, Pebble. I mean our conversation on the plane. Do you remember?"

She smiled, thinking back to their flight. "Yes, vaguely. I just remember there was this instant connection between us…we were so happy to get away from that place."

Thinking back to how desperate they were to leave Greenland made them both laugh.

"Yeah," he swirled his beer around in his glass. She knew he wanted to tell her more.

"You made me feel something I'd never felt before… I don't know how to explain it." He turned and looked at her. "You're so exciting, do you know that?"

"Me?" she laughed. "I don't know if you'd think I was so exciting if you heard about my life since I got back. The last few months have been impossible."

"Really? What happened?"

"Remember I told you I was a freelancer?"

"Yeah."

"Well, I'm not anymore."

"You mean you gave it up?" He was shocked. Part of the mystique of Pebble Beach was her independence. He'd never met anyone like her before.

"Well not exactly. It's a long story, Per, and I'd really like to tell you some day, but I can't right now."

"Why not?"

"Because I'm not sure what happened myself. Somehow I got involved in this scandal while I was away and I came back to a stupid mess. My whole career was in ruins."

"I don't believe it, Pebble. What did you do?"

"I'm not really sure, but I'll tell you when I find out. Until that happens, I had to take a job to support myself and my kids."

"You?"

"Yeah...actually I like it. It's funny, I didn't think I would, but I got this great opportunity and it's a lot of fun."

"What are you doing?"

"I'm working for the Republic Group."

"You are?" There was awe in Per's voice. Everyone in Denmark knew about the Republic Group; it was the biggest advertising agency in the country.

"Yeah, I'm Assistant to the Vice-President."

"God, Pebble, that's great."

Per was overwhelmed. He couldn't figure out what a woman like Pebble was doing in his apartment. Funny thing was, she couldn't either.

"What about Albert? Have you heard from him?"

"Yeah, he's doing okay. He calls me sometimes." She was silent for a while, looking at her beer and thinking about Albert. Every time she thought of him, she felt bad. The bond was still there.

"Do you still love him?" Per asked.

"Didn't I tell you he's an alcoholic?"

"You did, but you can love an alcoholic, too." He was wise enough for one so young. *Damn, I don't want to look at it. Albert's far away and he drinks like a fish.* Pebble got up and walked over to Per's stereo equipment. He had lots and lots of CDs. "Shouldn't we put on some music?"

Per followed her and they selected something by Robbie Williams...and Pebble thought, *Same music as my kids listen to...* But even music couldn't drown out the tension in the room; both of them felt uncomfortable. Pebble realized that Per was not going to sweet talk her into his bedroom as she'd hoped. He just didn't know how. He might not know her exact age, but he knew she was older – much older – and that knowledge seemed to inhibit him sorely. If anything exciting was going to happen, Pebble would have to initiate it herself. She went back to the couch and opened another beer. *Now's the time to forget what a good girl I've been all my life.* She'd never done anything like this before. *Why can't you act like a man, woman!* She moved much closer to Per. *If only Einar was half as pretty as Per, life would be so much easier!* But Pebble knew wishful thinking got you nowhere in the real world. No amount of creative visualization on her part would change Einar's face.

Moving closer helped. Per was eating his heart out trying to figure out how to get Pebble from the sofa to his bedroom. He knew instinctively they had to make love before there was any chance of their being friends. He couldn't explain why, he just knew it. He was so tense, Pebble almost despaired.

Maybe he's never slept with anyone besides Louisa – he's so young. Pebble cupped his face between her hands and kissed him gently, full on the mouth. Sparks illuminated the bare room. Per was so surprised and encouraged by her heat that his strong arms slid firmly around her. Now that the ice was broken, they snuggled and kissed for a while, enjoying the nearness and warmth of each other's presence.

Then Pebble freed herself from his embrace and got up. The look of dismay on his face melted when she stretched out her arms and said, "Come." She didn't know exactly where his bedroom was, but she was planning on leading him there anyway.

He stood up.

She pressed herself into him. She felt his hardness working perfectly. *He might be a kid, but that part of him works like a man.* "Per?" she looked up at him. "Where's your bedroom?"

They both laughed.

And somehow the laughter helped him rediscover the boldness he'd felt on the plane from Greenland. He dragged her to his room.

Their lovemaking started out so awkwardly that Pebble almost wished she'd stayed home. Once he'd gotten her part way undressed, the thought of how experienced she probably was – compared to him – almost paralyzed him completely. He fumbled around with her clothes and her body for ages. In fact he fumbled so long that Pebble had plenty of time to worry about her body and how she would look to him when she was naked. *What if he thinks I'm too old?* She wondered if her breasts were firm enough – or if they sagged. *Maybe he'll compare me to Louisa.* It wasn't pleasant to think about – a 21-year-old body is a hard act to follow.

And then it happened...finally! Her clothes were off and Per was deep in her... Only something was wrong...after waiting so long, everything was happening too fast...way too fast. Pebble had forgotten how young men are. His urgency gave her no time. He humped and thumped on top of her with gunshot rapidness, coming before she had time to find him at all. He was finished before she even tuned into his movement, or picked up his energy. Pebble was furious. *God what a waste! WHAT A WASTE!! After all that effort...and aggravation...the kid goes off like a rocket...before I even get started!* When he rolled over, Pebble was so mad she could have cried.

She stared up at the ceiling, stunned. *Damn, damn, damn! It just isn't fair.* She was ready to get out of bed, put on her clothes and say, *Thanks for nothing, kid!* when God gave her a miracle.

Per got another erection. He was, you remember, only 24.

And the amazing thing about this amazing erection was that it was just as hard as the first one, and just as perfect. And (God is Great) equally usable for a woman like Pebble Beach.

And this erection, being Per's second, lasted longer. Which gave Pebble ample time to forget her anger, her inhibitions and her age, and climb right up on top of him. Where she frolicked and danced and thoroughly enjoyed herself, while he, growing older and wiser every moment, waited until she was good and ready. And then, when he heard her moaning and groaning like the apocalypse was approaching, he knew that if he was ever going to have a chance with this marvelous, mellow fellow-creature named Pebble Beach again, it was now or never.

So he let himself go, and this time, his timing was perfect. And for that short moment, he was an absolute miracle. He let go of his youth, and his Danish shyness, and found the Viking in his soul, bellowing like a bull while Pebble grunted and groaned and enjoyed every lusty thrust of Per's iron rod in her pulsating womb. Then Pebble came with a full-blown, head-shattering, cunt-wrenching, body-twisting orgasm, and Per, wonderful Per, was right there with her.

Chapter 12

Thursday night, Pebble ate dinner with Slim at RizRaz on Store Kannikestraede, a lovely old street in the heart of Copenhagen. Jon and Adam weren't invited. "I want to talk to you," Slim said on the phone when he called and asked her out. "It's about the kids."

So she said okay even though she really didn't want to go. When he pleaded children, she couldn't see how she could refuse. *He is their father, even if he is a jerk.* And besides, Pebble's friend Fast Eddie, the copywriter from Santa Monica, always said the most important thing for kids from broken homes was to see their parents could be friends. "You know, acting like civilized human beings," was how Eddie put it. This was the first time Pebble had been alone with Slim in over a year and she didn't particularly like it. *Oh well, I guess that just because it's my duty, it doesn't mean I have to like it.* But she wasn't positive she was there because of duty either. Maybe the real reason was guilt.

You see, Slim had been mad at her for years. He was mad before they got divorced and mad afterwards, when she finally left him. It was a no-win situation for Pebble. Whatever she did was wrong. Slim wanted Pebble to be the woman he wanted her to be. When she turned out to be somebody else, it was just too much for him. Sitting with him once again at a table in the back of the restaurant brought the memories flooding back. They'd been married for 14½ years. Even if they were on opposite sides of the fence now, nothing had changed. She knew Slim would go for the jugular.

I guess Irene's right – I'm suffering from the doormat syndrome. Irene was a gentle prodder. On her last visit, she asked Pebble to explain what she meant by being a decent human being. Irene hinted that there were limits. *Why are you so nice to everybody, Pebble? Just tell me how far your decency quota goes.* When Pebble couldn't tell her, Irene gave her more homework. "Go home and find out."

"So, tell me about your life," Slim asked over the food they'd both collected from the buffet. He was thinner than she remembered – and older. *Or maybe it's just in comparison to Per.* Pebble was still high from making love to Per the night before. She still felt his smell on her body, even though she'd showered carefully this morning.

"I'm doing great." She didn't want to discuss her life with Slim. He invited her out to talk about their boys.

"Jon and Adam tell me you've got a new job."

"Yeah, it's terrific, I'm learning so much." She smiled at the thought. Einar was a great man to work for, especially now that she'd staked out her turf.

"Well, what exactly do you do?"

"Oh, I help my boss develop business plans and stuff like that." Pebble knew that Slim knew nothing about the advertising business.

"I'm just wondering," he chose his words carefully, "how you can work on shit like that... I mean after everything we've been through together."

She didn't want him preaching. *Damn, why did I come?*

"I don't have any problems with it." She tried to sound upbeat, but they knew each other too well. She remembered sitting by his bedside at the hospital after he'd gotten his head bashed after an Amnesty International demonstration. In an unusually violent episode in London, the police had banged up some of the kids who had chained themselves to public buildings in connection with the "Human Rights Tour" during the late 80s.

"I wonder what the kids think." Slim was wiping his mouth with his napkin. He ran away from home as a 16-year-old to join Greenpeace. Once when the police returned him (after an episode against Icelandic whaling in the North Sea) to his parents who were farmers in Jutland, they shrugged off his politics as temporary insanity.

Thinking back to their remark, Pebble couldn't help but wonder if they'd been right all along. There was something about Slim's politics that made him seem almost inhuman. *You can be on the right side and still be a mensch.*

RizRaz was not at all like the upbeat restaurants and cafes Pebble frequented in her new reincarnation. But Slim couldn't afford anything better and besides, he equated poverty with righteousness. The fact that he never had any money proved his virtue. He was into "just causes." His on-and-off employment teaching displaced minority groups just barely kept him going – another sign of his superiority. "I live outside the system," he declared proudly. Now that she was making money, he treated her like a sell-out, a traitor. He never mentioned the fact that she was single-handedly supporting his kids without any help from him.

"What do you mean?" she asked. "The kids think it's great."

"I'm surprised. I would think they'd wonder about having a mom who worked in an ad agency. Especially with their background."

"God, Slim, this is ridiculous." She sat up straight and put her napkin down. "I didn't accept your dinner invitation to have you lecture me. I thought we were going to talk about what we can do as parents to help Jon and Adam. If I'd known you were going to start in like this, I'd have stayed home."

"But you don't understand," he shot back, the righteous fury back in his eyes again, "my children are living with you."

"Slim, we're not married anymore..." but he didn't let her finish.

"My children are living with you and I don't approve of the way you're bringing them up. It's as simple as that."

All her impulses said "go!" But she forced herself to be calm and sit there. They'd had too many fights like this before. *Why can't we just be friends?* Fast Eddie's words (he was divorced, too and had three kids) went up in lights in her head, *It's so important for the kids to see their parents together, behaving like civilized human beings… It's so important for your kids…for your kids…* Pebble knew that Jon and Adam desperately wanted them to be on speaking terms.

"Slim…" she waited until her voice was steady, "…didn't you hear what I just said? We're not married anymore…and whether you like it or not, you can't tell me how to live my life anymore…" She stopped and laughed. "Well, obviously you can… but the point is I don't have to listen to you anymore."

Violent inner storms had left their mark on his handsome face. She watched him struggle once more with his anger. She wished he'd let it go, but he couldn't. He never really came to terms with their separation, and for that reason alone, she pitied him. *He should be stranded on a desert island with Irene for a couple of years.* Slim was so concerned with the world around him that he was incapable of facing the demons within. She was glad she wasn't married to him anymore.

"Now either we decide to behave civilly, or I think we'd better call it quits. The kids really want us to be friends. That's why I'm here." Her level-mindedness infuriated him.

"How can I be friends," he couldn't control himself any longer, "with the woman who betrayed me – who betrayed me and my children. You betrayed me, Pebble, yes you did! You betrayed everything I believe in. I still can't believe it. And now you're nothing but a hussy for some advertising bigwig who stands for everything we fought against all those years…"

She was hoping he'd regain his senses.

But he didn't, "And to think we stood on the barricades together. God I remember that morning when we met in Auckland. You were so beautiful. Beautiful." He stood up slowly, his fury making him larger than life. "And look at you now, it's pitiful to watch. You think money…you think freedom and going to bed with whoever you please, is going to make you happy – is going to make this world happy. Aren't you ashamed?"

Pebble just sat there without moving and watched him. It was like watching a movie she'd seen a hundred times before. It used to hurt, but it didn't anymore. Slim had lost his power to move or wound her. She was indifferent to the condemnation in his voice – dead to the ties that once bound them. Actually it was strangely liberating to sit there quietly and listen to him rant and rave. She might be a wounded bird, but at least she was free now. *Poor man – why is everything he sees so dark? How did he become so impoverished?* Pebble felt that something was desperately wrong with Slim, only she didn't know what. *Will he ever be able to sit down quietly and admit that he feels miserable – that everything's not right in his world?* She wished for him that he could reach out and touch someone – anyone – but in her bones she knew the earth would have to rotate on its axis many times before that happened. *The man's got so much heavy baggage with him. I guess nobody can help him but himself. God knows I tried.*

She watched him as if she was looking at somebody trapped in a fishbowl. She recognized his tactics – they were the same ones he'd used on her for years. He'd stomp and shout until he bamboozled her into doing whatever he wanted her to do. Most of the time, his routine was so refined that he managed to convince her that whatever it was that was wrong was her fault. He had a way of placing it right on her doorstep. And she let him do it – every time. That was their game. That was the devious, deceitful way – the sick way – they played with each other. Other people might play other games, but that was their game. *Name the blame.* That was their game. Whatever it was, it was her fault. *He manipulated me like this for years – by guilt.*

Sitting quietly and watching him bluster again brought her the precious gift of self-knowledge. *And I let him.* It exploded in her consciousness like a bomb. *AND I LET HIM!* If Irene had been there Pebble would have kissed her right on the lips. *Nobody – nobody was standing there pointing a gun to my head. Nobody. It was me all along! I let him.* She wished for an insane moment she could jump up and tell Slim. She felt like hugging him for letting her see. *He's been my teacher all along!* That was the irony of it, the ingeniousness of the ways of the world. *I guess Jon would say – you're learning, Mom.* She was glad she had a son who read all those New Age books. Sometimes he read her passages from Emmanuel's Book. Emmanuel said the world is a school and for the first time in her life, she really believed it. You just keep repeating your lessons until your learn them. *But it's taken me so long...and it's cost so much.*

Now she saw that Slim was a very insecure power person and what enraged him more than anything else were situations and people he couldn't control. Her insubordination was just one more sign of his impotence in a large and frightening universe. Their marriage had been fine until the day she questioned his might and his right. She interpreted his present rage as a sign that somewhere, deep in his subconscious, he thought he could win her back and regain his power. *This isn't love,* she saw it clearly, sadly, *and it never has been. What Slim calls love isn't love, it's a power trip. I'll love you as long as you do what I want you to do.* Now that she was independent and making money, he couldn't touch her – and that incensed him even more.

"Pebble, you know what I've always said." He was standing at the end of the table now, trembling all over. His lips seemed to curl with rage. She hoped his departure was imminent. She remained seated, watching their uneaten food turn cold.

"Slim, I really don't want to talk to you when you're in this frame of mind." She said the words carefully, quietly. "Why don't you just go?"

"You'll see." He leaned forward and pointed his finger at her. "You'll see. One day when the party's over and you have to pay, don't come crying to me."

She picked up her belongings and started to get up. *I don't need to listen to this anymore. If he's not going to leave, I am.* Irene was right; politeness does have its limits.

"Excuse me, if you'll just let me pass." She didn't look him in the eye, but clutched her purse to her breast as if it could protect her from his wrath.

"Just let me finish, Pebble." He blocked her path. The people at the other tables were watching them now. "Slim, stop it – please. Enough is enough."

"God damn it, Pebble, will you listen to me – for once in your life."

"Please get out of my way." She was mad now, too. She didn't want it to end like this, but she couldn't change the way things were. *I should have known better.*

She pushed herself past him, shoving him aside. If they hadn't been in a public place, she was sure he would have tried to restrain her. He'd never hit her before, but she always felt he came very close when she defied him. Today was no different.

She made a beeline for the door.

"Capitalist pig," he shouted at her back.

Chapter 13

"Well, what do you think?" Irene asked. Pebble was telling her what happened the other night when she met Slim. "Do you really think you've sold out?"

After contemplating Irene's question for a while, Pebble tried being ruthlessly honest and failed miserably. All she could say was, "I really don't know." Her answer was such a disappointment to both of them that Pebble plunged on bravely trying to come up with something that felt a little bit more satisfying. "You know, Irene, sometimes life is just so confusing. Here we are all safe and sound in this cozy little country, protected from much of what's going on in the world – with both the time and the opportunity to try and sort out our lives – and we still screw up. Sometimes it doesn't make sense. Anyway, when I was young in America, everybody with a social conscience freaked out. You remember how it was in the 80s; there was more than enough to get excited about. I was as much a part of that movement as Slim was back then. So when we met in Auckland during the Rainbow Warrior affair in '85, we had no problem communicating. I mean we knew all the same phrases – we shared the same mythology…we inhabited the same world. That's what brought us together. I mean it wasn't us, it was the world situation. We had this…well…common vision…but things change."

"Do they?"

"Sure they do, the world's not the same as it was then and I'm not either."

"Aren't they two different things, Pebble?" Irene adjusted her horn-rimmed glasses carefully. She dressed like so many other Danish women who regard themselves as fervent members of the intelligentsia – faded corduroy trousers, a sweatshirt and good running shoes. She wore her luxurious, gray-streaked hair pulled tightly back from her face.

"What do you mean?" Pebble was confused.

"I mean just what I said – the way the world has changed and the way you've changed – are two different things."

"Yeah, I guess so…"

"Maybe it would be a good idea to look at them separately…"

Pebble nodded, but in truth, she felt annoyed. *Sometimes Irene can be such a pain. Why do I always have to sort things out?* Pebble was starting to appreciate the amount of hard work that went into self-discovery. At times like this she wasn't sure she had what it takes. *All this responsibility stuff is enough to make you puke! … Maybe I should pack up and go home.* All of a sudden, Pebble was more interested in having a good time than in learning about herself. If Irene had known how Pebble was feeling, she would have agreed wholeheartedly. There was only one small catch – Irene firmly believed that self-discovery was a prerequisite to having a good time.

"Tell me about Slim's idealism." Irene knew Pebble needed prodding. It was usually like that when people had to look at something that was bothering them.

"What do you want to know?"

"Well, try to describe it to me first." Irene smoothed back her hair and settled comfortably into her chair.

"Well, it's hard to explain… Basically I don't think Slim's beliefs are any different than yours or mine. I mean he believes in social justice and racial equality and peace on earth and saving the rain forest and all that stuff. The problem is more what he does with those beliefs."

"What do you mean?" Irene kept on prodding.

"He's different from us."

"How?"

"Well, he's…" Pebble searched for the right word, "he's well…a fanatic. I think that's how you'd describe him."

"What do you mean by a fanatic, Pebble. Explain it to me." Irene wanted Pebble to nail it down.

"I don't know exactly." She paused again while she tried to find the right explanation. "I think Slim thinks he's better than other people – superior. I know it's hard to imagine, but I think he feels he knows what's good for other people or that he can solve their problems better than they can themselves. I don't know, sometimes I think it's like he looks down on other people... It's not a very compassionate attitude... I mean why should he be able to solve other people's problems better than they can?"

"That's a good question, Pebble. Especially when I get the impression, from what you've told me, that he's not very successful when it comes to solving his own problems." Irene usually didn't say so much, but she was trying to encourage Pebble to speak more freely. Pebble had a tendency to only say things when she was sure they were correct which greatly limited their exchange. Irene wanted her to dare a little more and to understand that she could verbalize her thoughts – and send them out into the world like little test balloons – without committing any crimes or making any judgments.

"Pebble, before we go on, I just want to say one thing. I know I've told you this before, but I think it's worth repeating. I am never going to repeat anything you say to another living soul. It's important that you allow yourself to speak freely. You're not passing judgment on anyone by discussing your ideas, emotions or reactions with me. That's why you're here. To test your ideas and feelings, and to find out a little more about yourself. This is a process of discovery and it's supposed to be fun. So try to let yourself go a little bit more."

Pebble thought about what Irene said for a minute. "I guess you're right, I kind of have the feeling I shouldn't say anything unless I'm sure it's right."

"But what's right anyway, Pebble?" Irene asked. "I mean there is no right here...what we're basically talking about is your experience – and who you are. By knowing yourself a little better, by gaining a little more insight into your own preferences and limitations, you should be able to navigate more successfully through life's complexities… What I'm trying to say is by understanding yourself a little better; you should be able to enjoy yourself a little more."

"Clare says she's happier since she's been going to therapy with you. At first I didn't believe her, because from the outside it looks to me as if her life is just as confused as it always was. But she says she feels better about herself and I guess that's something you can't always judge from the outside… I don't know if I feel any better about myself since I started coming here, Irene, but I do know I'm more aware of my inner processes…"

"Well, that's a good start," Irene smiled. Pebble was learning. "Now where did we leave off?"

"We were talking about my marriage," said Pebble and cleared her throat. "If you look at it, you'll see that we always had a big communications problem. I mean, it was hard for me to communicate with him. Well that's not completely true. In the beginning, when we both had the same youthful ideals, I could – or I thought I could. It was easy then and that's why I think it had something to do with the times – because in the 80s, we were both a part of the youth movement here – there was so much going on that held us together. But after our children were born, I started to realize how immature he was. He just couldn't seem to grow up. I don't know if it was because he didn't want to or what. But he didn't. It was like he didn't change. He was still this kid, instead of a grown man. He couldn't hold down a steady job and he was always changing his mind about things – going off on tangents. When you have your own children, you change. Or at least I did. Kids make your responsibilities change – but for Slim, it didn't. He figured it was my job to take care of all that – to adapt and deal with it."

"Why you?" Irene interrupted.

"I didn't understand at first, but later I realized it was because

I was the woman. Children, in Slim's world, are woman's work. Anyway…that's how it was. I mean I accepted his vision, too – and became the woman he wanted me to be. I accepted the responsibility for keeping us afloat, but he stayed the same. He had all these ideas, while I worked like a horse. Sometimes I thought he talked too much. I remember thinking – this man's got such a big mouth, if only he'd practice half of what he preached. But I was loyal. I had to be. He was my husband and the father of my two babies. He said I was supposed to back him up no matter what – and I did. Backing him up became my mission in life. (For quite a while anyway.) But how did he back me up? I was like this second-class citizen. Looking back I can see that somehow he convinced me that doing everything was my job. All the while he gallivanted around Scandinavia going to meetings and working for different movements. There was revolution alright in our family, but not when it came to women's lib. It was a strange mix. Sometimes when I think about the past, I get so mad. But then I think I've got it all wrong. I actually had this really strong feeling when I was sitting in the restaurant with Slim the other night that I couldn't just blame him… I mean, I let him get away with it. I agreed to it all. At the time, I mean, sitting there across the table from him the other night, when I realized all this, I almost jumped up and thanked him because I realized that he really was my teacher. I mean, on some very deep level our relationship had to go on until I was mature enough to say stop. I realized the other night that he never forced me to do anything… I did it all of my own free will. In the end, though I really wasn't conscious of it at the time, I guess I just got fed up with all his bullshit. I mean, I just couldn't take another word from him. The way he manipulated me… with his right-eousness. Now when I look back, I can't believe I let him browbeat me for so long."

"Seems to me he's still manipulating you, Pebble."

"Well, not really."

"Are you sure? Why did you agree to go to dinner with him in the first place?"

"Well, because he said he wanted to talk about the kids."

Irene laughed. "And?"

"And what?"

"He's always used your children and guilt to manipulate you...he's done it for years...what made you think he suddenly changed?"

"Are you saying that on some level I really do feel guilty?"

"Well do you?"

Pebble knew she did, but it was hard to admit it. She forced herself (ruthless honesty, right?) to speak. "Well, maybe I do, but having a broken marriage behind you is nothing to be proud of...is it?"

"Well I guess it depends on how you look at it," said Irene, "but it's certainly nothing to be ashamed of either."

"I don't think I'm ashamed, it's more like I feel bad about the kids. It's hard to explain. I guess I feel I let them down. I mean not being able to get along with their father. Everybody dreams about having a happy family. I just feel I failed."

"You weren't the only one in this marriage, Pebble. Slim was married to you, too. It takes two to make a marriage and a divorce."

"I know... I mean I think I know, in my mind anyway. But emotionally, it's not so easy. I mean I'm not sure. I really wish we could be friends. Lots of people get divorced and still manage to keep some kind of a relationship going because of their children."

"You might want that, Pebble, but what about Slim?"

"I know what you mean..."

"I get the impression that your ex-husband may not be that kind of person. He doesn't exactly sound like a person who can tolerate a lot of emotional freedom. You said so yourself. You said he was a fanatic, that he was immature, that he had difficulty dealing with his own problems...is that the kind of person who's going to be friends with his ex-wife, especially when he's such a stiff-necked, old-fashioned radical and she works for the most successful advertising agency in Denmark?"

Pebble laughed. "It doesn't sound good, does it?"

"No, it doesn't," said Irene and laughed, too. "Maybe you're just going to have to accept Slim the way he is, too, Pebble. I mean what makes you think that you can change him? And more importantly, what gives you the right to change him? That's thinking and acting just the way he does."

"I never thought of it that way."

"Well maybe it's time you do. You didn't want him changing you. Why should you be able to change him? It's a two-way street, you know. You've got to respect him for what he is, too, whatever that happens to be. Give him the respect you want yourself."

Pebble marveled at Irene's way of looking at the world. *How would things be if everyone treated each other the way Irene did?*

Irene continued, "Did you ever consider the fact that in spite of what you may or may not want – your ex-husband just may not be able to deal with you, or his feelings about you, at this moment in time... Perhaps he's never going to be able to deal with his feelings for you... Did you ever consider that?"

"You mean it's not going to get better? I keep hoping it's going to get better."

"Well maybe it will, and maybe it won't. Whatever happens, you have to go on living your life. Right?"

"Yeah." Life without any link or accountability to Slim was hard to imagine. Pebble didn't realize how connected she still was to her ex-husband. "I didn't realize how much he still influences me."

Irene got up and started pacing the room. Outside, the sun was shining brightly.

Pebble never heard Irene talk so much before. "Maybe," Irene continued, "you're going to have to stop feeling guilty about the problems Slim is having dealing with you. Did you ever think about that?"

"No, not really."

She's really giving it to me today. Pebble loved it when Irene allowed Pebble to see how intensely she cared about her clients.

"Well, if you never looked at it that way, then maybe you're still operating on the assumption that it's your responsibility to make things right, Pebble."

Once again, Irene hit the bull's eye.

Pebble smiled. "How did you get to be so insightful?"

"Being insightful is my business," Irene shot back. They both laughed. "If you're still operating on the assumption that you're the one who's supposed to make things right," Irene continued, "then why did you get divorced in the first place? You are divorced, aren't you?"

"Sure I am," Pebble nodded. "I mean I thought I was!"

"Well if you are, are you still responsible for his anger and hurt? Or for the fact that he's not a very successful person? Is that your responsibility, too? Why isn't he doing something about his problems himself? Who appointed you to be his caretaker?"

"I guess he did...and well, I allowed him to...and now that I'm not his caretaker anymore, he's furious." Pebble laughed. "Men are such jerks. Actually I just realized Albert's the same." It was another new insight.

"Let's not mix Albert into this yet," said Irene, trying to keep Pebble focused. "Let's go back to the capitalist-pig bit. He really got to you, didn't he?"

"Yeah, I mean it's just not true." Just thinking about it was enough to make Pebble mad again. "I work hard for my money. I really do – and I support our kids all by myself." She didn't realize how angry she was until she heard her own voice.

"Okay, okay, so how come this particular insult upsets you so much? You just told me the man was a jerk and you didn't care what he thought about you. But obviously you do."

"He ought to know me better." Pebble was irate. "We were married for 14 years. He knows how hard I've worked all my life to make a positive contribution to this planet – and he knows what I believe in…and now, just because we got divorced and I changed tracks, he accuses me of abandoning everything I ever stood for."

"So what?"

"I still want him to like me and respect me." She surprised herself.

"And what if he doesn't? What if he can't?"

"Well, he should."

"Why?" Irene demanded.

"Because I'm the mother of his children." Pebble wasn't in doubt.

"Well, what if he can't?"

"You just said that." Pebble was almost mad at Irene, too.

"I know, but you didn't really answer me. Just because you were married once and just because you're the mother of his children, it was still you who rejected him. Don't you understand that, Pebble? You rejected him. And you still expect him to love and respect you."

Pebble gazed out the window. Christianshavn's Canal looked quaint and lovely in the bright sunshine.

When she didn't reply, Irene continued, "Rejection is a very unpleasant experience. Very. And I think men probably have a harder time dealing with rejection than women do. You are going to have to recognize that no matter how nice you think you are, you were the one who rejected him. You were the one who said – I'm through with you, Charlie. He may never be able to forgive you for that."

Pebble didn't want to talk about it anymore. Irene had made her point, so she said, "I guess I must have some doubts about working for an ad agency, too."

"Well, maybe you do," sighed Irene, realizing they were

coming to the end of their session. "Now I don't know if you should, but the most important thing is to put the responsibility for the way you feel where it belongs."

"You mean with me?"

"Of course I mean with you! Who else could I possibly mean? The Queen of Denmark! Come on, Pebble, do you want to do the hot seat exercise again?" Pebble laughed. "You think I need it?" She was ready to go home.

"I don't know. Do you?"

"Nay," said Pebble, "I'll just end up saying the same things I said last time."

"Which is what?" Irene wanted her to say it again.

"That it's about time I got my act together and stop acting like a doormat."

Chapter 14

Late in May, Einar threw one hell of a party. The night of Einar's party was one of those extraordinary early summer nights you find only in Scandinavia. To truly appreciate the tenderness of such an evening, you almost have to live through a long, dark Nordic winter – a time of cold and gloom which can seem to have no end. Then a spectacular evening like the night of Einar's party can truly set the heart of the most hardhearted individual aflame with a crazy, inexplicable love of life.

On this particular Saturday, the sun didn't set until almost 10 p.m. The evening was surprisingly balmy and warm, pregnant with all the wonderful promise of the long midsummer nights to come and the incredible lightness of those dancing shadows. It was something all the sun-starved people of the North dream of. Einar couldn't have planned it better if he'd had a direct line to God himself.

Einar had reason to celebrate – the fashion show he produced and directed for Denmark's top furrier at the Hotel George Cinque in Paris earlier in May was a huge success. Somehow, Einar convinced the Danish Crown Princess to preside over the show's inauguration – quite a coup for the Republic Group – and the international fashion press was all over the event. Vogue magazine ran a four-page spread of the svelte Scandinavian models looking divine in futuristic furs on Einar's high-tech catwalk in this most famous of Parisian hotels. Pebble, who was suddenly lifted from anonymity to – Ms. Beach, l'assistant de Einar Bro – found the heady world of Paris fashion, a mad, charming frenzy after her quiet life as a newly divorced freelancer in sleepy Copenhagen. *And to think I recently spent 18 days in the wilds of Greenland, drinking with a bunch of cowboys.* The incongruities of her life amazed Pebble. *Or that I went to bed with a 24-year-old electrician from Taastrup and loved every minute of it.*

God – Molly should only know!

Obviously Molly was overjoyed when Pebble started working for Einar. "I'm so glad you've come to your senses, Pebble." Pebble's trip to Greenland almost worried Morris and Molly to death. Even Pebble was glad there was no chance of her parents finding out what really did happen while she was up there. In fact she was quite relieved nobody she knew would ever know. Her only problem was that she had a hard time forgetting Albert – and she couldn't figure out why. She didn't realize that Albert was a throwback, a memory, a long-cherished dream of hers that never came true. He represented an almost childish desire to find that one strong man who'd protect her from everything, and the successful Pebble – that competent business woman – was strangely incapable of cutting through the bullshit of her own little girl fantasies. She was almost afraid to admit (even to herself) that she wanted desperately to be in his arms again, no matter how crazy it seemed. She didn't even dare tell Irene.

Sometimes, longing for Albert almost made Pebble consider going to bed with Einar. Strange as it may seem, there was a connection, however illogical. Her very real physical need for Albert had a way of turning, at times, into a general mad yearning for male energy. When that happened, Pebble found herself even considering Einar, as unattractive as he was. But she never went further than the mental process – even though he gave her every opportunity to do so. She was well aware that she'd never forgive herself if she allowed him to move into the circle of her privacy. So Einar and Pebble continued to play their own special version of touch-and-go at work. It happened almost every day. It was as if Einar was so convinced he'd conquer her eventually, that he kept the pressure up. Knowing that Pebble respected him immensely certainly fueled his fire – and helped him continue to behave as the gracious gentleman no matter how many times she turned him down. He pushed, but took care not to push too hard, and bided his time enjoying the inevitable march towards intimacy with Pebble. He enjoyed the way she liked him more and more – enjoyed the way she often allowed herself to drop her guard, even though WonderLift still stood between them like an ugly barbed-wire fence. Probably Pebble would have been much more relaxed around Einar from the start if it hadn't been for WonderLift. She often wanted to broach the subject with him, but never quite dared. She didn't know where such a discussion might lead and wasn't sure she'd be able to control herself if she got very emotional. So she was torn between regarding Einar as her mentor/savior – *he gave me a job when I really needed it* – or as the man who did her in. *If it wasn't for WonderLift, I'd still be on my own.* The fact that she was having a wonderful time as Einar's assistant made the whole matter even more complicated. Not only was Einar a kind and brilliant mentor, he was her passport to another world. The trip to the fur show in Paris, being just such a case in point of the new worlds Einar opened for her.

Einar was in for some surprises too. He knew from the start that Pebble was a talented copywriter, but he never suspected she possessed such business acumen as she did. She was such a good assistant that he soon discovered she had the potential to be a top-level manager at the Republic Group or anywhere else for that matter. He thanked his lucky stars that she wasn't aware of it yet, but he knew she would be soon. With her brains, it was bound to happen. All he could do was hope he'd be her lover before she was ready to fly on her own. Being such a homely, awkward man didn't make things any easier for Einar either because basically Einar didn't want to be as attracted to her sexually as he was – it made life too complicated. But he couldn't get over her, try as he may. He really didn't want to hire Pebble – he was well aware that hiring someone he was so attracted to was like playing with fire, but he felt guilty about the WonderLift scandal, so he did. He knew Pebble would be out of work without his protection. At least, he was relieved when he noticed how happy she seemed working for him. It had to be a sign she was unaware of the ugly gossip surrounding her name.

The night of Einar's party, the usual coastal wind had disappeared (as if Einar Bro was truly in control) to some far corner of the globe while the Katrine Madsen Trio played sweet music on the terrace of Skovriderkroen. Skovriderkroen – combination brasserie, restaurant and discotheque – was one of the absolute trendiest places to throw a party of course, nestled as it was comfortably in fashionable Charlottenlund, close to the Sound which separates Denmark and Sweden – and only a short 15-minute drive from downtown Copenhagen.

A drink in hand, Pebble was weaving her way through the crowded terrace, making her way down from the inn towards the calm, glistening sea quietly lapping the shore. Pebble wanted to sit by herself by the icy waters of the Sound for a few minutes – away from the booze and the partying. Not that it wasn't one of those wonderful parties – the kind only Danes can invent when it's time to start celebrating the advent of summer. Einar was a serious party-maker – no person or detail, no matter how insignificant, was forgotten. Einar didn't just invite the select team of people who worked for him on the Parisian fur show – he invited every employee of the Republic Group (including the sandwich lady in the canteen), and everyone and their uncle employed by the Republic Group's growing subsidiaries in Sweden and Norway.

It was 11:30 p.m. when Pebble sat down on a wooden bench by the sea, a glass of Southern Comfort on the rocks in her hand. Far behind her were sounds of drunken laughter and the smooth music of the Katrine Madsen Trio. Pebble wasn't drunk, just very, very relaxed. The evening had been beautiful, everyone treated her like a queen as she laughed and flirted with countless dashing young men and women in the Republic family. Being Ms. Beach, l'assistant de Einar Bro, was more than fun – she had immediate access to the whole corporate culture of the Republic

Group. It was a whole new way of life.

Who would ever have guessed? Pebble sunk down into the comfortableness of being just exactly who she was. She knew she was experiencing something unique. *How many times in my life have I felt like this?* She couldn't remember when it had happened before. *Maybe never.* Pebble might have cried (for joy and the turn of fortune in her life) if Einar hadn't disturbed her special moment.

"Pebble," his voice was strange, "I've been looking everywhere for you..." He had come up behind her and put his hand on her shoulder.

She turned around in surprise – she wasn't expecting anyone. She thought she'd slipped away quite unnoticed. But Einar found her, pulling her from a special place she'd never visited before...no wonder she was stunned.

"Einar?"

"May I sit down..."

She moved over on the bench, making room for him. She was still not quite there.

"What a magnificent night." She tried to come back to the now.

"Pebble...?"

"Yes, Einar?" She could feel his warmth besides her. She'd never seen him drunk before.

"Isn't it a wonderful bunch of people...?" He waved his arm back towards the inn and the crowded terrace.

"Yes, really." She meant it.

"My people..." his voice was slurred. "Every one of them loves me... you know."

She'd never heard him speak like that. But that's the way liquor works... "They do..."

"Einar, let's go back... We can't just both disappear like this..." Pebble felt uncomfortable. "It's not polite for the star of the show to..." She was trying to be funny, feeling the darkness of his mood surrounding her.

"Oh come on, Pebble, nobody's going to miss us for a few minutes. And besides, it's not often I get to sit with you like this...we're always so busy when we're together..."

He moved closer. He was wearing one of those wonderful designer shirts he was so fond of. In the darkness, his frog-like features were softer.

"Pebble..." He tried to put his arm around her.

"Please, Einar..."

"Aren't you cold?"

"No. I'm okay..."

Einar gazed out towards the lights twinkling in the distance along the coast of Sweden. "You just don't understand, Pebble... my wife's still seeing Peter Cato..." Pebble was surprised at Einar's admission, *Why is he telling me this?* Since that dinner at the Hotel d'Angleterre, Einar never talked about his private life with Pebble again.

"Birgitte's still seeing him...after all these years." It was almost as if Einar was talking more to himself than to Pebble. "I thought they'd given up on each other... long ago..."

Pebble didn't know what to say.

"I know I've never been an attractive man..."

God, I wish he'd stop. Pebble felt sorry for him, but didn't know how to deal with his revelations. *He is my boss.* "Come on, Einar, it can't be that bad." She let him sit close. He smelled of cologne and booze.

"You know, Pebble, Peter was my best friend once. And now he hates me. And my wife hates me, too."

"It can't be true. I don't believe it."

"It is...it really is."

"Then why don't you get divorced?" Pebble asked. She surprised herself by asking. "I mean what the hell – I'm divorced. Jesus, everybody's divorced."

"Divorced?" Einar laughed. "Birgitte would never consider

it."

"Well, why not? Almost everybody I know is divorced."

Einar laughed, "You don't know my wife."

"No, I don't... but I don't understand, Einar. If she really hates you, why would she want to stay married to you?"

"Well, first there is my money..." He paused and took another swig of his drink. "Yes my money, Birgitte really likes money..."

Pebble had heard about their mansion up the coast in Humlebaek, but she'd never seen it.

"And then there are the children. Birgitte was brought up on the West Coast of Jutland – she comes from a very religious family." Einar turned and looked at Pebble. "But a New Yorker like you would never understand." He laughed bitterly. "I have the most wonderful daughter, Pebble. Wonderful. Christina is simply the apple of my eye... But I guess you can understand the money part...first and last, Birgitte loves my money."

"It can't be that bad..."

But Einar wasn't listening. He was drunk and mad. "It's just a crying shame...being married to someone who hates you. Nobody ever despised you I'm sure...so you'll never understand." Einar looked down into his glass and laughed again. "The two of them were made for each other...they really are."

Pebble wished she could extricate herself from the situation. *Einar's my boss. I don't want to know this.* But she couldn't just walk away.

"Einar, let's talk about something else..."

"You know why Birgitte isn't here? That bitch...do you know why?"

Pebble didn't say a word. *I guess I have to know.*

Einar put his arm around Pebble. As she turned to push him gently away, she noticed tears on his cheeks.

"Oh Einar..." He looked pitiful and forlorn in the light of the moon. *Poor little frog face.* The waves lapped gently on the shore.

Pebble wished they would comfort him. "Einar," she started out slowly, in her kindest voice, "this is a night to be happy – for you – and for everybody in the Republic Group... I mean, without you where would we be? You're such a talented person..." She knew it sounded corny, but she wanted to comfort him. "Look how successful you are..." She knew her words sounded empty.

"Talented – me?" He almost laughed. "What difference does it make, when I'm so lonely and unhappy?"

"Oh, Einar, just think of all the people who admire you." She tried, but her words just seemed to roll off his back.

"You're such a nice person, Pebble... but you can't imagine how it is being married to Birgitte – that bitch... Do you know...it's unbelievable...I could wring her neck..." Suddenly he laughed, but Pebble didn't like the way he sounded. She was glad they were so far away from the crowded terrace. *What if somebody sees him like this?* She didn't quite understand why, but she wanted to protect him.

"That bitch...do you know she was the one who betrayed Peter?" Pebble had no idea what he was talking about. *Must be some private matter I'm not privy to.*

"She betrayed him, she really did." It was almost as if he was mumbling to himself. "That two-faced bitch... Oh if only I could wring her neck...I'd do it gladly..."

"Come on, Einar, let's go back to the party. You're just getting yourself all worked up for nothing." She stood up and took his arm and tried to pull him up from the bench.

"No, no." He withdrew his arm from her grip. "Do you know what she did – what my wife did?"

"Einar, please... I really don't want to know..." But she sat down again, afraid to leave him alone in the mood he was in.

"Birgitte and I were having this insane fight – it was months and months ago – around the time I found out she was seeing Peter again... And I said to her (almost in jest) something like – 'what can you possibly see in that sweet-talking conman?' which really burned her up (of course) because according to Birgitte, Peter is God's gift to womankind. Well, anyway...she was defending him, she really was, telling me how smart he is...and all that stuff..." Einar kept pushing his hair back from his forehead nervously as he talked and rattled the ice in his empty glass. "And, Pebble, I just sat there... I mean I was just trying to be calm, and so I just sat there. I remember we were in the bedroom and I was sitting on the bed and she was ranting and raving – really hysterical, and all I could think about was how to end the discussion and get out of there. But she wouldn't stop. She just went on and on about me and about Peter. And when I finally stood up and told her enough was enough, she said 'Einar, you just don't have any idea how talented Peter really is...' and to prove it or maybe just to humiliate me a little bit more (like it wasn't bad enough she was seeing him again), she flings a bit of unpleasant business information right smack in my face."

"You've got to understand, Pebble, that even though Birgitte's got a good head on her shoulders, we almost never discuss business. Well Birgitte says to me – just like that – Peter's American copywriter developed this wonderful campaign for him so he's launching WonderLift soon, way ahead of time. You see Birgitte probably just heard in passing that both Peter and I were representing similar products and that we were competing for the same market. She probably didn't think anything of it at the time, but suddenly, when she was going for my throat, it dawned on her that she had a bit of information she could hurt me with.

"So I said – 'oh yeah?' And she said – 'yeah.' And I said – 'well, how do you know?' And she says – 'well I saw some papers on his desk the other day...' And I say... 'oh come on, Birgitte... why should I believe you, for all I know you're just trying to hurt me?' And the bitch says – 'you can believe me Einar because I can tell you that they're going to be launching

WonderLift on February 20^{th'} ..." and Einar laughed and laughed. "Isn't that amazing, Pebble?"

Pebble sat as if turned to stone.

Einar slapped his knee drunkenly and kept on laughing at his story. "So you see, my charming wife betrayed her lover, too..."

Einar was silent for a while. Then he said, "It sure does serve him right..."

Pebble stared out at the quiet sea. *So I didn't tell Einar,* she muttered to herself.

"And you know something," Einar was so drunk he didn't realize what he'd just told Pebble, "I called up YourLift the very next morning and moved the launch fast forward. Poor Peter...anybody my wife touches is in for trouble..."

So I didn't tell Einar!

Einar was quiet, lost in thought. The sea was utterly silent. "The funny thing is...since this happened, Birgitte's been behaving a little more civilly...she knows I can ruin her affair with Peter any day of the week. All I have to do is tell him it was Birgitte who told me the WonderLift launch date."

* * *

The next day Pebble told Irene.

"It wasn't me."

Irene had heard the story before, but at that time Pebble wasn't sure.

"Well, what are you going to do about it?"

"I don't know."

"Well, maybe you should think about it." Irene was surprised that Pebble was so subdued. As far as Irene was concerned, Pebble should be in a stark, raging fury. "I mean, we're talking about your career, Pebble. Your life."

"I know, but I'm just so stunned – I almost can't believe it."

"Believe what – that you were the fall guy?"

"Well, not just that – I mean the way this whole thing has changed my life."

"What do you mean?" Irene was puzzled.

"Well, I mean I'd never be working for Einar if this hadn't happened."

"So?"

"Well, the irony of the whole situation is that I love working for that man. He's a terrific boss and I'm learning so much. It's really changed my perspective on a lot of things."

"Like what?"

"Oh, I don't know...like about myself...like about how much talent for business I have."

"Why do you think Einar hired you?"

"Well, originally I thought it was because I was a talented copywriter."

"And now?"

"And now I'm not so sure."

"Do you think he hired you out of pity?"

Pebble was aghast, "I never thought of it that way... I just thought maybe he hired me to cover up the WonderLift thing... No, I never thought it was out of pity."

"And now?"

Pebble thought about it for a moment, "I really don't know." It was a weird thought.

"You really like Einar, don't you?"

"Yeah, I guess I do."

"It's nothing to be ashamed of, Pebble. You're not the first woman in the world to be fascinated by powerful men. But I think you should be aware of it."

Pebble was almost mad. *Irene doesn't understand a thing.*

"That's not fair, Irene, there's more to it than that. Einar's so intelligent and so capable. And he's given me so many wonderful opportunities."

"But, Pebble, you seem to forget, you're intelligent and

capable, too. Why should you always be dependent on other people? Why does somebody else have to give you the opportunity all the time?" Irene was big like a man again. The windows to her office were open wide. Outside, small groups of people were sitting along the canal, drinking beers in the bright sunshine. The leaves on the trees glistened green in the sunshine. "Why are you always servicing others, Pebble? Why you?"

Pebble couldn't answer Irene's question. *No matter how much progress I make, she always wants me to make more.* Pebble tried to explain the feeling she had on the bench just before Einar found her and disturbed her. "It was the most wonderful feeling I ever had in my whole life…I don't know how to describe it. It was like I was so whole…in a way I've never been before in my life. I was so comfortable being me. Sounds strange, doesn't it? But I've never felt like that before in my whole life."

"It doesn't sound strange at all," said Irene, sitting large and comfortably in her chair. "In fact, it sounds very good, Pebble, but it's just not enough…this feeling good. I mean what are you going to do about your situation now? It's not enough that Einar opens a lot of doors for you. What about your good name? You've got to think of your reputation – or have you forgotten what everybody else in the business must be saying about you?"

"I guess I've tried hard to forget." Which was true, Pebble was good at looking the other way when the truth was unpleasant.

"Don't you think Peter Cato should know it wasn't you? Or have you forgotten the panic you were in when all this happened? You were almost hysterical. Remember? You said nobody would ever give you work again. At that time, you felt you were forced into taking the job Einar offered you. So in a way, it's besides the point that you like it so much."

"But I can't just go in there and tell Peter."

"Why not?"

"Well, for one, why should he believe me? I mean it's an incredible story in a way."

"What do you mean?"

"Well, that Einar learned the launch date from his own wife. Peter didn't tell Birgitte or anything. She just happened to see some papers on his desk by accident. Can't you just imagine how it happened…"

"So what if it's incredible…" Irene was persistent; she didn't like having her clients slandered. "It's the truth, Pebble."

"Okay, say I do go to Peter and tell him the truth; what good will it do? It's not like I have any proof… I mean, Birgitte is Peter's mistress… I mean, how can I prove that she told him? Look, maybe Peter and Birgitte really do love each other – how should I know? All I do know is I don't see any reason why Peter should believe me…he'd probably throw me out of his office again." Pebble laughed.

"I see what you mean," said Irene, laughing, too. "But even if he throws you out, he'll have to think about what you said after-wards."

Pebble didn't reply. She knew Irene was right. She had to clear her name.

Irene tried a new tact. "Let's try something else, Pebble."

Pebble glanced at her watch before saying, "Okay." There was still a half an hour left of her session. *God, I've had more than enough of Irene for today!*

Irene got up and placed an empty chair before Pebble.

Oh no, not another one of her exercises.

"I want you to imagine that Peter Cato is sitting in this chair, Pebble."

Pebble sighed; she was getting wise to Irene's methods. "Yeah, and tell you what I'd like to say to him?"

Irene laughed.

"You know, I'd like to beat his brains out…"

"Really, why?"

"Well, he didn't treat me fairly."

"Are you sure? Remember he thinks you told Einar the launch

date, right?"

"Yeah, that's true." Pebble was crestfallen.

"Actually, what I wanted you to do was complete the encounter you had with him the day you came back from Greenland. You were so stunned by his accusations that you practically didn't defend yourself, did you?"

"Well, I tried...but I was so surprised by the whole thing."

"Right. Well, looking back, what do you feel like doing? I don't care if it sounds immature, irrational, overly emotional or whatever, now's your chance to have it out with Peter – scot-free."

"Well, I'm still mad at him for misusing me two years ago."

"Two years ago?"

"Yeah."

"What happened two years ago?"

"Well, I did some ghostwriting for Peter; it was just after I split up with Slim and didn't have a penny to my name. So I worked for Peter on the cheap. God, Irene, I was so naive then. Anyway, I did the entire English language campaign for him for a company called Nordkyst..."

"Nordkyst? Sure I've heard of them. They make those neat clothes for kids, right?"

"Yeah, that's them. Anyway, I did all this work for him and the campaign I created was an enormous success. Nordkyst became a booming business in the United States because of me, but Peter got all the credit for it."

Irene was silent.

"He was lauded to the sky in the press – but he never mentioned me. Peter was the creative director at DDB Needham at the time – and basically I think he was rewarded so lucratively for the Nordkyst campaign that he used the money to start Fem-Ads."

"You never told me this before, Pebble." Irene's voice was unusually stern.

"Well, I didn't think it was relevant before now."

"Relevant!" Irene almost shouted. Pebble had never seen her so mad. "You help a guy make a million bucks without getting any credit for it – and you don't think it's relevant…sometimes I don't believe what women…" Irene stopped herself short when she saw the look on Pebble's face.

"My uncle Mel in New York who's a big shot at Young & Rubicam was furious when he heard about it. He wanted to go to Nordkyst in New York and tell them it was me who did the campaign, but I was so insecure about myself that I made him promise not to do it. I guess I should have let him."

"You guess…" Irene voice was heavy with sarcasm. "So what do you really want to say to Peter Cato?" Irene pointed at the empty chair.

"Well." Pebble paused. "I'm not really sure."

"Oh come on, Pebble." Irene made no effort to hide her impatience. "Isn't it about time you grew up?"

Pebble blanched. "I don't need you to tell me what to do." But instead of confronting Irene, she bit her tongue and walked over to the window. She stood for a while looking at the crowds of happy people enjoying the warm May sunshine.

Pebble turned towards Irene. "You know," she said, her face pale and her voice trembling slightly, "sometimes I think you're just a little too pushy. I know you want me to grow up and take charge of my own life – and I know you're right. But I've got to do it in my own way and not yours!"

If Irene was pleased, she didn't show it.

Pebble walked over to her chair, grabbed her purse and marched out of Irene's office.

Chapter 15

About a week later, when Pebble was all alone in the office, Einar called her from Frankfurt because he'd forgotten to take some highly sensitive market information with him to the Odenweiss & Hauser meeting that day.

"Pebble, I need the figures from the consumer electronics survey we did for Odenweiss & Hauser." Einar's voice rumbled over the line.

Einar, and his secretary Marianne, had taken an early flight to Frankfurt that morning to negotiate a deal with Odenweiss & Hauser Gmbh, a German high-tech company, who were going to start marketing their pricy camcorders in Scandinavia. The Republic Group was the front-running agency pitching for the account. Apparently, an extra meeting had been arranged in great haste and when Einar and Marianne charged out of the office that morning to catch their flight, Einar forget the results of the market research the Republic Group compiled to pinpoint the possible marketing strategies in relation to the tastes of potential buyers in Scandinavia.

"Pebble, the figures are in my wall cabinet. Go into my office and I'll tell you how to find them."

Pebble shared a large suite of offices with Einar and Marianne. Marianne occupied the cream-colored front office, while Einar had a large conference room and office (with a breathtaking view of Copenhagen harbor) directly behind hers. Pebble's small, but bright office – she had a large skylight in the ceiling – was to the right of Marianne's. Nobody else had access to these rooms on the top floor of the Republic Group townhouse in Nyhavn, the picturesque harbor district of Copenhagen.

Pebble went into Einar's office and sat down at his black lacquered desk. "Are you sitting at my desk now?"

"Yes," said Pebble and almost sighed. This was the first time she'd ever surveyed the world from Einar's point of view. *Wouldn't it be nice to sit on a power spot like this?*

"Okay, now open the third drawer on the right-hand side of my desk and in the middle of all my odds and ends, you'll find a little silver box."

Pebble opened the drawer and saw the box in the jumble of paperclips, rubber bands and fountain pens.

"Open the box."

She did and found four slender silver keys inside.

"Do you see the key that's slightly larger than the other three?"

"Yes." She picked it up.

"Well, that's the key which belongs to the black cabinet on the wall to your right. Now go over and find the file marked 'Hauser' and come back to my desk with it."

Pebble opened the cabinet (it was more like a vault) and quickly found the Hauser file. She brought the thin file back to Einar's desk.

"Okay, now find the papers marked 'consumer electronics' on top. I want the figures from the test we ran in the Stockholm area."

All in all, it took about 20 minutes. Einar had an exacting mind and an eye for detail. He'd obviously studied the Hauser file carefully before, so he knew exactly what information he needed to close the deal with them. By the time Einar was finished, he'd made Pebble flip back and forth between the various sections of the survey so rapidly, that she was all hot and sweaty. After she said goodbye, she kicked off her shoes, leaned back in his comfortable ergonomic chair, and promptly put her feet up on his desk. While she was relaxing, she scrutinized Einar's office carefully, taking in every detail. *I must say – the man's got marvelous taste.* There was a huge, fiery Jackson Pollock-like painting on the opposite wall, and polished wooden beams stretched across the ceiling of the restored top-floor office space.

The burnished tan leather sofa arrangement in the corner had a splendid view of the harbor. *I wish I had an office like this.* That was when Pebble remembered Irene's words: "Why does somebody else have to give you the opportunity all the time? Why are you always servicing others?"

Pebble put her feet down and started collecting all the Hauser papers she'd scattered all over Einar's desk during their conversation. Then she placed them carefully in the file and walked over to the open wall cabinet. Without thinking, she put the folder under H and started to close the sliding door, when something caught her eye. *No, it can't be right.* The door was already closed by the time her brain processed the information. She stood staring at the black wall cabinet, debating what to do. *It wouldn't be ethical.* She turned and started to walk towards Einar's desk to put the key back in the little silver box. *So what if it's not ethical. Was Einar ethical when he let everyone believe it was me who told him the date of the WonderLift launch?* Pebble stood still before Einar's awesome desk and stared at the silver box in the open drawer. *I'm sure I saw my name on a file. I'm sure.* She turned slowly and walked back to the black cabinet. She opened it again, only this time her hands trembled slightly. *I've never done anything like this before.* She flipped through the folders, and sure enough, there was a file entitled Pebble Beach.

Pebble raffled rapidly through the pages in her file. Einar had jotted down various notes about her background, age, talent, her uncle Mel at Young & Rubicam, etc. *Not particularly interesting for a secret file!* Then Pebble's eyes stopped dead in their tracks. *So Einar knows I did the Nordkyst campaign two years ago!* She couldn't believe her eyes. *How did he find out?*

She rushed back to the wall cabinet. *There must be a Nordkyst file, too.* There was. She pulled it out and hurried back to Einar's desk, hands trembling. There was a brief history of the company and some basic data about Monica Soderland, the designer who started Nordkyst seven years earlier by sewing kids' clothes in her Hellerup basement. Plus all kinds of figures tracing the company's explosive growth from a tiny Mom-and-Pop enterprise to an aggressive, upmarket Scandinavian clothing manufacturer which was doing phenomenally well in the United States. There was brief mention of the DDB Needham campaign which launched Nordkyst on their road to success in the U.S. On the last page of the file – Pebble could see from the date on the top of the page that it was added recently – there was some startling information. Nordkyst was developing a new product line of bright-colored cotton sportswear for pre-teens. The line, which was very similar to their existing signature line for smaller kids, was intended to capitalize on the fact that the kids who'd been wearing Nordkyst clothes for years were now growing up. *What a brilliant idea! And so obvious!* Einar had already run a pilot survey in the New York area to ascertain the market potential for a pre-teen line. The results were promising. On the basis of these initial figures, Pebble could see that Einar had already allocated generous funds to develop a new Nordkyst campaign. At present, the Republic Group pitch that Einar sketched in his notes was to include a sample storyboard, some initial copy and layout. The Republic Group presentation was tentatively scheduled for June 29th at Nordkyst headquarters in Hellerup.

On the next page, Einar had scribbled some wry comments on the likes and dislikes of Monica Soderland. *Why does the woman always come across sounding like a cross between a kindergarten teacher and a racing-car driver?* Pebble chuckled thinking of all the stories in Danish press about Monica with her bobbed red hair and her white Porsche. *Danes sure do have a strange way of treating their fellow countrymen when they're successful abroad – they like nothing better than picking them to pieces.*

Pebble continued to flip through the file, her mind racing crazily. *Why didn't Einar tell me about this? It doesn't make sense.* Pebble couldn't figure it out. *If he knows I did the first U.S. campaign…you'd think he'd want me in on this one, too.* That was when she noticed that Einar had scribbled "Pebble" in the margin of one of the pages where he was jotting down random ideas about the campaign. *Wonder why he wrote my name there? Maybe he is going to involve me after all.* She read on. Another bit of interesting news popped up. *So Peter Cato is pitching for the new account, too.* A chill ran up and down Pebble's spine. *I wonder how Einar found that out? Maybe Birgitte told him that, too? Nothing would surprise me now…* Peter Cato and Einar Bro locking horns again… The feud between the two seemed to overshadow everything Pebble touched.

Peter Cato, Peter Cato. Einar's probably got a file on him, too. Pebble almost ran back to the cabinet this time. Sure enough, there was a file on Peter, too. She raced back to Einar's desk with it. Suddenly she thought of what would happen if somebody found her in Einar's office looking through his files. *Nobody's going to come in here…but what if somebody does?* She felt uneasy and apprehensive. *What am I doing…going through my boss's files like this?* Furtively, she crept out to the empty front office where Marianne usually sat and locked the door.

She went back to Einar's desk. Reading the Peter Cato file was like reading a cheap novel. Somehow or other, Peter had wrangled his way into Nordkyst – Einar seemed to think Peter was some kind of secret (or silent) partner in the Nordkyst emporium. The whole murky business was quite beyond Pebble's grasp, or else Einar's notes were incomplete. *Maybe Einar doesn't know either.* Whatever the case, Pebble gathered from the bits and pieces in Einar's file, that Peter had some undisclosed ties to Monica Soderland's empire. For example, Peter's sky-blue BMW roadster was apparently a gift from Monica. *Amazing isn't it – the only hold Peter seems to have on Nordkyst is the campaign I developed and the copy I wrote. Monica's probably convinced Peter has golden fingers – when the fingers are really mine!* Pebble was astonished at the amount of power and influence Peter had managed to gather as a result of her work.

Mel was right – I was a jerk. And Irene's right, too – I'm still a jerk! It wasn't pleasant to realize she'd given up a unique shot at fame and fortune because she wasn't gutsy enough to grab the chance when she had it. *But Peter's got to be in desperate straits now.* Pebble chuckled. *What a heart-warming thought.* It was obvious. *Nordkyst is going to expect him to deliver more of the same – in the same style – and he won't be able to!* Peter could hardly write a complete sentence in English, let alone create a whole advertising campaign! *He's going to have to find somebody else to do it. And without me, who in the world is he going to use? Who will be able to copy my style?* Pebble hurriedly reviewed the styles of the other copywriters she knew in Copenhagen who wrote in English. *Their styles are so different from mine – and most of them are men anyway!* The copy Pebble had created for Nordkyst had a definite feminine touch. *Nordkyst's going to be wanting something similar – something with the same tone and style...* Pebble smiled. *Poor Peter...looks like his chickens are coming home to roost...*

Chapter 16

As soon as Pebble got home from work that afternoon, her phone rang. The reception was lousy, but there was no mistaking the voice. It was Albert – from far-away Greenland.

"Albert?" Pebble's heart thumped loudly in her breast.

"Ma chérie." His voice was husky with emotion, too. The letter he'd sent her over two weeks ago lay open on her desk. When she received it, she read it promptly; then crumpled it up and threw it in the trash. Five minutes later she fished it out again and lovingly pressed it flat against the surface of her desk. Since then she must have read the letter at least 100 times.

"I'm coming to Copenhagen on Friday," he said between the long-distant echoes of himself on the line, "and I want you to go with me to an island off the coast of Croatia for a week's vacation."

"Oh, Albert…" Pebble still hadn't recovered from the shock of his letter. After visiting him, she'd written him as kindly and honestly as she could about how she felt about his drinking. He'd written to her several times since and said in this last letter – the one still open on her desk, "I know you worry about my drinking, darling, but you worry needlessly. I am not an alcoholic, I promise you." Then he underlined, "I am sure of it. Perhaps I drank a little too much when you were here – but I guess the joy of being with you made me forget myself. I promise you it won't happen again." Pebble hadn't answered his last letter yet simply because she didn't know how to. *What can you say to a drunk who doesn't believe he has a drinking problem?* She wished she could free herself from him, but she couldn't – strangely enough he was still the fleeting star in her life. *My impossible love.* At least her new job didn't give her much time to think about combining impossible love with the business of life.

"Ma chérie, are you there?"

"Yes, I'm here." But she didn't answer his question. Instead she sat at her desk smoothing out his crumpled letter with her free hand. His handwriting was fine and gentle for so strong a man. "I don't know what to say, Albert."

"What do you mean? Say yes! I'm not asking you to marry me – I'm just asking you to go to an island paradise with me for a week!"

"Be serious, Albert, please."

"But I am serious; I just want you to go with me. We'll have plenty of time to talk then…" And when she still didn't answer, he added, "I need you, Pebble, you must know that."

"But, Albert," she tried to formulate her fears, "I can't handle your drinking… you know that… I told you that…it scares me."

"Didn't you get my last letter, Pebble?"

"Yes, but…"

"But what, didn't I explain it to you. I'm not an alcoholic if that's what you're worried about…" He sounded almost hostile. "Okay so I drank a little too much…I admit it, I did…but what's a man supposed to do? I was so happy when you were here…it's so lonely up here without you."

"Oh, Albert…"

"Would you feel better if I promised never to drink again? Is that what you want?"

"Well…I don't know…well…yes. I guess I would," she stumbled, trying to say what she felt. "I don't mean you can never drink again, but I don't want you drinking so much…it scares me…"

He laughed. "How much is too much, Pebble? Is too much a couple of beers at a party – two or three glasses of wine when we go out to dinner?"

"You know what I mean," she shot back, irritated at his pig-headedness.

"No, what do you mean, seriously? How am I going to know when you think I've had enough? What you're really saying is you don't want me ever to have a drop to drink again."

"I didn't say that...I just meant..."

"Ma chérie," he laughed, "you don't know what you're talking about, you little goose. You've never lived in the wild places I've lived in. Men drink a lot – they do – it's completely normal – and perfectly harmless. Don't you remember Martin's party?" Unfortunately, Pebble remembered all too well. "Did I drink anymore than anyone else?"

"Well...no." As if that's any comfort. *The man just doesn't understand.*

"Listen, Pebble, I'm sure this is all one big misunderstanding. If you love me, you've got to believe me and trust me. You've got to give me one more chance. Okay? Just one more time. You do love me, don't you?"

"Yes." She did, but she felt uneasy about it.

"Well, if you love me, you must believe in me, too. I mean what kind of love is it if you don't trust me?"

Pebble really didn't know.

When she didn't reply he asked, "Are you still there?" It was as if he was trying to reach her all the way from Greenland. "My darling?"

"Yes, Albert, I'm still here."

"How is your new job going?"

"Oh great. Just great."

"Do you think you can take a week off?"

"I don't know, I guess so." Her heart was torn in two.

"Then it's settled. I'll order the tickets and pick you up when I get to Copenhagen on Friday."

Chapter 17

"Why is it always me?" Pebble didn't realize she was almost ranting and raving. "Why am I the one who has to pick up the pieces, and then get left holding the bag? I mean why me?" She was pacing up and down Irene's office, gesturing helplessly in the air. Tears were streaming down her cheeks. "Why can't things just work out? For once in my life. Why can't they?"

Irene didn't reply.

"It's like I'm never in control of my life – it's always somebody else."

"What do you mean, somebody else – like who?"

Pebble felt fine when she arrived at Irene's that grey, rainy morning for her weekly session, but, to her own surprise, halfway through recounting her conversation with Albert, she started crying. Irene just wouldn't understand that Pebble wanted to love him. It was so frustrating trying to explain her life to Irene.

"Well, take Albert." Pebble was making a serious effort to calm down. "I really did want to love him. Now does that sound crazy?"

"No...why should it sound crazy?"

"Well, I mean, I wanted to love him and so I do. But now that I do, I don't want to anymore."

"Well why not?" Irene was right there. She was almost beautiful today.

"Well, he's an alcoholic... Do you realize what a hopeless situation being in love with an alcoholic is? And I'm so mad at myself for accepting his invitation to go on vacation with him." Pebble walked over to the window. It was still raining outside, a gentle early June rain; the kind that brings forth summer flowers in the Northern part of the world. "Why can't I be strong like you – and live alone – without a man...?" She didn't really know if

Irene lived alone – she just kind of took it for granted. "Well, do you?" Irene was so masculine; Pebble couldn't imagine her sharing her life with a man.

"No, I don't live alone. My husband's a recovering alcoholic."

Pebble was stunned. Stunned. "Your husband was an alcoholic?"

"Yes, he was. So I know how challenging and sad it can be."

Pebble couldn't believe it – Irene – who she thought was so strong – who seemed so in control of her life, was married to an alcoholic!

"Just because I'm a therapist, it doesn't mean I don't have problems of my own."

This was the first time Irene said anything about herself. Pebble sat down and stared at Irene. "Who knows, maybe I became interested in psychology because I was so fucked up myself. I mean look at me. I'm not the best-looking woman in the world."

"But you're so in control of your life," Pebble shot back.

"That's what you think, probably because that's what you've been fighting for your whole life. You know, Pebble, your problems are not so special. Most of the women I know, including myself, have the same feelings. We all feel like we've been put here on earth to take care of other people and then when we decide we want to start taking care of ourselves, we feel like we just got put in a meat-grinder." Irene laughed. Pebble thought Irene had the kindest laugh she'd ever heard.

"Why didn't you ever tell me about yourself before?"

"That's not what you're paying me for, Pebble. You're paying me to help you focus on your life. I'm supposed to help you get the right perspective, you know that."

"But maybe it would have been easier for me if I'd known you were just another woman like me."

"Are you sure?" Irene asked: she was wearing a faded sky-blue cowboy shirt with pearl buttons and blue jeans. She didn't look feminine at all, but she looked grounded and whole. "You seemed to need somebody with authority, just to begin to open up. That's how I read you anyway. But you've changed since then."

"Have I?" Pebble smiled.

"Oh yes, pretty soon you're not going to need me anymore. You're doing very well, Pebble."

It was as if a loving mama had patted her gently on the head. Pebble wished she could hold onto this intimacy – wanted Irene to be her best friend for the rest of her life, but intuitively, she knew she couldn't.

After she held onto the moment for a while, she let it go. "You know, I feel like I'm on the verge of finding out something important. But it keeps eluding me."

"Remember the last time you were here and I asked you what you really wanted to say to Peter Cato?"

"Yeah, and I walked out..." Pebble laughed.

"Well, not so much that...the walking out was fine... It was more...I'd like you to try to express what you really feel about the three men in your life who seem to be bugging you. Somehow, I think they're some kind of symbols who represent something deep for you. As far as I can tell, there's Peter Cato, and then there's your ex-husband and now Albert. Einar doesn't seem to be one of them, but maybe he is... Did you ever notice you never tell me about your women friends when you come here? I know you're friendly with Clare...how come you never have any complaints about Clare?"

"Oh, Clare's different...she's a woman!"

They both laughed.

"Well there you go..." Irene continued when their laughter died down. "What is it about your interactions with men that make you feel so weak and helpless? You don't seem to feel that way about women..."

Pebble knew Irene had touched a nerve. *Men! Men!*

"I don't know, I guess I never thought about it that way before..."

"Well, maybe it's about time you do."

"Yeah, well..." Pebble was trying to put her finger on what it was that always screwed up her relationships with men, "...it's like I'm always arranging my life around pleasing them. It sounds so dumb when I say it that I hate to admit it... How come women are like that?"

"Don't you think it's more important to figure out how come you're like that?"

Here she goes being pushy again. Pebble groped for words. "I seem to spend an awful lot of time and energy thinking about how things are going to affect them, I mean if it's not my husband – or my ex-husband – then it's my sons or my boyfriend or my boss. I don't know why, but for some reason, they're always more valuable or more important than I am. It sounds so stupid when I say it out loud...doesn't it?"

"Sort of..." Irene was kind again in blue. Today her steely grey hair was loose around her face. She wore no make-up.

"Why can't we just grow up?" *I wonder if Irene has a little girl somewhere inside her, too.*

"We can," Irene answered slowly, "but it's hard. It's a long difficult process, this process of growing, it doesn't just happen overnight. It takes time and sometimes it's painful, you know that."

"How am I ever going to thank you for helping me so much?"

Irene laughed at Pebble's sudden mood swing, "Being able to participate in your growth...do you have any idea what a privilege that is?"

Pebble never thought of it that way. "No, I guess I don't... I wish I was your friend." When the words were out, Pebble was sorry she said them.

"Well you can be, you know. In fact you already are, even if you are my client. You might be surprised, but I know you didn't really like me very much before."

"How did you know?"

"It happens all the time. Right now you're fond of me, because you're going through a period of rapid growth, but if you get stuck again and I push too hard, you might hate me again."

This time Pebble laughed, too.

"So why don't we give it another try!" Irene got up and placed three chairs along the wall. "Now let's imagine that Peter Cato is sitting here, and Slim is over here, and Albert's right smack in the middle. I think it's best we leave Einar out of this for the moment. Okay?"

"Okay," Pebble settled down in her chair – her friendship high with Irene was gone. *This Irene is too much, first she gets me to fall in love with her and then she puts me through the wringer again…*

"There's something about your interactions with these guys that's bothering you…"

"There sure is…"

"Well what is it? Do you know?"

"The three of them all have this picture of me as this helpless little girl…"

"Are you sure that they're the ones who have this picture of you as a helpless little girl? Are you sure you're not the one who sees yourself as a little girl?"

Pebble considered Irene's question for a moment. "Then why do they make me feel like…like God's sole purpose in putting me on this earth is to please them? Like I'm the guilty one if I don't arrange my life to please them. It's always their pleasure which comes first and I'm the one who's supposed to adjust. It's my job to support them."

"How do you know they feel like that? Did they ever tell you they did?"

"No, I guess not, but you know what I mean, Irene. It's always been like that. I'm not the only woman who feels this way. God, it makes me sick – sick!"

"Why?" Irene was really pushing again.

"Because I've got a right to my own life, too. I've got a right to my own feelings and needs and wishes. I'm not just here to please them."

"Well, did you ever think about telling any of these people how you feel?"

"No."

"Well, why not?"

"I don't know." Pebble was mad and thought, *Now she's getting pushy again.* Then she said, "Well, maybe I do have a problem. I mean, I know I have a problem, but it's like even if I know it, I can't help but let it happen anyway…"

"What are you saying, Pebble?"

"What do you mean?"

"I mean I want you to tell me what's really going on – okay?"

Pebble still didn't know what Irene meant.

"Take a good look at those guys." She pointed to the three empty chairs. "What's really going on inside you when you meet them? Why are you so afraid of displeasing them? What kind of a hold do they have on you?"

Pebble was silent for a while, not liking the thoughts in her head.

"Come on, Pebble, tell me. Say it out loud… You'll feel better if you do…"

"If I don't do what they want," Pebble blurted out, "they won't like me anymore, they won't love me anymore. And if they don't love me anymore, they'll leave me…"

"And…"

"And…" Pebble started crying again. "And…and I'm so terrified of being alone…so terrified…" She hated herself for telling the truth and being so weak.

Irene let her cry for a while.

Then she said softly, "And what's so terrible about being alone,

Pebble?"

"Well, who will take care of me?" It just flew out of Pebble's mouth. "Who?" And she sobbed even more.

"Well, what about you?" said Irene again, as soft as a feather.

"Me?"

"Yes you."

The room was very quiet. Very very quiet. You could have heard a pin drop.

Irene must have thought that was enough for one day so she got up and walked over to Pebble's chair and started massaging her shoulders. "You're so tense, Pebble. So tense. Why don't you let me give you a massage..." Part of Irene's treatment was 'healing massage', but so far Pebble had only had talk sessions with Irene. She remembered the shiny brochure Clare gave her about Irene before she started going to therapy – *A unique combination of gestalt therapy and intuitive massage.*

Pebble was so shaken that she crawled up on Irene's massage table without the slightest protest. It was covered with dark green leather and raised high enough so Irene could walk around it easily.

"I'm going to start with your head and neck – okay?" Pebble was lying on her back staring up at the painting Irene had hanging down from the ceiling. She hadn't noticed it before. *What a strange place for a picture!* But actually it was rather nice. The splash of blue color on the huge piece of plexi-glass was suspended by four chains and the name of the leaping blue and silver tones was *Magnificent Dream. Some name for a painting hanging over a massage table in the middle of the universe.* Pebble felt she was somewhere she'd never been before. Everything felt strange, including herself.

Irene quickly homed in to the points of tension in Pebble's neck and shoulders. "I'm going to turn your neck very slowly. I don't want you to do anything, just relax."

Irene lifted Pebble's head between her hands and started

turning her neck very carefully. It felt great, for a while. "Now I want you to try to imagine yourself sitting before this big screen – like you were sitting in a movie theater – and I just want you to let yourself watch all your thoughts passing before you on this big screen? Okay?"

Pebble sighed.

"I don't want you to try to censor them or pass judgment on them or anything. Just let me massage you and try watching your thoughts as they pass before your eyes on this big screen…"

Irene placed her hand on Pebble's chest. "You're breathing way up here…" She moved her hand to Pebble's abdomen. "Now try to move your breathing down here…"

Pebble tried, but it wasn't easy. It was like something was blocking her breath, keeping it from going down there.

"There's no rush," Irene said. "Just relax and try again." Irene moved to the side of the massage table and held one hand over Pebble's navel and the other over her solar plexus. Then she moved her hand again. "It's here, isn't it?" she asked, referring to the tightness in Pebble's chest.

How does she know? I didn't even know – before now.

"Just imagine…" Irene's voice was soothing. "Just imagine there's no rush…nobody is waiting for you…nobody's expecting you to do anything… I just want you to relax as much as you can…and to breathe nice and easy…don't worry about me, either." Irene kept her hands on Pebble's navel and solar plexus. They were warm through Pebble's olive-green T-shirt. Pebble closed her eyes and breathed. It felt kind of nice but the tightness was still there. The tightness almost felt like a cry.

"Just let it go…just let it all go… It's quite okay."

Pebble sighed, a long, slow sigh. She was breathing easier now.

"Good, very good." Irene lifted her hands from Pebble's abdomen and stomach and went back to her head. "Now just keep on breathing deeply and slowly." She didn't do much except turn Pebble's head very slowly – first all the way to the right, and then all the way to the left. The funny thing was it made Pebble feel like crying. There was something about the slowness and the gentleness of Irene's movements that touched Pebble deeply.

What's wrong with me? Pebble fought back the tears until she realized that she couldn't cry because she was lying on her back – and crying, lying on your back, is pretty difficult to do. But mainly, because the tears weren't in her eyes, but in her soul. *Irene is giving me something wonderful. Up until now I've spent my whole life doing for everybody else – for my husband and my parents and my kids and God knows who else. But right now Irene's doing something for me.* She wanted to embrace Irene, but knew she shouldn't. She knew the most important thing about this moment was to allow herself to receive from another human being. *I've been tense my whole life, trying to please others.*

"Now, remember what I said about the big screen. While I'm massaging you, I just want you to relax and let all your thoughts flow through you – just let them go – just like you were watching them up on the big screen…" Irene kept moving Pebble's head very gently.

Pebble let herself go and saw herself schlepping four plastic bags stuffed with groceries up the two flights of stairs to her apartment across from the park. *Adam and Jon always manage to disappear miraculously when I need help – the funny thing is they have no problem emptying the refrigerator… Kids are so…well my kids are so… I guess I raised them to be just like everybody else I know who's male…or is it just because I'm…* Pebble had almost forgotten Irene's touch. She felt safe now. *Can't you just see me winning The Mother of the Century Award?* She smiled, watching the pictures flashing rapidly on the big screen in her head. *I'll get the award from the local supermarket, and it will be a gold medal with the following citation engraved on it – FOR BRAVERY BEYOND THE CALL OF DUTY. Or something like that. Something which conveys all the effort involved in schlepping all those grocery bags up all those flights of stairs..."In honor of this major, lifetime effort".* The big screen was chock full of plastic grocery bags filled to the brim with cheese and milk and orange juice and potato chips and bread. Lots of bread. Especially the healthy kind. Good old-fashioned (and heavy) Danish rye bread, the kind growing boys are supposed to eat if they want to become movie stars or soccer players with MBAs. And tomatoes, too. Don't forget the tomatoes, or the lettuce or the mustard and mayonnaise for all those wonderful sandwiches that helpless teenaged boys are so good at fixing and eating when they get home from school and at all times of the night and all weekend long. (Without cleaning up afterwards either!) And what about spaghetti? And pizza, of course pizza! How can you raise teenagers without pizza? *No wonder my arms hurt. It's all these groceries I schlep up the stairs every other day. I must be qualified for The Mother of the Century Award...*

She saw herself standing on the podium, the band playing bright inspiring music while the most incredible commotion was going on around her. The red and white Danish national colors were flying – even Queen Margrethe was there. *But where's the American flag? Where's the president? No president? At least his wife ought to be there... We're not talking small potatoes... We're talking Mother of the Century here.* The whole ceremony was being transmitted live worldwide and online so that no matter where you lived in the world, no matter what your race, religion, sex, age or country, you could be a part of this wonderful ceremony. *And here she is... Da, da, da, DA! ... SUPERWOMAN!* Pebble was shocked – at cross-purposes with herself. *But I don't want to be SuperWoman anymore.* The bright, inspiring music seemed to fade. *Being SuperWoman sucks!* "Ladies and gentlemen, announcing the winner of *The Mother of the Century Award,* the SuperWoman of all times..." *But being SuperWoman not only sucks – being SuperWoman is a real drag. I hate baking homemade cookies and being the perfect wife and mother. Am I going to eat humble pie all my life and accept this shit? Why am I allowing this to happen? I don't want to be Mother of*

*the Century ever again. What about Pebble Beach for Pebble Beach?
Isn't that a better award? Pebble Beach for Pebble Beach!!*

More ugly thoughts flashed across the big screen. *Slim! He'll
always blame me, even if I do win The Mother of the Century Award –
nothing's going to help there. Let's face it, if the slightest mishap ever
befalls Adam and Jon, if they so much as trip and skin their knees –
however slightly – it's going to be my fault. So why try? I mean who
are you kidding, sister? To Slim you'll always be to blame. Nothing –
not even eternal sacrifice – is going to tip the scales in your favor... So
you might as well forget it...*

Molly was standing there, too, with her newly lifted face,
saying, "Pebble, this is your life! Your life." She saw her father
Morris, but he didn't say anything, he was too old to get
involved. *God... Time is running out. Why am I spending the best
years of my life being a single parent, dreaming of the perfect romance,
the one I've never had?*

She heard the sounds of the Anti-Single Parents League
marching loudly across her inner screen. The Anti-Single Parents
League was the hoards of people who vehemently objected to
single-parenting. They were mortified to discover the prestigious
Mother of the Century Award was being given to a single parent. So
they were picketing Pebble's event, bearing signs reading – "Is
this an immaculate conception?" Pebble was dismayed. *This is
my day – my special day and they're going to spoil everything. They'll
cast a blemish on my accomplishment. How come these jerks are
incapable of imagining the enormous effort that goes into single
parenting? Is it because everybody in the Anti-Single Parents League
lives uptown, is married, has a live-in maid and owns two cars? They
should only know the cross single parents have to bear.* Pebble was
enraged at the injustice. *We're not just talking about my award, even
if the Queen of Denmark is here. What about all the people who are
divorced nowadays? I mean divorced is almost normal... Who ever met
a kid in downtown Copenhagen who actually lives with his real honest-
to-God biological father and mother anyway? The poor kid would*

almost certainly be regarded as some kind of a freak of nature! At least in this part of the world...

Pebble watched this poor kid – the kid who shared space with both his biological parents – march across the big screen right before her eyes. His friends teased him on the way to school saying mean things to him like: "You who, you who – you've got two parents, too. WHAT THE HELL IS WRONG WITH YOU?" The authorities would be forced to send the poor kid to the school psychologist whose first question would be, "Why aren't your parents divorced?" Having married parents would be a serious emotional handicap. Much sensitive counseling would be necessary to help this child be accepted in the world of divorced kids. The school shrink would have to wait until he was sure he had the kid's confidence before popping the awful question, "Okay, Joey, now tell me the truth – are your parents really living together because of you?" Just think of the guilt. The poor kid would be a potential suicide case. A walking time bomb. He wouldn't want to live. Pebble saw this poor desolate creature wandering aimlessly down the cold, snow-covered streets of Copenhagen, hoping his parents would be divorced by the time he got home. She saw him moaning and groaning and saying to himself, "My parents are living together because of me... Please God, forgive me..." *Well at least I don't have to worry about Jon and Adam slitting their throats because I'm still married to Slim. Oh Slim.* She saw him watching her receive *The Mother of the Century Citation for Bravery Beyond the Call of Duty* on TV. *It'll burn him up. But I guess things can't get much worse than they already are between us.* She saw him raise his fist and fume at her on TV, pontificating about how this traitorous woman was bringing up his kids. In his white rage, he said encouraging things to himself like, "Look at the wild life they're living, running the streets at all hours of the night." *But this is modern times...modern times...* But Pebble's defense was too weak, as usual, too lame. *Everybody knows that. Modern times. When 12-year-olds drink vodka at home with their friends at four o'clock in the afternoon before going out to smoke hashish in their tattered jeans. At least Jon and Adam aren't that bad...or maybe they are and I just don't know. Besides, is that bad? Besides this is modern times...besides.*

By now Pebble had drifted away on a cloud of safety while Irene continued probing gently, looking for tension and carefully massaging it away. Every bit of tightness carried a vivid, living picture with it.

Even if it hurt, I'm so glad I'm not living with Slim anymore. Pebble let herself remember the pleasant surprise she felt when he finally moved out. *It was such a relief...* And the relief turned into the comfort of Irene's hands, working carefully on her neck and shoulders. *The house didn't cave in or anything when he moved out. Nothing really happened except things got awfully, awfully quiet.* She saw herself up on the big screen packing up her geisha gear. All the sexy underwear went straight into the garbage. *I wasn't Japanese anyway, so the role never suited me... I'm a true-blue child of the 20th century...with no credentials or authentic training in man maintenance anyway. I've got too many dreams stuffed in my head...and now they changed all the rules... Only SuperWoman can be the absolute geisha while holding down a full-time job and raising kids with her left hand.*

And suddenly, it was there, clear as day: *I don't want it!*

It was such a relief to find out. *I just don't want it. I'm not SuperWoman, never was, and Lord have mercy, never will be. And the best part is I don't even want to try anymore. So much for Mother of the Century!*

"I never thought I deserved things from other people," Pebble said suddenly to Irene who was still there. "And now you're giving me this wonderful gift of caring about me." Irene stopped massaging Pebble and walked around and looked down into her face as she lay there on the green leather massage table.

"Well, you deserve it," Irene said simply.

And after a long pause, Pebble smiled and said, "Yeah, I guess I do."

Chapter 18

Irene's touch opened a well of vulnerability inside Pebble that she hadn't perceived before. A rawness.

When Jon came home from school at four that afternoon, he found his mother sitting, all alone, on their faded sofa, crying.

"Why aren't you at work, Mom?" The lanky 16-year-old plopped down on the sofa besides Pebble, his face still flushed from running up the stairs.

Pebble looked at her number-one son and smiled. "I decided to take the afternoon off – that's all." But she couldn't fool him, even if she liked to think she still could. Those times were gone and Jon was almost a man.

"Is anything wrong, Mom?"

"No, not really."

"Well, why are you sitting home crying like this? I thought you liked your new job so much." Sometimes he was wise beyond his years.

"I do."

"So what's the matter then?"

"Oh, I don't know… I'm just such a nerd…I guess," she laughed between her tears. "My life's such a mess."

"A mess? Oh come on." He took her hand. "I've been reading more Emmanuel stuff, Mom." He pulled the book out from under the stack of school books he tossed on the coffee table when he sat down. He flashed the title in her face: *Emmanuel's Book, A manual for living comfortably in the cosmos*. Pebble just loved the title of that book. It never ceased to amaze her – the concept of "living comfortably in the cosmos". She wondered if it was possible. She stopped crying and wiped her face with the sleeve of her bathrobe. "Living comfortably in the cosmos – that's what everybody's trying to do I guess," she said and sighed.

"Where did you get this book anyway?" she asked. Jon had

talked about it before, but Pebble never really paid much attention before now.

"Oh, David gave it to me. It's really something, Mom, you should read it."

"What do you think Emmanuel means by...living comfortably in the cosmos?"

"I guess he means just that." Jon was flipping through the pages, trying to find something – but he stopped and looked up at Pebble. "You see, Emmanuel is this wise spirit who speaks to us through someone here on earth and gives us guidance."

Pebble smiled at her gentle son and the perspective he had on life. *He sure didn't get these ideas from his father!* She was proud to have a son who thought about things like this.

"Emmanuel says that this earth is a schoolroom and we've all come here to learn the lessons we need to learn. If you look at the things that happen to you like that, it kind of looks different...you know what I mean?" His face was slender and his green eyes glowed with inner conviction. If his brother Adam had been there, he would have said, "Oh come on, Jon, stop acting so holy..."

"You know," Pebble said, "whether or not it's true, it sure is a comfort..."

"Well...why were you crying...really? You've been so much happier since you and Dad split up."

"It's not that." Pebble was always in doubt when it came to talking to Jon about her problems. *He's only a kid.*

"Well, what is it?"

"A lot of things," she almost started crying again, but didn't.

"Like what."

"Like Albert..."

"Albert?"

"Yeah, he called me the other day and asked me to go on vacation with him to an island off the coast of Croatia for a week...and I said yes."

"Gee, that's just great, Mom! An island in the Mediterranean…it'll be wonderful…"

"I don't know how wonderful it's going to be. In fact I don't even want to go."

"You don't?" He didn't understand. "Why not?"

"Albert's an alcoholic."

Jon was silent for a while, processing this new information. Then he said, "An alcoholic? That's weird. All the times I've ever seen him, he was never drunk. I mean, he visited us a few times before he started working up in Holsteinsborg."

"Yeah, I know. I mean, I didn't realize it until I visited him either. He drank the whole time I was up there. Constantly. He just couldn't stop."

"I've never known anyone who was an alcoholic," Jon said thoughtfully.

"Me neither. That's the odd part about it. I just didn't realize he had a drinking problem before. I mean, I really like the guy, but it looks hopeless to me."

"Can't you talk to him about it?"

"I've tried, but he won't listen."

"So why are you going with him to Croatia?"

"That's what I just said…I don't know why I'm going. It's like I'm torn. I know it's best to break off our relationship, but I just can't seem to do it."

Jon got up and paced around the small living room like a young tiger. The view of the King's Garden across the street was beautiful at this time of the year. The morning's gentle rain had made the old chestnut trees look even greener than usual as the sun tried to poke its way through the afternoon's clouds. Pebble's potted plants were growing happily in the windows; in fact they needed a good trimming.

Suddenly Jon stopped and started flipping rapidly through Emmanuel's Book, searching for something. "Emmanuel says all our relationships are a learning process. Listen to this: … 'when a relationship no longer serves, if you have scraped the bottom of the barrel to find the meaning, to find the lessons, to find the essence of why you have come together, and this has not brought forth what you are seeking, what more can you possibly do? Can you not let this go with your love and your blessings so the next time you meet this soul again there will be more compatibility, more compassion, more understanding? For you will meet again. Since all will ultimately come to Oneness, there is not one person you encounter in your life you will not see again. Think about that."

"The words sound so beautiful – but I don't know if I'll ever really understand that or be wise enough to live like that."

"Oh come on, Mom, I think you're doing pretty good. Look how well you managed when Dad was here. I know that was real hard for you." His insight surprised Pebble. *Sometimes this kid just knocks me out.*

"Emmanuel also says in answer to the question why so many marriages are ending in divorce... 'It's because people have accelerated their growth processes. Souls come together, not to remain together in physical contact, but to grow. When this has taken place – the gifts have been given and the lessons have been learned. So why don't you agree that it's time to move on?' It makes sense, doesn't it?" He fidgeted shyly with the pages, wanting to comfort his mother, but not really knowing how. Then he got a bright idea and his whole face lit up. "Come on, Mom, let me make you some tea – okay? Besides, I'm starved." Pebble laughed, suddenly thinking how thin Jon was. *It looks like he never touches food. People should only know how much he eats!*

"Come on out in the kitchen with me." He couldn't handle any more sadness from his mother.

She understood and said, "Okay," glad to accept his invitation. She gathered herself and all her 40+ years together and followed Jon. He was almost a head taller than she was. *At times, children can be such a blessing. Funny, it's always when you least expect it.*

The sun finally came out from behind the grey clouds and was streaming through the kitchen windows. She drank tea with Jon who stuffed himself with four Danish open sandwiches, a banana and a generous piece of pound cake. When Cynthia called his eyes shone brightly. "She's a grade ahead of me at school…you've just got to meet her." He ran down the hall to the bathroom to take a look at himself. When he turned up in the kitchen again, he was wearing a clean white shirt. *She really must be something,* Pebble thought.

"Don't expect me for dinner, Mom. I'll probably be late."

He was gone before she could thank him for keeping her company.

Chapter 19

"Albert."

"Pebble, ma chérie."

Through their open window, the shimmering blue Adriatic sparkled in the background. But they didn't care. Albert's hands were already inside Pebble's pale yellow blouse – their suitcases thrown hastily inside their airy suite at Le Chateau du Mer. They didn't notice the open windows or the spectacular view of the crystal clear Mediterranean below. They were in too much of a hurry.

Albert sought Pebble without words.

And Pebble was there – with all her defenses down.

This is a time outside time.

She'd lost her memory and had no past or future. Only Albert's strong hands holding her breasts, awakening a maddening passion in her.

He was a bird winging down from the frozen North to thaw in her warm sun.

She quivered at his touch.

Only the slightest hint of a breeze moved the white chintz curtains in the late afternoon heat that day. Outside, under the clear blue sky, everything was quiet. People had already left the beaches, scurrying to their hotel rooms, smelling of sun and sea, to rest and shower before going down to the village for dinner and music under the star-studded sky.

Albert sat on the bed, pulling off his jeans, hot from the long trip behind them. He'd been moving for almost two days now (Pebble thought travel only made him more handsome). He picked her up at the Copenhagen airport on his way down from Greenland. From there, they flew directly to the airport on the outskirts of Split, an old Croatian coastal town, took a taxi down the mountainside to the old fortress harbor, and finally the hydrofoil to the village of Hvar on the island of Hvar.

So far, only their lips, hands and eyes had touched. The journey generated much body heat and many penetrating glances – but they didn't talk much. This was not the first time in Pebble's life that she was allowed the privilege of savoring the agonizing tension of wanting Albert so badly. The memory of her trip to Greenland was still vivid in her mind. Both the flight up, filled with wonderful expectations of loving him, and the flight back, when she was elated to escape the ice prison. The memory was so vivid, that several times during the flight to Croatia, Pebble wondered if she was losing her mind. *Why am I doing this again?* She knew it was the pull of his body. The power of those cells again. There was no other way to explain it – in all honesty – even to herself. *Some things are beyond mind. Beyond understanding. I don't even want to be with him...but still I do...my body does... Unless it's like Emmanuel says – we keep repeating our lessons until we learn them. But I thought I knew...what I wanted...and it's not this. I'm a big girl now, or at least Irene says I am. I could have said no to this whole thing – at anytime – instead of agreeing to one more crazy episode of Life with Albert. And now I'm going off the deep end for the second time in my life – and with the same cowboy... So how can it be a mistake? Or is it so obviously a mistake that everybody can see it but me? Damn I wish I didn't want him so badly... So maybe I'm not what I thought I was... Maybe I'm not your normal hard-working career woman... Maybe I'm some kind of aberration... Or maybe not. Maybe all your other normal-looking women – the ones who don't scream so much but seem to be in such control...maybe they're just like me inside...* But there wasn't time to think. His smell was in her brain making her shake with expectation...anticipating undiscovered heights of pleasure. *There's just something about the man's hands, eyes, body... Albert's hands, eyes and body...* She could never quite put her finger on it. *It has to be in my cells. My brain's not involved in this at all. It's something stronger than I am. Every woman dreams of sleeping with a Greek God once in her life – and I've done it*

more than once. Even if my Greek God is French and drinks like a bottomless pit. And even if I know before I start it will never work...
She didn't want to consider anything but the ripple of muscle in his bare back as he took off his jeans. She was already there, standing by the bed, close to him, warm and naked. He undressed slowly, or so she thought, deliberately folding his jeans before throwing them on the chair by the window. Moments before, he had undressed her hurriedly, and pressed her naked body against his. He'd taken off his shirt, but his jeans were still on, and she enjoyed the hot feel of his manhood through the faded blue denim.

Jeans off, he suddenly grabbed her and pulled her down on the bed, pinching her nipples hard between his fingers. She moaned. He was on top of her, his body firm as his breath quickened. His heat matched her heat.

In one swift movement, his throbbing penis found its way into her – like a ship finding safe harbor in the storm – and she was so hungry that her wetness allowed him to find the full depth of her need immediately. She spread herself wide, hiding nothing, laying herself bare. With all her years, Pebble had finally left shyness behind on the dusty road of life for other women to waste precious moments on. Whatever else he was or was not, Albert was a man of power, and for the moment, he was hers. Life had given Pebble enough wisdom to know at least that.

Gather ye rosebuds while ye may.

And Albert, his flashing French eyes closed, surrendered to the sensualness that was his heritage. His mind went blank as he plunged himself into her depths, no longer able to wait for her to follow. He had watched her body, her lips, her eyes for far too long – to be able to control his need any longer. But Pebble was right there, matching his simmering need and lightning speed – like a sleek racehorse plunging recklessly forward when the gates are finally opened.

All at once, everything was perfect. Their rhythm, their

bodies, their need. Everything. Whatever else was in this world, whatever else would be, at that split second in time and space, Pebble and Albert finally found each other in all their infinite depth as the stars exploded in the hot afternoon sun. Every cell, muscle, hair and heartbeat was locked together tightly. And for one intense moment, Pebble and Albert were as close as two human beings can be.

* * *

The next morning, Pebble felt more than a little ridiculous as she spread her battery of sun potions out on the towel before her. This impressive arsenal of anti-aging, anti-wrinkle sunscreens was the result of one mad rush of shopping the day before Albert was scheduled to meet her at Copenhagen airport.

Now on the pebbled beach of Hvar, Pebble surveyed her investment in eternal youth in amazement. She couldn't quite decide if it was comforting or not to know that all over the world women Pebble's age were like weather vanes – predicting the mood of millions while the prosperous cosmetic industry chuckled madly at the advent of all the wrinkles appearing on the faces and bodies of women around the world. *The prospect of aging is just no fun at all.* Pebble hated the thought of other people cashing in on her fear of aging. *But what's a woman to do? Especially when she's over 40 and she gets a look at the competition parading around half-naked on every beautiful island and beach in the world? It's just not fair…*

Pebble had invested (wisely or not) in every one of Clinique's anti-wrinkle sunscreen for the body and face preparations plus Clinique's targeted protection stick (SPF 45) for the sensitive areas like the nipples, nose, lips and cheekbones. *The secret is to get brown without getting old. Not that anybody knows how to accomplish that.*

When she was racing around spending all her money on sun

potions and a new bathing suit, she kept repeating her slogan from that day at Irene's – *Pebble Beach for Pebble Beach! Pebble Beach for Pebble Beach!* A basic part of Irene's therapy was that Pebble was supposed to learn to do good things for herself and discover the joys of taking care of "her". Which was more difficult than it seemed.

Irene said astonishing things like, "Splurge, Pebble, splurge! Life's a party."

And when Pebble countered with tales of her limited budget, her two teenaged boys, her always-empty refrigerator, Irene had bounced back, "Life is a party. And You Deserve Some Fun." Irene always asked Pebble what she was waiting for? "Are you going to wait until you're 92 and can barely see, hear or walk?" But surely Irene didn't mean such expensive extravagance as buying tons of idiotic sun potions which promised eternal youth? *Will I end up looking half as good as Catherine Zeta-Jones if I do? Oh please God, yes...please!* Pebble knew something was fishy in the state of Denmark, but didn't have time to question the logic of all the things in her head that were screaming for attention. Irene insisted that Pebble buy herself two new things every day. *Two new things – the woman must be mad...* But Irene insisted – even if she had to force herself. "It's high time you discover that you can be the source of your own pleasure, Pebble...and I don't just mean masturbating..." Pebble had trouble daring – risking pleasure for herself. She had trouble doing for herself... She remembered racing out of Magasin du Nord clutching all her jars and tubes and lotions thinking, *Irene would never spend so much money on anything so frivolous as anti-aging sun block...or anti-wrinkle aftersun...just think of the practical shoes the woman wears...any fool can see she's never dyed her hair or gone on a diet...so how can she possibly know?* Pebble was becoming a little more selective (and critical) when it came to Irene's advice. *After all, I'm the one who's got to pay the bills, right?* Following Irene's advice to the letter could lead to catastrophe...

Just think of what will happen to us if I'm this good to myself more than once every ten years... The thought was positively unnerving.

But now, sitting on her big blue beach towel, right smack in the middle of the nudist colony Albert insisted they go to, Pebble was glad she'd binged on beauty the way she did. A stupendous array of tits and ass were promenading along the beach before them. It was absolutely disheartening. *And they're not only young – they're younger than I'm ever going to be again in my whole life.* The thought was positively alarming. *It's just not fair, after all I've been through, after all I've learned...that I'm never going to get a shot at being young again... For the first time in my life, I'm better equipped to be young than ever before...and now it's too late.* She knew it was a fruitless line of thought. Her brain felt like an old, worn-out strainer anyway, the holes too big to catch a single worthwhile thought.

Last night's repeated lovemaking, and the wine, the music and the lovely balmy air of the Mediterranean, were much more than Pebble could handle. Suddenly being so far away from Copenhagen and the heat of battle made her feel unreal. The bone-hard struggle to find herself and support her sons had evaporated like a bad dream. She felt disconnected, disoriented, happy, free and confused. Albert's body was the only reality she could touch. So she covered herself from head to toe with suntan lotion as Albert sat chatting with an equally naked French couple who parked themselves and their voluptuous teenaged daughter right next to Pebble and Albert.

They were speaking French and Pebble didn't understand a word they were saying, so she didn't pay much attention to them...but instead allowed herself the splendid luxury of drifting off in the sun-filled world of her own thoughts... As soon as she closed her eyes and relaxed, the battleground of her daily life appeared brilliantly before her eyes. *It's like the big screen exercise I did with Irene.* And since she had already tried it before, she decided to let it happen again. To just let her thoughts appear at random on the inside of her mind without editing or judging or anything. The first person she encountered was Peter Cato. *What is with that man...?* Then, being so far away from home, she suddenly saw it wasn't him, but her relationship with him that was the problem. *I've been much too submissive... I let him take advantage of my talent and become successful because I have some kind of inferiority complex. Basically, I guess I don't really believe in my own worth...that I'm a valuable person – so instead, I acted like a jerk... And now I'm mad at myself because of what happened because of my own insecurity. Today, I wish I'd behaved differently...but it all happened two years ago when I was somebody else... I can't keep on blaming myself for what I did then. Now is now. Now is different, and I'm different, too. Everything's different. Even the Nordkyst campaign I did then is old hat now. Nobody remembers a thing, it's all dead and buried... Or so I thought...until I started talking to Irene about it. She says it's not dead and buried – that it's not over, that it's never too late. Not as long as I feel the way I do... She says it's not a question of winning anything or of getting back at anyone – it's my own self-esteem we're talking about... But how can I bring it all up now? Won't it seem pretty ridiculous? Won't I seem pretty ridiculous? Besides, the thought of facing Peter practically scares me to death... I wonder why he makes me feel like that? I mean where's all my courage gone off to?* But the thought of confronting Peter wasn't at all pleasant to imagine. *What would I say?* She saw herself standing in his office, like a tongue-tied little school girl – when the big screen in her head went blank. *At least Einar's different. Maybe he's manipulated me too, but I know he respects me because he treats me like a human being – and not like a second-class citizen.* Still, she wasn't quite sure this was true. Pictures of Einar the Worm panting heavily, pawing all over her naked body as he did in her dream flashed through her brain. *I know the man would like nothing better than to touch me all over...and maybe I wouldn't mind so much if he just wasn't so physically repulsive...which is pretty embarrassing since I'm supposed to be this enlightened, modern woman...and see beyond the exterior to the inner soul... I guess when it comes to being spiritual I'm just a miserable failure. I'm just as concerned about looks as anybody else... I wonder why it's like that...I mean, Albert's so good in bed and so good-looking – but what do I really see in him?* Her inner turmoil and confusion were frightening to contemplate, so she got up and plunged headfirst, right into the cool water. *Oh this is life...* She felt the sea wash away the battles raging inside... *Life really is so simple.*

When she finally emerged from the world of cool blueness, Albert broke into her reverie by shouting happily, "Come, Pebble, I want you to meet someone..."

She was surprised at the excitement in his voice.

"Gilbert and Claudine are from Chamonix," he said gesturing towards the couple he'd been chatting with. "Isn't that a coincidence?" Pebble smiled in amazement. Chamonix, a small village and famous ski resort in the French Alps, was Albert's hometown. "They even know my sister and her husband and the little ski hotel they own on the outskirts of town."

"Really?" Pebble picked up her towel, and in an attempt to hide her naked body a little from these complete strangers, she pretended to dry herself as she walked towards them.

Albert introduced Pebble formally to Gilbert, Claudine and their daughter, even if everyone was naked. "And this is Stephanie, their daughter."

Pebble shook hands with the three of them. "I'm sorry, but I don't speak French." Pebble was quite content with the fact that she had such a good excuse not to be sociable – she preferred lying in the sun by herself. Albert, who'd been stranded on Greenland for almost a year, seemed to relish their company. The conversation became animated. Pebble nodded and smiled occasionally and noticed that Claudine's fading Gallic beauty was fully revealed in her stunning daughter stretched out close by. *I know I must be a little dazed by the sun, but I wonder why Stephanie persists in lounging about with her legs spread a little too far apart. I guess it's just my imagination.* Looking at Albert, she noticed how his eyes followed every female shape on the beach. *Well, why shouldn't he? I just wish this had been a regular beach and not a nudist colony... I'd really rather hide some flesh.* Pebble would have felt more comfortable wearing the tight black bathing suit she'd bought in Magasin du Nord.

But since there was nothing she could do about anything, she rolled over on her stomach and let the warm sun beat down on her back. *At least I won't get wrinkles on my face in this position.* She was almost asleep when visions of the power struggle in Denmark came to mind again. *I wish I could get to Monica Soderland... I wonder how she would react if she found out that I created that first successful Nordkyst campaign...maybe she'd give me a shot at their new one...* The thought jolted Pebble awake. As she sat up to think about it, she noticed that she could see a little too much of Stephanie's vagina from where she was sitting. When she turned, in one sweep, to look at Albert's eyes behind his sunglasses, she realized he had discovered the same thing.

What difference does it make? Being philosophical didn't work, she was furious. *It does make a difference – damn it!* At that very moment, as Albert laughed about something Gilbert was saying, Stephanie shifted her golden thighs a trifle...and the deep rose-colored lips of her young flower opened a tiny bit more in Albert's direction. Pebble watched his eyes follow her movement behind his dark glasses. *She ought to be shot.* Pebble felt much hotter than she should have in the afternoon sun. *Only a young girl would do something like this to an older woman!* Pebble turned over on her towel and pouted. Unfortunately, it was much too easy to imagine Albert holding onto those young, perfect thighs...

Chapter 20

Two evenings later, when the air turned balmy, they went out to dinner with Albert's new friends. Pebble was luminous after another day of sun and sea, spiced by another afternoon of hungry lovemaking on their soft, wide bed at Le Chateau du Mer. So Pebble wore white with amazing grace, not only because it highlighted her new suntan, but because it accentuated the deep sensuality she was experiencing as well.

She enjoyed looking at herself in the mirror – and the glimpse of Albert behind her. He was a strong, vigorous man, and the movements of his body as he buckled his wide leather belt around his waist gave her great pleasure. When he saw her watching him, he smiled back at her image in the slightly tarnished mirror, "This is better than slaving away in Copenhagen, isn't it?"

She returned his warm smile, but deep in her heart, she wasn't sure. There was no way of getting around it – she was at a critical point in her career. The little voice inside just wouldn't roll over and die. Not for love or money or blissful orgasm. The fundamental need to take control of her own life was too strong. *And it's not just my career – this is a critical point in my life, too!* She didn't talk about it with Albert, though. He wasn't a man of all seasons, so how would he understand? His winter world of he-men and Eskimo women was a world of black and white, inhabited by good guys and bad guys. That was his way of dealing with reality. Make things clear cut. Though he never mentioned it, Pebble was sure he considered her boss a bad guy. *Albert's not all that different from Slim when you think about it.* She hadn't realized it before. *Getting away from your life for a few days sure does put things into perspective.* Not that she particularly wanted to cultivate that perspective right then and there. *I'm here to have fun...remember, kiddo?* Still, his remark made her want to tease him a little, so she playfully threw her arms around him and said, "How come you don't like my job?"

He smiled and kissed her gaily on the check. "How come?" He didn't want to deal with the hot potato she chucked at him either. "You don't really want to know... do you?" He held her at arm's length and regarded her well-proportioned figure. "If you had any idea how jealous I get thinking of you spending all your time in the office next to Einar... How do I know you won't run off and marry him... The guy probably makes more in a month than I make in a year..." He glanced at his watch. "Come Chérie, we're late."

The first glass of wine at dinner, before any food arrived, made Pebble strangely lightheaded. *I forgot we were going out with a bunch of people I can't talk to.* It irritated her suddenly, to be cut off from Albert like that. This was supposed to be their week of romance together. Not her sitting at a table with a bunch of people gabbing away in French. The conversation was animated indeed with everybody stuffing hot crusty bread into their mouths and talking at the same time. Pebble was only an outsider, sitting silently, sipping her wine. *What am I doing here?* Again, she realized it wasn't her choice. *So this is my whole life in a nutshell? Or what? I let the other guys do the choosing for me...and I just kind of let myself get carried away until I realize I'm not going in the direction I want to go in...* It was a strange, upsetting thought. To be forty-something and not in control...

Gilbert looked much better with his clothes on, no question about that. He had graciously pulled back Pebble's chair for her and was now seated on her left. They smiled occasionally at each other, and he tried his few words of broken English out on her. Claudine seemed more elegant and relaxed, too and Pebble wondered if they'd made love that afternoon, too. Stephanie, cheeks flushed and dressed in a tight-fitting, low-cut, red dress, eyed every man who entered the restaurant.

Why did everyone drink too much?

Why did Pebble feel left out?

Why was the moon almost full in the sky above?

"Albert?" Pebble said when they'd finished their dessert.

"Yes, my dear?" He turned towards her, his face warm and alive with the pleasure of being with people from his home town.

She was planning on asking him to wind up their conversation and leave. She wanted to go walking through the village with him in the moonlight, but looking at his face, she knew she couldn't. He just wouldn't understand. To him, the night was young, and the release of strong wine and good company made his eyes sparkle. He would only think Pebble was acting like a sour puss if she asked him to leave his newfound friends now. "It's nothing..."

It never occurred to him that she might feel left out. But it did occur to her that Albert, who was on her right, had Stephanie to his right, too. Was he really turning more and more frequently towards Stephanie, or was it just her imagination? The imagination of one insecure woman in her 40s who had just woken up and realized her life was out of control...

What am I doing here? It was a bad time to ask because suddenly she realized Albert was more than flushed and happy, he was drunk, too. *Oh no...not again.* Her whole life seemed to come tumbling down on her head. Her heart beat – boom, boom, boom – loud and strange in her chest.

What would Irene say? Pebble wasn't in doubt. *She would just stand here – if she was here – with her hands planted firmly on her broad hips and say (without batting an eyelash), you asked for this yourself, Pebble... A lot of good knowing what Irene would say does me...*

A volcano of emotions exploded inside Pebble.

Her mind did somersaults and on the big screen behind her eyes unkind messages flashed menacingly. *Why did I have to travel so far to realize that I'm my own worst enemy? Me and nobody else? Me and not 42 other people and most of all not Albert. It's not his fault that I'm out of control... Maybe I just never wanted to admit it...maybe it was always too scary.*

Pebble almost turned green with envy when she saw Albert's strong muscular arm on the back of Stephanie's chair. He was leaning towards her, directing the full, hot blast of his manhood into her every pore. Obviously enjoying his attention, she laughed huskily and tossed her young head so her jet black hair fell gracefully on her full bosom. *God, she's pretty. Can't blame him for liking her.* Stephanie's red mouth was full and open, her young lips warm and sensual. The image of Albert holding those young perfect thighs returned from the beach to haunt her once more.

She wished she could disappear from her life.

This can't be me.

She wished she was sober, instead of sloshing around in the strong red wine they'd shared. It was a mistake. Everything was a mistake. *I don't belong here.*

She stared down at the crumbs on the table before her.

In an attempt to save the situation, Gilbert (who was sober enough to figure out what was going on and who probably didn't want his daughter getting involved with an older man anyway) motioned for the check. "Pebble," he struggled in broken English, "we go for a walk, non?"

Pebble appreciated his wanting to help.

"I would dearly love to see the moon." She knew it was almost full. *I wonder if he thinks his daughter's a virgin?* It was obvious she wasn't, even a doting father should be able to see that. *That is, if he wants to.*

"The moon...ah...la lune, mais oui..." He spoke rapidly to Claudine, Albert and Stephanie. They all nodded; then looked at Pebble as if they were considering a child who needed entertaining. *I wonder what he said to them?*

Even though the night was splendid, walking didn't help.

Albert had his arm around Pebble on one side and around Stephanie on the other. As they walked towards the shoreline, he swayed from one woman to the other, humming merrily to himself. *He sure is feeling good.* Claudine and Gilbert followed in silence.

Pebble wished he would let go of her, but couldn't seem to make it happen. The little voice inside said, *You will be hammered until you do.*

"Albert," Pebble turned towards him and said, "let's go back to our room, darling."

"Back to our room?" He stopped, amazed by her suggestion, but didn't let go of Stephanie. "The night is young, darling, are you tired?" She could see life pulsing hot in his veins.

Claudine and Gilbert, sensing danger, joined the discussion. Claudine spoke with a mother's authority to her daughter who protested violently. *Maybe she doesn't want her daughter hanging out with a guy like Albert either. Smart woman.* Gilbert looked uncomfortable. Stephanie, who had moved away from Albert, stood besides her mother, pouting. Her full red lips glimmered defiantly in the moonlight.

Albert, who seemed not to hear the discussion between Stephanie and Claudine, said, "Mes amis, let's go down to Bill's Bar for a nightcap." Pebble wondered how he could be so unaware of the tension around him. *Maybe he chooses not to see it.* The moon was big and shiny in the night sky. It was still early.

Pebble stood still contemplating her fate as Albert approached her. When he stood directly before her, he placed both his hands on her shoulders. *He might love me, but he's a bum.* She didn't want to be around him anymore.

"I've got a headache…" the words spilled out of her mouth with infinite slowness. The eternal excuse; instead of saying to the bum – why are you acting like such a jerk? But she didn't, because she couldn't. Because in the final analysis, she was too civilized to do it.

"Oh poor you." He fumbled in his pants pocket and pulled out the hotel key. "I'll be back soon."

She knew he wouldn't.

"I just want to have a little nightcap with my friends, okay?" Pebble smiled pathetically, like a wet cat.

"A walk in the night air will do you good," he continued, pointing towards their hotel on the hill overlooking the sea. *Give me a break, will you please... I don't need night air, I need consideration...* She turned away from Albert and said goodnight to Claudine, Gilbert and Stephanie as politely as she could. *I wish I'd never laid eyes on the three of you.* But she knew in truth it wasn't them. *If it hadn't been them, it would have been someone else.* Then she walked away quickly, heading up the curvy road towards the hotel on the hill. She felt her anger everywhere. After a few minutes, she turned and looked back at them. They were headed in the other direction, down the hill towards Bill's Bar and the crowded harbor. Albert had his arm around Stephanie once more, and now that Pebble wasn't there, Stephanie leaned her head freely against Albert's shoulder.

Tears welled up in Pebble's eyes.

Just as Pebble was about to turn and continue on up the hill, the four figures stopped to talk. Pebble wondered what they could be talking about, until suddenly she understood perfectly. Claudine and Gilbert turned and started walking down the pathway that branched off to the right in the direction of their hotel. Albert and Stephanie, bodies close together, continued down the hill towards the milling crowds of vacationing tourists.

Damn them all to hell. The vision of Stephanie's perfect golden thighs flashed vividly before Pebble's eyes. *Damn, damn, damn.*

So he's going to fuck her – so what?

The full weight of what she'd done with her life came crashing down on her head.

It's not Albert, it's me. It's my screwed up life. I don't care who he is or how drunk he gets or what problems he has... I'm just not interested...I hate him... He can drink himself to death for all I care...and believe me, I couldn't care less... It's me I care about – me. It's me I've got to care about. And all I know is I keep putting myself through this senseless anguish over and over again... She looked up at the sky with tears of rage in her eyes. *Can somebody please tell me why?? Because that's the rub – I can't see it...I can't fathom it...why do I keep doing this to myself, over and over again?*

She turned and walked slowly towards the top of the hill, the white heat of determination flowing through her. The little voice inside said again: *You're going to keep hitting yourself over the head with the same hammer until you learn your lesson. Remember?*

Where is Irene when I really need her?

Pebble felt the full weight of her aloneness in the universe when she realized that though Irene might not be walking right besides her, she was some place far more important – *she's inside me. Because she's been there all along – a reflection of me.* The clarity of her vision pierced her aching heart. *So why am I standing all alone on top of this hill somewhere in Croatia, crying my eyes out? Does that make sense?* But the little voice was right there: *You're going to keep hitting yourself over the head with the same hammer until you learn your lesson. Remember?* She wanted to scream shut up to the voice, but didn't dare – the voice, after all, was inside.

Maybe I should thank him for treating me like shit and making me see what a fool I am... Maybe I needed somebody just like Albert in order to learn... maybe...well, obviously I needed somebody just like Albert because if it wasn't Albert I needed I probably would have ended up with Luke or Jack. How come things are always so simple when you get them straight?

Pebble plopped herself down on a deserted bench on the hotel terrace and surveyed the panorama of sky and sea before her. Now that she was calmer, she felt the fires of freedom and courage burn hot inside her. For the first time in her life, she knew for sure she had it in her. *I'm going to cultivate my own power because I am not only talented, I'm tough, too. Real tough.* A big mean grin spread slowly across her well-lived face. It was a grin she'd never tried before. *And I'm me. Yes I am. I'm me and I ain't never going to be anyone else, ever again. I'm not going to be younger or prettier or braver or wiser either. Cause I've got what I've got and not a drop more. So it's either use it or lose it, sister.* The big mean grin spread wider and felt very comfortable on her face. *Life is an adventure and this happens to be my very own personal adventure and I'm right smack in the middle of it, and you know what – I'm starting to like it and who I am, too.*

So she sat there, free as a bird on the wing and liked herself mightily – maybe for the first time in her whole life. That was when she hit pay dirt, too – because right then and there Pebble knew exactly what she was going to do when she got back to Copenhagen. It was so obvious that all she could do was sit on the bench in the moonlight and laugh and laugh and laugh, and wonder why she hadn't figured it out before.

Chapter 21

Albert came barging noisily into their hotel room at nine the next morning, just as Pebble was getting ready to leave. He caught her off guard, trying to stuff more clothes into the battered, navy-blue suitcase on the bed than it was meant to hold. She looked at him in shock. She forgot that he might suddenly turn up.

His face was flushed, and his luxurious, black hair fell forward onto his forehead, slightly unkempt; but he looked happy enough. Pebble could tell by his unsteady gait that he was still drunk.

Oh no... The realization made her tingle with fear.

"Pebble, what are you doing?" he asked cheerfully. *Thank God he seems to be in such a good mood.* Great, powerful beams of sunlight illuminated their room. The bright, blue Mediterranean sparkled outside their open windows.

Even though he seemed relaxed and happy, she found herself at a loss for words. Having made it through the night in perfect harmony with herself, she somehow forgot to consider the fact that Albert not only still shared this lovely hotel room with her, but that he had every right to turn up at any time and probably would do so again soon. After all, why shouldn't he? For some mysterious reason, she failed to consider how the world must have looked to him when they went their separate ways the night before. She said she had a headache. He'd been politely and fittingly sorry about her headache, but decided no harm could come from going down to Bill's Bar for a drink with his new friends. Nothing more had passed between them.

Unfortunately for Albert, Pebble wasn't that kind of woman. Maybe he met her at a bad moment in her life. Or rather at a momentous moment in her life. But no matter how one looked at it, something inside Pebble had snapped that night, and in the process of snapping, which happens very fast when it happens, she'd written Albert off – once and for all. There was only one problem; Albert knew nothing about all this. While he was out having a good time his whole world changed. Up until 9 a.m. that morning, Albert had been innocently following his ordinary life script, doing what mountain men always do in his world when they came down from the heights to mingle with ordinary mortals and muck about in the perilous world of civilization – they go out and get drunk. So how could she expect him to understand that while he was out doing what he always did – that is, coping with a fearful world by trying to drown himself in booze – she turned from hot to cold. Maybe, if he'd been sober, he would have shook his head and smiled (because after all he was a kind man), remembering how temperamental Pebble Beach was at times. But drunk or sober, there was nothing in Albert's world to prepare him for the fact that something final might have, could have, and in fact did happen. Something very final indeed.

Not only was Albert suddenly, irrevocably, a closed book for Pebble, but Pebble thought closing the book, and leaving him, just like that, was as good a way of dealing with the hurt of loving him as any other way she could figure out. *Stop wasting your time and your life. Forget him. Forget all about it. Nothing you can ever do or say is going to change it anyway.* The picture of him wandering off into the tender night – on their vacation – with a very young and very beautiful girl on his arm wasn't easy to swallow. Even if he was a jerk and an alcoholic and a mountain man. She was too new at being divorced and too old to take him anymore. She had invested too much of her emotional life in him. Now all she wanted to do was blot him out of her existence forever.

"Albert?" The shock of his unexpected arrival threw her off balance.

"Planning on going somewhere?" He acted as if he was truly mystified by the sight of her suitcase on the bed. All she noticed was that he was standing before her, blocking her path towards the door.

When she didn't reply, he said, "I thought you had a headache last night...?"

"Well..." She looked down at the floor, like a little girl who wasn't good at lying. "Oh I don't know..." But she knew that 'I don't know' wasn't good enough. *Get your act together woman and grow up.*

"It's hard to explain, Albert," she pulled herself up to her full height and forced herself to look him in the eye, "but I just had enough... that's all."

"Enough?" He swayed slightly. "What are you talking about?"

"Oh, Albert, you'll never understand."

"Understand what?"

"I don't want to live like this..." her words hung like tiny crystals in the air between them.

"Like what, what are you talking about?"

She didn't want to tell him, and besides, she couldn't. All she wanted to do was get out of there.

"Look at me, Pebble..." The slight change in the tone of his voice sent a wave of panic through her. "Look at me..."

Suddenly, she was afraid.

She was standing right before him, watching him wallow slowly in the confusion she'd created in him. There was about a foot of hot, pulsing space between them.

Suddenly, he got it right. "So you are going to leave me...just like that?"

"Albert..." There was pleading in her voice – and fear. "You don't understand..." As the tiny crystals, the fragile crystals of her words and thoughts crumbled, things were turned crystal clear. *This is what happens when you're not brought up to be independent... So tell me, Irene, now that I understand; what to do now...*

"What don't I understand?"

"You don't understand anything… I've got things to do." The minute she said those words, she knew she shouldn't have. She tried desperately to calm herself. *Anger will never get me out of here.* She never wanted out so bad in her life before. He was still standing between her and the door. Her over-stuffed suitcase on the bed still wasn't closed.

"Things to do… What do you mean?" The drunken slur in his voice grated harshly on her nerves. He swayed more than a little on his feet. The top two buttons of the beige shirt she'd given him for Christmas were undone. "What kind of a woman are you…anyway? You were going to run out on me without so much as a goodbye…" He stared at her with hurt, angry eyes. "Women are snakes…" he muttered. "That's what Travis always said…and when I told you…you said you were different, but you're not, you're just like the rest of them…sneaking and lying…you bitch…I thought you were…but no, you're a snake, too…" He swayed as he spoke.

Before she had time to fully realize what was happening, she saw his right arm moving through the dense air between them towards the right side of her head. *I can't believe this is happening to me – I can't believe he's going to hit me,* but it was already too late to duck. He was that fast. A split second later, Pebble found herself on the floor, stunned, her right jaw aching from the force of his blow. His fist was clinched.

She moaned softly and edged slowly backwards towards the open door and the balcony beyond, trembling all over and holding her aching jaw. Her heart was pounding furiously.

When she saw him approaching her, she pleaded, tears streaming down her face, "Oh no, please don't hurt me…"

He looked at her curiously, as if he was surprised at what had happened. Then he bent down slowly towards her as she cowered in fear. "Mon amour…" Suddenly he was by her side, stroking her hair gently. "Mon amour…"

Pebble shook like a leaf. *God help me, please.* She would have run if she could, but she couldn't. He had her cornered. She didn't like to think of what he would do if she displeased him further. *He's so strong.*

"Ma chérie," his voice was soft and kind. "Please forgive me, I didn't mean to…" Tears of remorse welled up in his eyes. "But the thought of you leaving me…it was more than I could bear…"

She couldn't speak, hating every inch of him. *I'll hate you till the day I die… if only you knew how much I hate you. Please God get me out of here. Please…* Still she didn't move. She didn't dare. His drunken breath was all around her and his hands too were suddenly touching her everywhere. He fingered her jaw, where he had struck her, then went back to caressing her hair. "Does it hurt? Look at me Pebble, please." But she couldn't, wouldn't. Everything inside her was pure hatred and fear. She was out of control, out of her head, in an uproar, still shaking like a leaf. No man had ever hit her before.

His hands found her breasts. *No please God, not this.*

"Albert," but she bit back her words, fearing his strength.

He misunderstood her, thinking she had forgiven him. "Ma chérie," he was unbuttoning her blouse, undoing her brassiere. Fondling her nipples.

Suddenly there was urgency in his hands; he bent forward, kissing her neck. *He might kill me if I don't cooperate.* His hot, drunken breath was everywhere. When she arched her neck backwards, trying to escape, the curve of her body only ignited him further.

He removed her blouse and brassiere and she let him. And let him lift her up to the bed and remove the rest of her clothes. When she was naked, he sat besides her with a wild look in his eyes, one hand fondling her vagina, the other unbuttoning his shirt. She tried to stare beyond the need in his eyes to the open sky and the infinity it contained beyond the open door and the balcony overlooking the sea. When he finished unbuttoning his shirt – and it seemed to take forever – he stopped fondling her clitoris and inserted two fingers deep inside her vagina. He kept them there for several moments, probing her deeply and hurting her. She moaned, but not with pleasure.

"Un moment, ma chérie, un moment." Again he misunderstood her signals. He bent forward and kissed the lips of her vagina. Then, thinking she wanted him badly, he removed his lips and his fingers and stood up, pulling off his shirt and pants as quickly as he could in his present state of intoxication. Then he stood for a moment besides the bed, swaying slightly and breathing heavily, regarding her nakedness. He must have picked up her true frame of mind because suddenly his face twisted into an ugly snarl again, and he muttered, "Women like snakes..."

Pebble, still fluttering like a leaf in a storm, caught his change of mood and panicked, picturing herself battered beyond recognition...

"Albert? Please...please darling...make love to me... please..." Her voice was like mountain honey...smooth and sweet. *This is rape...dear God...please, protect me...please...*

The sound of her sweetness brought him down upon her in a rush, his hands and lips everywhere, seeking her breasts, her buttocks, her cunt. "Never leave me again...Pebble...never..." He was rough and drunk as he smothered her with kisses. She felt his powerful arms surround her as the hot ramrod of his need penetrated her, finding the depths he knew so well. That was when she began to moan, surprised at how the fear and ice in her melted suddenly and mysteriously into quick, liquid fire. She did not want him, with her mind, she hated him, despised him, loathed him. But her body and soul opened hot to him as his power and fury forced her to find in herself, some twisted, ecstatic state of need, of hunger she'd never experienced before.

The fact that she hated him, the fact that he hit her, the fact that he had overwhelmed her and was now forcing his way into her innermost depths had nothing or everything to do with it. By some demented, roundabout path, Albert guided Pebble to a place where nothing except total surrender was possible. She was no longer Pebble Beach with an identity worth protecting or preserving. He had robbed her as thoroughly as any man could of whatever it was she was. He had stripped her bare. Left her with nothing she could identify with, and in that strange, naked state of being no woman she knew, she found herself connected to a sexuality so powerful that it jolted her beyond everyday reality to some awesome cosmic plane she did not recognize. *This is not me. This is not anyone.*

He plunged headlong, headstrong, into her, finding in her an intensity she did not know she possessed. She spread her legs wide, baring her soul, allowing him entry everywhere – allowing him anything, everything. And when he raised himself up above her, supporting himself with his powerful arms, staring down at her like a madman – she understood him perfectly.

Just when you think you've got it all figured out. For one short moment, the real Pebble Beach, the Pebble Beach inside the writhing, aching body of Pebble Beach, laughed. And though no one else in the entire universe heard, she laughed heartily and joyfully at herself, and at Albert, and at her life, and at her search for wisdom, too. *It's almost too funny.* She stood perched, perfectly poised, before that formidable plunge into the cosmic void when all that light hit her. *He is the most strange and powerful man I've ever known.* And right before she let go and jumped, heart first and ecstatic, in the nothingness before her, she knew, once and for all, now and forever – that nothing in her life would ever be completely clear-cut and understandable ever again. Then she closed her eyes and let the passion – his passion and her own passion, and the passion of loving and fearing and being alive all wrapped in one – finally carry her over the edge. And as she flew fast, hurtling through space towards her infinite self, she screamed, delirious as a sacrificial lamb suddenly released from the agony of an evil spell... *And this is exactly the way it's supposed to be.*

* * *

Later, when Albert fell into the deep, undisturbed sleep of a drowned man, Pebble hastily put on her clothes, locked her suitcase and left, a strange smile on her lips.

Chapter 22

"Mel?" Pebble's tense, eager voice reached across the Atlantic to her uncle in New York.

"Pebble?" He would recognize his favorite niece's voice, no matter where in the world she was calling from. "Where are you?"

"Me? Oh, I'm in Copenhagen, where did you think I was?"

"I don't know, last time I spoke to your mother, she told me you were on vacation in Croatia with some Frenchman."

Pebble laughed, amazed at how well-informed Mel always was. "Well, I came back early."

"Really?"

"Yeah, things didn't work out too well."

"How come, sweetheart – what happened?"

"Albert's a jerk, that's all. I really don't want to talk about it."

"All of a sudden, just like that – the guy's a jerk? According to Molly, you were pretty hooked on this guy... Isn't he the one you went all the way to Greenland to visit?"

"Yeah, but I found out he's got a drinking problem."

"Oh..."

There was a pause.

"I know..." Pebble sighed, wanting to get on with the conversation, "alcoholics are bad news. Look, Mel, you don't have to tell Molly and Morris, okay?"

"Sure, I guess not..."

"I mean there's no reason for them to know, it will just upset them. Don't even tell them I called or that I'm back early. I'm calling you about something else anyway..."

Mel yawned. "What time is it anyway in Copenhagen?"

"It's two in the afternoon here. Did I wake you up?"

"Well, yes you did, if you really want to know." It was 8 a.m. in New York.

"I'm sorry." She was. "The only reason I called this early was it's important and I wanted to be sure to get you. I figured if I waited till you got to your office I'd never get a chance to talk to you..."

Mel laughed.

"How come you're still in bed at this hour anyway?" Mel was a notorious fast-tracker. "I thought you went jogging in Central Park at six thirty in the morning come hell or high water..."

"I usually do, but last night I had to go to this big shindig...you know how it is – a big client. The whole thing just went on and on and since it was my account, I couldn't leave early..."

"I didn't know."

"No problem. In fact, I'm glad you woke me up: I've got tons of work waiting for me anyway. So let's hear it, Pebble. What's on your mind?"

"I want you to get me in the door at Nordkyst, here in Copenhagen."

"Nordkyst?" Mel laughed. "Isn't this a bit late in the game, Pebble?"

"No, you don't understand," Pebble lowered her voice. "I found out something – something important."

"Yeah? Like what?"

"Nordkyst has developed a new product line. They're branching out into the pre-teen market."

"That's interesting. But how do you know?"

"Well, one day when Einar was in Germany, he called me and asked me to pull a file for him and give him some data over the phone. When I put the file back in place, I stumbled over his Nordkyst file."

"Well, well, well – my talented little niece is finally growing up..."

"Come on, Mel, I know it wasn't ethical, but look how they've treated me. All this stuff with Peter Cato's made me change the way I look at things. And besides, a lot's happened to me in the past two years... I've changed, you know. I always wanted to tell you, you were right then, I should have gone public, but I guess I didn't have enough self-confidence at the time. So I acted like a jerk, all right? I admit it. I never told you before how bad I feel whenever I think about it. It makes me mad as hell. Somehow I always feel like I passed up this golden opportunity."

"Well, you did... I'm glad to hear it makes you mad. It should."

"The thing is, Mel, this is another golden opportunity. It's got to be. Einar and the Republic Group are in the process of developing a campaign for the new account and from Einar's notes I can see that Peter Cato's doing the same thing."

"Clever, clever girl." Mel chuckled. Pebble enjoyed the honest warmth of family in his voice.

"Mel, I want a crack at it, too. And you've got to help me!"

"You? Whoa, whoa, slow down a minute, sister." Mel was now fully awake, processing Pebble's information. "Just backtrack a second and tell me exactly what you know about this new line..."

"Well according to Einar's notes, what they're basically going to do is take their signature line of bright-colored cotton kids' clothes – and modify them slightly and sell them to pre-teens. It's a brilliant idea, isn't it? And an obvious one, too. Just think about it. All the kids who've been wearing Nordkyst stuff for the last couple of years are growing up. They're not going to want to dump their neat image..."

"Hmm...not bad... Monica Soderland's real smart, isn't she?"

"Yeah, and tough. Anyway, Einar did a pilot survey in the New York area to check the market before deciding whether or not he wanted the Republic Group to work on developing a new campaign for Monica. From what I gathered from his notes, the results must have been quite promising or he wouldn't have decided to go for it in such a big way."

"How come you're not involved in developing this new campaign? You'd think somebody with Einar's nose would know you were behind the first campaign. He's seen plenty of your work – or he wouldn't have hired you."

"I thought of the same thing, especially when I discovered he does know it was me... Do you believe it..." Pebble still couldn't, "that Einar's known all along I was the one?"

"Doesn't surprise me in the least. To tell you the truth, Pebble, I suspected he knew. Things make a lot more sense now. I mean, him hiring you to be his assistant – and all that. Maybe you don't realize what a good job you landed there. What doesn't make sense is Einar not involving you in the creative team who's developing the new campaign."

"Well, all I can tell you is he's got my name scribbled in the margin on one of the pages where he was kind of brainstorming about the pitch, so maybe he is thinking of involving me. I don't know. The other thing I thought of is that maybe nobody's started working on the presentation yet. Or let's put it this way, as far as I know, nobody's doing any work on anything that could be even vaguely related to Nordkyst at the moment in there. I guess you're used to ad agency hysteria. But I'm not yet. It seems to me everybody's pretty much gone off the deep end because we've got so much new business coming in. And so many of the new accounts are such other high-priority clients – like the big Odenweiss & Hauser deal they just finalized – that maybe Einar simply hasn't had time to pay any attention to Nordkyst yet."

"When is the Republic Group supposed to make their presentation?"

"They're scheduled for June 29th at Monica Soderland's headquarters in Hellerup."

"June 29th, June 29th. That doesn't give you much time, Pebble. What's today's date?"

"The ninth."

"What makes you think you can do it, Pebble?" She was glad

he asked.

"I've been thinking about it day and night, Mel. I know I can do it. I just know. I've got the whole thing in my head. All I need to do is get it down on paper."

"You're going to need more than a concept and copy, kiddo. You're going to need the visuals, too."

"I've already thought of that. One of my friends is this great graphic artist – Steffen Kellerman. He spent some time in New York at the Parsons School of Design. I'm positive I can get him to work up some visuals for me. At least some preliminary stuff. But I don't dare go to him with the idea until I'm sure I can get my foot in the door. It wouldn't be fair to Steffen."

"No, you're right, it wouldn't be."

"And there's one other thing, Mel…"

"Which is…?"

"Peter Cato's got to be in deep trouble."

"How so?"

"Everybody thinks he did the last campaign, so everybody will be expecting more of the same from him. The thing is – the poor man can't do concept or even write a complete sentence in English. So he's going to have to hire somebody else to ghost for him, like he did the last time."

"That shouldn't be too hard to do."

"No, there are plenty of copywriters in Copenhagen who do good work in English, but the problem is the style and the tone. Don't you remember my stuff?" Pebble was insulted. How could her favorite uncle, her mentor, the hotshot from Young & Rubicam forget? "You told me at the time, you thought my work was terrific."

Mel laughed. "So I did, so I did. I was just wondering if Monica Soderland would go for exactly the same style again – now that they're so successful over here. Maybe it's got to be a little bit more sophisticated than the last time. Don't forget the kids – and their mothers – are slightly older now."

"I've been thinking the same thing...it's going to need a new twist. Something which is subtle, but which is an obvious development of the old theme..." Pebble replied, grateful for his advice, but impatient for a commitment from him to help her. "Mel, please...please, you've got to help me. Please! You can get me in the door. I know you can."

"Well, it's not going to be easy, you know. Unless you let me tell their vice-president over here that you did the first campaign. That would change everything."

"No, no, you can't. You promised you wouldn't tell Richard, remember?"

"But things have changed, Pebble. You said so yourself. Why should Monica Soderland give you the time of day, unless she knows you were behind the first campaign?"

"You've got to find another way, Mel. You've got to."

"Give me one good reason why."

"I don't know; I just have this feeling that it won't work. Peter Cato will deny it and Monica will believe him. Somehow, I've got to prove myself first...and besides there was some funny information in that file I didn't really understand."

"Like what?"

"Something like Peter Cato being Monica Soderland's secret partner. Some of Einar's scribblings were unclear, and besides how could Peter be Monica's partner. It just doesn't make sense. But according to Einar's notes, Peter's sky-blue BMW roadster was a gift from Monica, too."

"You should have had the car, you know."

"Yeah, I should have."

"Richard Davis tells me Monica's quite a character. The other day while we were playing golf, he pulls this picture of Monica out of his pocket – from some Danish gossip rag – she looked absolutely wild driving this white Porsche with the top down and her short, flaming red hair plastered flat by the wind."

"That's her all right. She's the talk of the town."

"She might just go for you, Pebble. She might." There was a hint of irony in Mel's voice.

"Thanks a lot." Sometimes Pebble loved her uncle so much.

"Look, kiddo, I'll see what I can do. I'll call you back as soon as I've thought this through... You're sure I can't tell Richard it was you..."

"I'm sure..."

Chapter 23

With so little time to develop her concept and put together her presentation, Pebble was working around the clock like a woman possessed. And in fact, she was. She barely found time to sleep or eat. For some reason, she knew that this was her time, her moment. She had to grab it before it vanished from the face of the earth, never to appear again. *Nordkyst is my call to arms. There isn't a moment to waste, a second to lose. If I'm ever going to make it, it's got to be now.*

When Albert socked her on the jaw, he socked her out of her Sleeping Beauty slumber forever and ever.

Goodbye days of innocence. This is my time, my life. I can do it.

In a way I'm lucky Albert hit me. It gave me enough steam, enough anger – and most important of all – enough time to get home and do this stuff while Einar thinks I'm off vacationing in sunny Croatia. He's not going to like my suntan!

Fortunately, Pebble still had her comprehensive notes from the first Nordkyst campaign. Peter Cato had briefed her extensively. Since she was ghosting for him, she never got to meet Monica personally or visit Nordkyst – and it looked like it would be pretty much the same this time. So her copious notes stood her in good stead. She had filled reams and reams of paper with her scratchy, sprawling, American handwriting – a bizarre collection of all kinds of data about Nordkyst. Not knowing what would be relevant, she wrote down everything. That was her technique – to dive in headfirst, trying to get a feel of the company and its product, instead of trying to see and analyze it first. During the time when she was unable to meet Monica and sniff around her factory located outside Odense, she bought a whole bunch of Monica's kiddie clothes and sent Peter the bill. When he hinted that she might be going overboard, she replied, *I've got to feel the stuff. And smell it.* Peter had trouble connecting smelling and feeling with writing advertising copy, but she knew she had to have more than the company's history and strategic goals. She had to get inside Monica and her concept for a while. Peter's approach was so masculine, so intellectual. He could provide a shotgun rundown of Monica's life story, but it wasn't enough for Pebble so she kept grilling him. She needed personal insights, stories. She wanted to know how Monica wore her hair. It wasn't enough to know what; she wanted the why and the how, too.

That was when Pebble started digging into the whole startup phase in Monica's basement in Hellerup. She wanted clues to the woman's psyche. Why Monica, why Monica, what was it about her, about specifically her that made her products so successful? Peter felt more comfortable describing Monica's production methods, and showing Pebble Nordkyst's phenomenal growth curves. For Peter it was a matter of matching design types with the right target groups, it was as simple as that.

But if Pebble was going to deliver gold, she needed more. She needed a handle, a hook, she needed that special magic that would trigger her special Nordkyst campaign. Peter was of no help there. He couldn't follow Pebble's womanly intuition or give her a whiff of what she needed, but at least he provided her with detailed information whenever she asked for it.

Oh, the Soderland trademark. Pebble sat flipping through the pages of the first American catalogue, the one Nordkyst built around Pebble's up-close-and-personal approach. Her original campaign set the tone that ran through everything Nordkyst did. Young urban parents' passion for high-quality cotton, their willingness to cough up substantial sums of money for traditional natural fabrics. That was what Nordkyst's trademark was all about – the obvious quality of long-lasting cotton clothes alive and well in all the vibrant colors of Scandinavia.

Her job today would be the same as it was two years ago – to cut through to the bone and communicate Monica's clean Scandinavian design and sense of quality with the same sure distinctiveness as she did in the first campaign. She had to startle and be personal again... *The kids are growing up now. Right? Your kids...* She knew she could do it. She was still talking to the same people. She'd gotten inside their skins once before. What was to stop her now? But Mel was right, something had to be different...somewhat, slightly, or very different. *Growth! That's it, growth. The world's changing, you're changing, your kids are growing up. But some things remain the same. Some values never change – like your desire for quality, like wanting the best for your kids. Even if they do smart talk you at times...* She was singing in the rain. Ideas were just popping out of her sleeves. Why shouldn't the same people be willing to continue spending that extra buck for their pre-teens? Einar's market research demonstrated that a large part of Monica's present success was based on repeat customers anyway. Pebble chuckled, it was all there. All the memorabilia, all tucked away in the big blue cardboard box she just lugged down from up on top of one of her bookcases. The box was so ugly and annoying that every time Pebble dusted (which was rarely) she thought about throwing it away – but for some reason she didn't. Now she thanked her lucky stars she didn't.

She almost sang. *Albert Audibert, you blessed jerk.* It was all coming together for her, suddenly, like a divine miracle. Her life was a revelation. She wished she could kiss Irene. *I will kiss her, next time I see her. Irene always asked me why I spent my life servicing others. And now that I finally understand what she was talking about, I just can't figure out why it took me so long to get the message. I must have been blind...* Pebble, like most people who receive the gift of sudden insight, was high, doing her own thing and enjoying every minute of it. Insight like that has a way of setting people free. *Even if I don't win the account, it'll be okay.* But she wanted it badly. More than anything, she wanted to prove to herself that she could do it.

Still she couldn't blot out Albert completely. He'd creep up on her while she was working in the middle of the night. Suddenly she would feel his hands on her body. The memory of his violence was that strong. Every time it happened, her insides would contract in misshapen desire, until, shaking like a leaf, she was able to put things into the right perspective again. Remembering the force of his blow to her jaw helped. Every time she thought of how he hit her – and how hard he hit her – she'd stop in midair as if stunned by life itself. *Was that really me?* It was so appalling, so atrocious, she could hardly relate to it or believe it really happened.

Still stunned in midair (it happened more than once), she would vow (for the hundredth time) to forget it and him and everything that went with it. But she couldn't. Something permanent that the universe could not erase happened between them. Some karmic bond, however despicable, now existed even if Pebble never wanted to think about Albert Audibert again. *If only I could forget him… It's just so confusing. It makes no sense at all. Nothing makes sense.* She vowed to call Irene as soon as she had her concept and outline down on paper. *I needed that French mountain guide like I needed a hole in the head.* And she'd try to laugh, but other more unpleasant thoughts bubbled to the surface of her restless mind. *But what if he turns up one day – and rings my doorbell? What'll I do?* The very thought made her shiver. She saw herself, caught off guard, in her baggy jogging pants without a trace of make-up on her face, opening the door and looking deep into those eyes. The same eyes she saw and understood so well the day they coupled like fierce, wild animals. She saw herself, trembling like a young deer, while he stood there, sober or drunk, but solid as a rock. *Will I be ever be strong enough to deal with him?* She wasn't sure. *I don't think so. I'm just not like that. Never was.* She hated herself for being timid in the face of strife, but she knew she was. *I might want to change, but there are just some things about being me I'm not going to be able to change.* She couldn't explain to herself how she knew this, but she knew it was true. *And besides, I'm afraid of conflict.*

Maybe I'll never be able to disengage myself from Albert completely. Maybe it will never go away, no matter how long I live. Maybe it's karmic and I knew him before. It was the only way she could explain the sneaking suspicion she had that she'd never forget him, or be free of him, because of the strange moment in time they'd shared. She knew it was more than just sex. *Albert hurtled me into space. The man is my karma.* No matter how much she hated him, he showed her unexplored depths within herself. *But the man violated me – and hit me.* Strangely, on some deeper level, she knew it wasn't his fault - even if he was a jerk. *We're not talking about jerks here – or blame.* She couldn't forget the strange lightness – or the delirious high – she discovered and savored that savage morning before she left him sleeping on that wide, untamed bed. *Nothing in life is ever that simple. There's always a twist. A flaw. A tiny break in the logic of things, in the flow of events, in the linear explanations that say this is life.*

It was too hard to think about it, and Pebble hated confrontations. *No, no, no... let me go... I can't take it anymore... okay?* Pebble buried herself in her work.

Mel called her late the next evening.

"Okay, doll, you're on."

"Oh, Mel," she shrieked with joy into her slim, white mobile, the ultimate in Scandinavian design.

"Whoa, sister...whoa...aren't you even going to ask me when?"

"Yeah, when?" She was beside herself with joy.

"June 29th at one thirty in the afternoon...and don't ask me how I did it."

She danced around her tiny office, shrieking into the phone. "I promise you my stuff is going to be soooo good...I'll do you proud Mel, I will..."

"You better, or my name is going to be mud over here with a whole lot of very important people..." He laughed, enjoying her joy.

* * *

She took time off on Friday to visit Irene.

"But I thought you were on vacation."

"I was, until Albert hit me..."

"He did what?" Even Irene paled at the mention of violence. Pebble told her everything, or as much as she could of everything, in as much detail as she could, until she found herself weeping and shaking and unable to describe what happened the morning she left.

Irene didn't push her.

In fact, Irene treated Pebble differently – like a new person. Like somebody she really respected. She had a nose for change, and she knew some major, important change was taking place in Pebble's life. When Pebble found herself blocked, stuck, she started talking about other things. "I decided to pitch for the new Nordkyst account myself."

"Good for you!" Irene smiled her most significant smile. "I can't tell you how pleased I am to hear it."

"I owe you so much, Irene; I'll never be able to thank you."

"You don't have to. This is my job...and my pleasure..."

"You said it all along, only I didn't understand it before..."

"Said what?"

"Well you used to ask me why I was always servicing other people. Remember? And I used to get so pissed off at you because of course you were right. Only I didn't see it before now. I didn't understand that I could do things by myself. And I didn't believe in my own talent. I just didn't or couldn't see who I was or what I can do. But something's changed... I don't know how to explain it but for some reason I feel more alive than I've felt in years. It's like I'm high, on a roll, so whatever happens, whatever the outcome of all this I'll be OK because I'll know that I'll have given it my best shot."

"I'm so glad for you, Pebble, I really am. Congratulations, this is such good news." Irene waited a moment and then added, "But I don't understand if everything feels so right, why did you need to see me so badly? You sounded desperate on the phone this morning."

"It's Albert."

"Well, what about him? Why are you wasting your energy on him? You told me you left him."

"I know... but I didn't tell you everything..." They were back to the moment Pebble couldn't talk about. It was like a huge lump in her throat, choking her. "How can I be so powerful, Irene, and be so weak at the same time? It just doesn't make sense..."

"What are you talking about?" Irene asked kindly and then added, "and where does it say that when you're a powerful person, when you're your own person, you're supposed to feel powerful all the time? You've just been through some very traumatic experiences, and I gather you haven't told me every-thing yet about your latest adventure.... Do you want to tell me about it now...?"

And when Pebble nodded, but didn't speak, Irene said, "Well?"

"I don't know...I'm so...so ashamed..."

"Ashamed?" Irene's voice was very soft. "Why, Pebble, we're all just human beings on a learning curve towards greater insight and understanding. Usually what we're ashamed of is just one of the areas of our lives that we haven't yet explored and don't yet understand. And besides, shame is such a non-productive feeling; it doesn't do anyone any good. Now tell me what happened. It always helps to bring things out in the light and talk about them."

"After he hit me..." She started to weep. "After Albert hit me...I was so afraid..."

"What did he do, after he hit you ...?" She was the midwife, again, kind and helpful, but firm, very firm.

"He raped me..." The words gushed out. "He forced me to make love to him and..." Pebble looked up at Irene as the hot tears poured down her cheeks, "and the worst part of it was I liked it...in fact I loved it...it was the most powerful lovemaking experience I've ever had in my whole life...and it was absolutely sick."

Tears of anger and pain erupted from somewhere deep inside Pebble Beach. "And I hate him for what he did to me."

Irene didn't say a word for a long time. She sat very quietly and let Pebble cry.

When she thought Pebble was able to take it, she said softly, "Who did what to you?"

Pebble looked up in surprise. "What do you mean? Albert of course!" Pebble felt her cheeks flush with anger.

"Are you sure it was Albert?"

Pebble gasped. "What are you saying, Irene?

"I'm asking you who did what to you?"

Pebble began sobbing again. "You mean I did this to me?"

"I'm just asking who did what to you, Pebble. There's no need to be so hard on yourself," Irene's voice had softened even more.

There was a long silence.

"You mean I did this to me?"

"Even though you're a modern woman, Pebble, it's obvious you weren't brought up to take care of yourself. It seems you never learned how to set limits and take care of you. And now you're learning..."

"Oh, why does it have to be so painful?" Pebble cried some more.

"Well, the way I look at it is...it's like you're getting rewired. And when this happens, when people undertake this process of self-discovery and relearning, they keep getting themselves into situations that make them face whatever issues they need to face. That's how the universe works. We always seem to attract exactly what we need."

Pebble was quiet for a while, contemplating what Irene said. "But why did I like it so much – even though I hated it?"

"Even though you are in the process of learning to follow your wisdom, it's not that easy to just step out of patterns of compulsive behavior and suddenly make wise choices. You seem to have a pattern of making choices that obviously are not good for you because you are still projecting your need for safety and protection onto the men in your life, when taking care of you and protecting you is your job. Haven't you ever heard about addictive relationships before?"

"Well, no, not really. What does it mean – addictive relationships?"

"Well we call a relationship 'addictive' when a person gets into or stays in a relationship that they know is bad for them…that goes against their better judgment. And they do this because they are projecting some quality or qualities they believe they need onto this person. And when this happens, even though the relationship obviously goes against their better judgment, the addicted person has a compulsive desire to stay in a relationship which he or she doesn't understand and can't control. Just like an alcoholic or a drug addict feels a compulsion towards substances which he or she knows are not good for them. There's something deeper going on in addictive behavior. There is an unmet need that the person is trying to get fulfilled, unfortunately in the wrong place – and until the person understands this, they keep getting themselves into unfortunate relationships and situations."

There was a long silence then Pebble said slowly, "It does sound a lot like me, doesn't it?"

"Well there certainly seems to be a compulsive quality to your relationship with Albert because on the one hand you keep saying you know he's not good for you and yet you keep running off with him and getting yourself into situations that you don't really want to be in."

Pebble looked very thoughtful, as if seeing her relationship with Albert in a completely new light.

"So you mean I am looking for something in Albert that isn't there?"

"Well are you?"

"Yeah, I guess so," said Pebble laughing.

"Well what are you hoping to get from him?"

"Isn't it obvious? Impossible love – and protection and safety and all the stuff he can never give me..."

Again silence.

"You know, Irene, now that all this happened, I'm afraid Albert will get really drunk one day and come knocking on my door."

"After what you tell me, I'm sure he will – and probably sooner than you think."

"The thought absolutely terrifies me. What am I going to do if he shows up drunk? I'm so terrified of him when he's been drinking. He's impossible to deal with."

"Pebble, now that you are getting rewired I am sure you will know exactly what to do."

"Really? But the thought absolutely terrifies me."

"Are you sure, Pebble? Let's go through the scenario, Pebble, and see what happens. Imagine he comes to your door, drunk out of his mind – or you meet him drunk on the street outside your building. What will you do? Close your eyes for a minute and go there."

Pebble closed her eyes and breathed deeply. It wasn't pleasant to think about, but she did it anyway. She was quiet for a couple of minutes, but then she smiled. "You know you're right, Irene, I'll know exactly what to do."

"And what's that? Tell me about it."

"I'll take care of me..." said Pebble slowly.

"And what does that translate into?"

"Well it means not opening the door if he comes to my

apartment when he's drunk and if he calls, it means saying no or hanging up. And it means getting a pepper spray or some kind of alarm in case I meet him on the street. And if he keeps coming around, I will call the police."

"Good, Pebble, good. So you see you know exactly what to do. There is no excuse for violence or abusive behavior – none whatsoever. But you are the one who's got to take care of you. You are the one who must set limits. You are the one who must say no. Nobody else can do it for you."

"Yeah, I can see that now. I guess I should have never gone on vacation with Albert."

"But the reality is you did, Pebble."

"But I could have stayed home…"

"Well, until you get more insight into the compulsive nature of your behavior and learn to make better choices for yourself, you obviously can't because you went."

"But I still think it's so perverted that I actually liked the sex." Pebble was staring out into space again…

Chapter 24

Pebble hung the bold, colorful, comic-strip figures Steffen created for her presentation at strategic positions around Monica Soderland's bare conference room at company headquarters in Hellerup. His drawings were huge, and fun, roaring with vitality. *They're perfect. Perfect!* Pebble loved them. Felt they were her babies. Her fat black portfolio, the one she had so carefully groomed for days, lay pregnant and silent on the big, red conference table. The dramatic white room with the bright red, oval table in the middle, and the spectacular view of the Sound, was exactly the way Pebble expected Monica's domain to be. Nor would she have been surprised in the least if an honor guard of rock musicians playing Madonna's latest hit ushered Monica in when it was time for her to arrive.

She still didn't know what Mel had done to get her in the door, all she knew was she'd gotten in – inside the holy sanctuary – and now one thirty and Monica Soderland were approaching very fast. The keepers of the gate – all of whom seemed to wonder who in the world she could be, because obviously a woman alone couldn't be an entire ad agency and also because nobody had ever heard of Pebble Beach before, except of course one of the sporty gatekeepers who knew Pebble Beach was a famous golf course somewhere in California. Still, magic words must have been spoken because they bowed and allowed her to enter the inner sanctum about 15 minutes before her appointment to get organized. She used the time to arrange Steffen's figures in just the right order and spread out the smaller comic strip sketches and primitive storyboards, while eying her watch nervously. *I'm no ad agency – so how in the world am I going to pull this off? If she doesn't like my comic strips, I'm dead.* She looked at her primitive storyboards for the hundredth time. *Jerk, they're wonderful.* She smiled to herself. *And so funny. Monica's going to love them.*

Everyone's going to love them. They're perfect. She'd already tried some of her ideas out on some of the kids she knew.

She had no idea how many people Monica would bring with her. *God, I hope it's not a whole entourage.* Presentations are usually like that. She felt tiny beads of sweat forming under her arms.

All the pretty words in the world will get you absolutely nowhere if you haven't got the chutzpah to stand up and deliver it, sister. Pebble prayed for power.

Monica entered suddenly, with no band or fanfare whatsoever. She was all alone, too, and much taller than Pebble expected her to be. Her bright, red hair had grown a little since the last picture Pebble had seen of her, but otherwise she looked just like she was supposed to. *She's powerful, alright.* Monica strode firmly over to Pebble and stuck out her hand. Pebble grabbed it and pressed it resolutely. *God help me.* Pebble knew she was face to face with a true Viking.

Steffen's comic-strip sketch of the 11-year-old kid with braces and freckles caught Monica's eye. She smiled.

"I don't know who you are, Pebble Beach, or why you're here, but Richard Davis can be very persuasive when he wants to. He said I wouldn't regret giving you an hour of my time." She stood very still before the 11-year-old cartoon kid. In the bubble over his head, Steffen's comic-strip figure was saying, "Emily is going to love me when I let her borrow my new iPod." Monica's eyes flashed, and when she did, Pebble forgot her carefully planned introduction.

"Can't you just see him – his name's Luke – wearing your clothes?"

When Monica didn't reply, Pebble rushed on. "Of course, I couldn't put your new clothes on Luke yet because I haven't seen them. I only know they exist and knowing you I'm sure they're a lot like your kiddie line. I figure you just developed your basic concept a little further and modified the designs to fit the pre-teeners. It's such a brilliant idea. It really is. The Americans are going to love your new clothes – just as much as they love your kiddie line. But you've got to present it to them just right, in just the right language, with just the right slant. And I figure, creating a family of characters who look and act and talk just like kids do in America would be the perfect vehicle. Can't you see it? Even the kids will like to read your ads and your catalogue. It'll be a whole lifestyle thing. That's why you're so terrific over there to begin with. You've got to capitalize on that…the whole mystique you've built up in the last two years…you know the purity thing.

"Do you realize how much those Americans need you? When I say those Americans, I mean the urban professionals. Because those people, that whole group, are really quality hungry. And quality is something you can give them. You and your products are synonymous with quality to these people. And sanity, too."

Pebble rushed on, without taking a breath or waiting for Monica to answer. "You can believe me, Monica, because I know what I'm talking about. I'm an American myself, so you can take my word for it. Quality, the kind of quality we have here in Scandinavia, is something so many American professionals long for. It's like a blessed antidote to all the hype they have to put up with over there. But they need a clear image of what real quality is; what it looks and feels like, and what it means – also for their kids. And when you consider the almost totally unethical consume and discard attitude that is so prevalent over there, you can understand why they need it so badly. Do you have any idea of the amount of junk that gets produced and sold at a profit over there every year? People are just so much more down-to-earth here. And real.

"Your first campaign hit pay dirt because you were right on target. You had the right product, you developed the right image, at the right time – your copy even had the right tone. You spoke to these people in their own language. You understood them."

"How do you know so much about me and my product?"

Oh no, did I say too much? thought Pebble, almost panicking.

"I've been following your career and Nordkyst for a long time. You're a pretty interesting person, you know."

Monica laughed and it eased some of the tension her question raised. She moved from Luke towards the next figure. "Umm…" she said and tilted her head to one side and as she stood before the drawing of this most astonishing little girl with bright, orange curls. She was an absolute bundle of energy, radiating mirth and mischief. She could have been a cross between a London punk, a Spice Girl and Monica Soderland. Monica laughed. "She looks just like I wanted to look when I was 10."

"Yeah? Well, I can tell you, you're not the only one who's ever wanted to look like her. Millions of pre-teens in America do, too. Her name's Emily. She lives on Long Island, as you can see from her school bag."

"Manhasset Junior High?"

"Yeah, that's on Long Island. You see, I think we've got to make her real. The way I look at it, Luke and Emily and the whole crew, whoever they turn out to be, can go everywhere, in your catalogue, in your ads, however you want to do it. But they've got to tell a story, too, wherever they go. They've got to relate. And amuse, at the same time. I want them to explain to their moms, who are still paying for the clothes, that even though they're growing up, they've still got this quality thing – this quality consciousness – the one their parents tried to instill in them. After all, that's why they buy your clothes. And that's why now – when these kids are starting to be old enough to pick out their own clothes – they still want to wear your stuff. 'Cause your stuff is not only ecologically sound, your clothes are neat, too, and cool and awesome. And all that other stuff kids want them to be. And they have that special look the kids want – and still they feel as good as their old kiddie clothes did."

"What's Emily saying?"

"She's saying – awesome, man awesome. That's one of those words over there among kids. We've got to get it right and use the right words – their words. I'm in New York enough, I was born in New York, and my family still lives there."

"Oh really?" Monica seemed to think it was important.

"Sure, I'm a true-blue New Yorker, so I know how people talk over there. But language is something which changes constantly, so I listen to people talking wherever I go whenever I'm over there. That's the only way you can create real, living, meaningful images and copy. You've got to get inside people – you've got to know them."

I can't believe the way I'm talking to this woman, thought Pebble. *I'm talking like me and not like the uptight person I used to be at meetings.* For whatever reason, Pebble let herself go, blabbering away, a mile a minute, off the cuff, her carefully thought out strategies gone and forgotten. She knew Nordkyst in and out and was telling Monica not only what it was she loved about Nordkyst, but what it was she knew she could deliver. She only forgot one thing – Monica Soderland had no way of knowing how or why Pebble Beach knew so much about her company.

"You see we could create these comic-strip characters, dress them up in your clothes, and have them doing the quirky little things every kid, from the kind of background we're talking about, does all the time. And whatever they say, or do, whatever, your clothes will be an intricate part of them – of their image – of their lifestyle. I want to get where they won't even question it or notice it. Their moms will automatically take them to the boutiques that carry Nordkyst if they don't already buy your stuff online. It's almost got to be something they take for granted – that you – that Nordkyst – understands them. Knows them – and their needs and can deliver just the right quality, with just the right touch, to make them feel right."

Monica continued surveying the figures on her walls. "Who did these drawings?"

"Steffen, he's a good friend of mine. I briefed him in detail because I knew he could get it just right. He's a Dane, but he's lived in New York for a while, so he knows the scene. I couldn't afford to get him to invest a whole lot of his time on this, but I wanted you to be able to get a glimpse of what I've got in my head. I know I'm not an ad agency or anything, Monica, but I know I'm the right person to develop your new campaign."

Monica went over and sat down. She started flipping through Pebble's fat portfolio.

"An impressive amount of work you've done. I like the fact that you're an American, too. It really makes sense. Actually, that's why I agreed to meet you in the first place. Richard and I have been talking about the possibility of using an American agency for this campaign anyway, but I wanted someone who was here who I could work with on a daily basis. I don't want to have to fly to New York every time I get a new idea. But Richard keeps telling me a Dane won't be able to get it right. He says it's got to be more New York, more American. Apparently somebody from Young & Rubicam recommended you highly to Richard."

Pebble smiled.

"But what I still don't understand, Pebble, is how you know so much about me and my products. And your language sounds so familiar – almost like it grew out of my last campaign – the one Peter Cato did. It doesn't make sense, it just doesn't. The way you talk about my work, you'd think you've known me for years. I have the feeling you almost know my strategies better than I do."

At first Pebble didn't know how to answer, but then she made up her mind, "I used to do a lot of work for Peter Cato. In fact, I should be driving a sky-blue BMW roadster now."

* * *

On her way out, in the parking lot, Pebble met Einar's people, unloading a truckload of stuff for their three o'clock presentation. They were surprised to see Pebble there, but she didn't care.

* * *

The next day at the office, Einar was furious. "Just tell me what you were doing there, Pebble – that's all I want to know." He called her in as soon as she arrived at work, and was now pacing up and down the polished wooden floors of his office, hunched over, his hands buried deep in his pockets. The striking view of Copenhagen harbor, jammed with sailboats of every description and powerful motorboats and hydrofoils, was right behind him. Pebble could see flags from all over the world flying from the masts of countless sailboats. Einar's toad-like face was all puffed up in anger. Pebble preferred looking at the fiery painting on the wall, the one that reminded her so much of Jackson Pollock, to looking at Einar's face.

"Don't try to intimidate me, Einar, because I'm not going to let you get away with it anymore."

"Intimidate you? What are you talking about, Pebble? Jackie and Bert told me they saw you leaving Monica Soderland's yesterday just before they went in to do their presentation. Did it slip your mind that you happen to be my assistant? My assistant? That I happen to pay your salary and that you work for me?" When she didn't answer, he continued in a slightly more friendly vein, "You've been acting mighty strange since you came back from your vacation, and I'd like to know exactly what's going on." Pebble was relieved that at least some of the steam seemed to have gone out of him.

"I guess it's about time I tell you that I don't want to work for you anymore, Einar. I'm through with you."

"Through!" he almost shouted, smelling deceit. "I know you told Monica you wrote the first Nordkyst campaign, didn't you?" He was livid. His eyes bulged in his head. He wasn't a pretty sight.

"You know why I'm mad at you, Einar; you know why I've been mad at you all along – because you never cleared my name."

"What are you talking about?" His mind was full of Nordkyst; everything else was either forgotten or irrelevant. WonderLift didn't even exist as far as he was concerned.

"You know what I'm talking about," Pebble shot back. *Just listen to me,* she thought, *you'd think 'conviction' was my middle name.* She was proud of herself. *Keep clear, sister.*

"I'm talking about WonderLift, Einar, or did you forget all about it already? Ever since your little party at Skovriderkroen, I've known the truth. You probably don't even realize you told me. But you did. You were so drunk that night I'm sure you don't remember a thing."

She could tell by the look of surprise on his face that she'd caught him off guard. *So he doesn't remember telling me.*

"Come on, Pebble, let's stop shouting at each other for a minute and sit down." Realizing that something serious had happened, or was about to happen (Einar wasn't sure), he motioned towards the tan leather sofa in the corner of his office. She accepted his invitation, pleased with this sign of respect on his part. But she was still determined to get it right. *Whatever you think, I promise you, you're not going to manipulate me out of what I know.* Pebble sat down.

"What did I tell you that night, Pebble?"

So, suddenly everything's coming up roses? she thought. He was acting too rational, too innocent all of a sudden. She knew he was as sly as a fox.

"You told me," Pebble said, hesitating slightly, "that...well...we were sitting on the bench down by the sea... and you told me that your wife, Birgitte, was the one who told you the launch date of WonderLift. You were pretty drunk at the time – do you remember?"

Pebble paused, waiting for Einar's response. "No," he said and shook his head, "I don't remember what I said, though I remember sitting with you there and...feeling absolutely miserable..."

His quiet manner, the way he curled up like a hurt animal, was like a red flag. Pebble rushed on, afraid to lose her momentum. "Well, you started telling me all kinds of things, sometimes you can be...so..." She didn't want to say pitiful, so she hurried on, "and well...I tried to get you to go back to the party, but you just went on and on Einar, about your life and your marriage. Then you told me about this awful fight you had with Birgitte and that you discovered she was seeing Peter Cato again. God, Einar, I didn't want you to tell me all that stuff, but you did. But there was one good thing about it all. In the process, I found out that it was your own wife who gave you the information about WonderLift."

Thinking of the injustice of it gave Pebble, who previously did everything possible to avoid a confrontation, even more courage. "How could you do that to me, Einar? How? Peter Cato thought it was me, and everybody else in this town thought it was me. You were the only one who knew all along it wasn't me. You knew, and yet you never said a word. How could you do that to me, Einar? How ...?" Pebble's voice shook with anger. "You even got me to work for you because you knew for sure nobody in this town would ever give me an assignment again."

She had to stand up, unable as she was to contain her anger any longer. "It makes me sick, it really does... You make me sick. The way you manipulated me, Einar. I just can't believe it." Now she was the one pacing furiously up and down the polished, hardwood floors. "I just can't believe it. How could you do that to me? I mean, you could have cleared my name. Why didn't you?" She almost spat the words in his face. And when he didn't answer, she rushed on, "Was it because you were afraid I wouldn't go to work for you unless I was sure I'd never survive as a freelancer? Was that it?"

"Pebble," he tried, wanting to calm her. But he couldn't get through to her.

"Well let me tell you something, Einar. If that's what you

thought, you had it all wrong. It would have been so much better if you'd been honest with me and with everyone. Just think if I had become your assistant because I wanted to – out of my own free will, instead of the way it happened. Because I had no place else to go…" She was silent for a moment because the rest of what she had to say was even more difficult to say. *But I want him to know the whole truth,* she thought.

"It might surprise you to know this, Einar, but the truth is I really have loved working for you. You're one great boss and I'm going to miss working for you. Why did you have to be such a jerk?" She laughed. "Funny isn't it, especially considering the fact that you're almost brilliant, Einar."

"You know, Pebble, you'll probably never understand how it is to be me…" he said slowly. "I wish you knew how fond I am of you."

But Pebble didn't want to know, didn't want Einar's feelings for his wife or for her to cloud the picture. "I'm not interested, Einar, really. And you ought to know better than that. We're not talking about your unhappy marriage or mine. We're talking about ethics here, plain and simple. Not about how your wife treats you. That has absolutely nothing to do with the way you manipulated me. So don't try to sidetrack me." Pebble knew that being mad was the only way to deal with Einar, now that her cards were on the table. "If you treated the people around you with a little more respect, if you were a little bit more honest and straightforward, God, people would do anything for you. I know I would. It makes me sick that you can't see it yourself."

"Pebble…"

"I'm really not interested in your excuses, Einar, and trying to make me feel sorry for you isn't going to work either, because I don't feel sorry for you. As far as I'm concerned, I don't owe you an explanation for anything."

Chapter 25

Pebble spent the next couple of days of sudden unemployment wandering around in a strange state of mind. She almost felt unreal. Summer, hot and wonderful, had finally arrived, and most Danes were busy packing up for the traditional move to the summer cottages which line the thousands of kilometers of Danish coastline. On this particular July the third, Pebble couldn't bear staring at her silent office telephone a moment longer, so she took herself and her strange state of mind down the two flights of stairs from her apartment to the King's Garden across the street where sunbathers lined the grass and the dark green benches, enjoying the hottest day of the year so far.

Pebble didn't want to sit in the sun so she chose an empty bench in the shade under the mighty red beech tree and stared at Rosenborg Castle sheltered behind the iron gates and the surrounding moots.

Pebble was truly surprised that she'd quit her well-paying job without any substantial source of income in the wings. If Nordkyst didn't come through, she didn't know what she was going to do in the future. Everything seemed strangely new and different. *I don't know what's come over me,* she thought. *Meeting Monica must have really gone to my head. What was I thinking? The woman didn't promise me anything... Not a thing. Did I think I had her account in the bag or what? And what made me think I could possibly handle such a big account as Nordkyst on my own anyway?* Pebble tingled all over at the thought, but she wasn't upset, rather surprised. So surprised that she was beginning to find it amazingly interesting to watch her own life unfold – almost as if she was someone else sitting far away watching her.

Adam and Jon had just gone off to Hornbæk Beach, north of Copenhagen for the day with their friends. They begged Pebble to go with them (quite unusual for them), but she declined.

"Oh, come on, Mom," they said, "you've got to get out of here sometimes and have some fun, too." They were worried about her, coming home from vacation the way she did, in a strange mood, after being away only four days, and then working day and night like a mad woman on some crazy project. She was so wrapped up in her own world, she hardly ate or slept – or even spoke to her own kids.

The boys whispered to each other and exchanged glances in the hallway more than once after Pebble's hasty return from vacationing with Albert. Finally, after powwowing about it, they decided it was time to talk to her about it.

"Mom," Adam, who was approaching 15 fast, took the lead, "is anything wrong?"

They surprised her, at her desk, deep in thought.

She looked up, startled.

"What do you mean?" She didn't realize the sun was shining brightly outside. Jon was standing behind his brother, almost a head taller.

"You've been acting so..." Adam didn't know what to say.

"Strange..." Jon finished the sentence for him. "What's going on, Mom? Are you okay?"

"Oh," she was touched by their concern. "So much has been going on in my life...I don't know." She sighed, not knowing how to explain. "I guess I should have talked to you guys about it. I didn't mean for you to worry..."

"Well, why don't you tell us about it now?" Jon said. He was mature now, she could tell.

"Well..." She didn't quite know how to begin. "It's hard to explain, but...well I guess I've changed a lot lately. You know since I got divorced from your father, I've been trying to support us and build up my reputation as a freelancer. You guys know all about that. Everything was going pretty okay until I got involved in that WonderLift campaign. You remember when I got back from Greenland and Peter Cato accused me of telling Einar the launch date and all that... Well after that, Einar offered me a job and I took it because I didn't think I'd be able to make it anymore as a freelancer because Peter said he'd tell everyone in town I wasn't trustworthy. It was an awful experience, it really was. But looking back what I think really happened was that I realized that I needed to take a closer look at the things I believe in and at the way I was living my life. It's hard to explain what I felt and I didn't really know what it was at the time, but I knew something wasn't right. And I knew I needed help. That was when I started going to Irene... And going to Irene was like starting this process of taking a closer look at my life in a way I've never done before. Looking back, I guess I just felt really lost – like I wasn't really in control of my life and...well...it was kind of scary."

"And now..." Adam didn't want this explanation to go on forever. They had friends waiting for them across the street in the park. It was almost noon and they were going to the beach.

"Well now, even if it might not look that way, I'm feeling better. A whole lot better. Things are rearranging themselves inside me and that's why I quit my job and decided to start working for myself again. Only this time, I don't just want to be just a freelance copywriter anymore – what I really want to do is start my own company."

"You do? Gee, that sounds great." Jon was impressed. He was slightly sunburned already and stood, tall and handsome, in the doorway to her office, twirling his black sunglasses. "What kind of company are you thinking about starting?"

"Well I'm going to call it *Pebble Beach Talk* – and I want to start a company that specializes in creating English marketing material for companies in Denmark and Scandinavia who want to make it in the global marketplace. International marketing is my specialty you know, and I found out I'm damn good at it, too. Working for Einar also taught me a thing or two about running a business. So I think I can swing it. Anyway, I hope I can, if I can get off to a good start."

"I just don't understand," Adam chimed in, "when you came home from Croatia you worked like crazy, day and night, until you went back to work. And then you quit your job and now you're just sitting here doing nothing."

"I guess it does look kind of strange, but what happened was I made a pitch for this really big account and I thought I was going to get it, only now I'm not so sure. Anyway, that's why I'm sitting here. I'm waiting for a call from those people. As far as Einar is concerned, I quit working for him for two reasons. First, because I thought I was ready to make it on my own. And second, because I'm absolutely furious at him for not clearing my name in the WonderLift thing. You see, I found out who really told him that confidential information about the launch date and I realized he could have cleared my name from the very beginning, but he never did. It was a bad thing to do. It really was. Completely unethical. I just felt I couldn't go on working for a guy like that. And besides I also feel that now is the time for me to stand my ground and speak up – and take care of myself. And I figured starting with Einar was just about as good a place to start as any."

"Why don't you go to the beach with us?" Pebble could tell Adam was getting a bit impatient with this discussion of business ethics. "Nobody's going to call you on a day like today anyway. Everyone's going on vacation, you know that."

"Yeah, I know. It's nice of you to ask, but I'm still hoping to hear from these people about that presentation I made. And besides, I know you've got your friends waiting for you. Look, I really do appreciate it, but go with your friends, okay? I'll be okay. Don't worry. I just need to be alone and think…okay?" She hugged Adam first and then she hugged Jon. "We're going to be okay. You know it's great having you guys for sons…" But they hardly heard her because they were hightailing it out of the apartment almost before she finished what she was saying. She smiled as she listened to their footsteps as they charged down the stairs.

After they left, she sat staring at her desk a little while longer. Then, deciding that Adam was right – *nobody is going to call me on a day like this* – she switched on her answering machine, put her mobile phone in her pocket, and wandered over to the park across the street and sat down on the bench in the shade under the mighty red beech tree. She knew she probably should have felt bad, but she didn't. She knew in the past she would have been sitting there on that bench feeling miserable and confused, but for some reason today she didn't. For some reason she felt happy, blissfully happy and okay and at peace with herself, life and the world in general. It was strange, but she did. And the more she thought about it, the more she realized that that was exactly how she was feeling – blissfully happy. It seemed there was a sparkle in the air – and in the world – and in her. Yes, a sparkle. A newfound sparkle and peace and quiet that had nothing whatsoever to do with success or failure or anything else. It was just there. And it was a most peculiar feeling – because it was quite independent of outside events. The feeling was in her and it was hers. Yes it was; it was really hers – lodged as it was deep inside her. Meaning that this feeling was free and independent of everything else. Meaning it had nothing to do with anything except her. In fact this feeling was her. It was who she was, in truth. It was the suchness and niceness and sweetness of her. Of her very own self. Of Pebble Beach herself. Which is why it sparkled like it did. And it was something that no man, no outside event, no job success or career could possibly ever give her.

So she sighed in contentment and inhaled the suchness and niceness of life – of her life – and of being her – for no special reason whatsoever. And that was when our own dear Pebble Beach knew she had come through. Knew she had somehow managed an important rite of passage. A rite of passage from being a lost little girl to becoming a woman of her own. A real true-blue, true-blooded woman, who might not be perfect and who might not know all the answers, but who now knew with a certainty that she'd never known before that she, Pebble Beach, could and would navigate her own life – all by herself.

Yes that was it.

She could navigate her own life. And not that it would necessarily be smooth sailing – but just that she could do it. She could navigate her life, whatever was up ahead. Which was the real triumph, no matter what else happened. And suddenly it didn't matter whether she won the Nordkyst account or not, or whether her mother ever understood her or not, or whether she found the man of her dreams or not. She'd be there for her. Now she knew it and felt it – maybe for the first time in her whole life. She'd be there for her. She'd show up for her, whether or not she knew what to do.

And so the sky sparkled and Pebble Beach sparkled. And the red beech sparkled. And this was her day – with all its bittersweet suchness and uncertainty – and she loved every minute of it, sitting on the park bench as she did, with nowhere to go and nothing to do. Knowing quite certainly for the very first time in her very own life that she was okay – that she was in fact very very okay.

* * *

When Pebble returned to her apartment later that afternoon, there were two messages on her answering machine. One was from Albert; the other was from Monica Soderland. Monica said, in her clear, earthy voice, "Hi, Pebble, I'm sorry it took me so long to get back to you. Will you please call me at my office right away; I'll be working late, so call me as soon as you get in – please."

Pebble listened to Monica twice, to make sure she heard the message right. Then she sat down and punched in the number, trembling slightly. *Oh dear God, make her say yes.* She saw herself being ushered into the inner circles of power, driving a sky-blue BMW Roadster, the one that was rightfully hers.

"Monica?"

"Yes?"

"This is Pebble Beach."

"Oh hi, Pebble, I'm sorry it's taken me so long to get back to you. You really must forgive me. But I wanted Richard Davis to see your stuff before I made my final decision. Richard is over here right now. In fact, he wants to meet you before he goes back to New York."

Pebble's heart thumped loudly in her breast.

"The problem is, Pebble, as you know; you're not an advertising agency."

Oh no, thought Pebble, *here it comes*.

"And as you also know," Monica continued, "we've become a very big company. Both Richard and I think your comic-strip concept with the kids and the lifestyle stories is terrific. We feel it's exactly what we're looking for. And now that we know you were Peter Cato's ghostwriter, we understand better how you were able to pick up our story and carry the ball forward so perfectly for us."

"Ask her," Pebble heard a man's voice in the background. Monica laughed. "Pebble, Richard's sitting right here, and he wants me to ask you something. Do you know a chap at Young & Rubicam in New York, a senior account director named Mel Rossen?"

Now it was Pebble's turn to laugh. "Sure, Mel's my uncle."

Monica must have turned the speaker on because she heard Richard laughing in the background. When Richard stopped, Monica continued. "I don't know why, Pebble, but Richard seems to think that's very funny. Anyway, we've come up with what we think is a compromise solution and we hope you'll like it. Let me just sketch our idea for you briefly now, because we'd like you to come out here tomorrow and discuss it with us in detail. Okay? Our proposal is this: we'd like to put you on a three-month retainer. We can discuss the amount tomorrow, if you're interested. Anyway, we feel that since you're not an ad agency – and don't have all the facilities an ad agency has – we'd like you to come out here and work together with me and Richard and our art department and see if you can develop your ideas into a full-blown campaign with the help of our people out here. I know you haven't met any of them yet, but we have some very talented people out here in Hellerup. I, for my part, am willing to invest in you for a three-month period because I think you've got what we're looking for. I know this is a bit irregular. But to be perfectly honest, I was terribly disappointed with the Republic Group's presentation and with Peter Cato's stuff, too. They were both way, way off the mark."

Pebble's heart beat so loudly in her breast she was sure Monica could hear it.

"When the three-month period is up," Monica continued, "and who knows, maybe we won't need so much time to come to a decision. But Richard thinks it's important to lock our agreement with you into a specific timeframe, especially because we want to launch our clothes next spring in New York (but we'll get back to that later). Anyway, when the period we agree upon is over, Richard and I will have to sit down and decide whether or not your stuff is good enough or not. If it is, we'll give you the account. If it isn't, I hope you'll feel that our arrangement was fair enough so that we can part as amicably..."

Pebble listened to every word that Monica said with this big, blissful grin on her face. *I'm glad she can't see my face.*

"Well what do you think, Pebble? Are you willing to give it a try?"

"I think it sounds...just great..."

"Good...well why don't you come out here tomorrow so we can talk?"

"That would be fine." Pebble tried not to sound too happy.

"What about for lunch. Richard wants to get to know you and to be quite frank, I do too. The weather's so great right now, why don't we drive up along the coast somewhere and have a leisurely lunch and discuss it all? Okay?"

"Sounds good to me, Monica... Shall we say twelve thirty?" Pebble didn't trust her voice to say more, but when she finally put down the phone, she allowed herself the infinite luxury of trembling merrily all over for a moment. Then, still grinning blissfully, she ran out of her tiny office and into the wide open space of her living room and leaped mightily into the air, like the true Princess of the Universe she really was. Then she shouted at the top of her lungs for all the world to hear "WHOOPEE!!!!!... I DID IT!!!!!!"

Epilogue

Richard Davis turns out to be a bright, fairly good-looking, newly divorced New Yorker. Pebble can see why her Uncle Mel likes him so much. Richard has two children of his own in New York who live with their mother on Long Island. He's very close to his kids. Pebble and Richard (who are about the same age) hit it off immediately, and every time Richard is in Copenhagen (which is more and more frequently) he invites Pebble out to dinner. After several dinner dates, they start seeing each other more seriously. Sometimes they talk about the future, and Richard brings up the idea of Pebble moving back to New York. When Richard mentions this, Pebble decides to tell Richard about her plans to start her own company in Scandinavia – *Pebble Beach Talk*. Also about this time – and well before Pebble's three-month agreement with Nordkyst is over – Richard and Pebble go to bed with each other for the first time.

Albert Audibert shows up at the door of Pebble's apartment one night when she is home all alone. He is very drunk and pounds on her door and hollers at her. She doesn't make a sound, but watches him through the peephole, horrified. After ranting and raving for almost 25 minutes, he turns away from her door, muttering, "Women are like snakes..." and leaves. Irene, who started losing weight and wearing make-up for the first time in her life, says Pebble is making good progress at understanding her addictive behavior and the compulsive drive behind her fatal attraction to Albert. She also says it's important that Pebble doesn't dive into another relationship right away because she'll just repeat her past behavior if she does.

As far as Pebble can tell, Slim doesn't change at all.

When Einar calls her one day in late September and asks her out for dinner, she says yes – to her own great surprise.

Peter Cato's new agency Fem-Ads files for bankruptcy. When Pebble meets him at a party, he walks right by her without saying a word.

Jon and Adam continue to consume enormous quantities of food. Every once in a while, when Pebble is least expecting it, they reward her efforts to become Mother of the Century with a rare flash of kindness or brilliance. Sometimes, too, without her asking for it, they wash all the dishes and vacuum clean the entire apartment. When this happens, Pebble is quite sure she died and went to heaven.

Pebble's mother, Molly, never mellows, even with age. But when her brother Mel tells her that Pebble is dating Richard Davis, and that Richard Davis could, perhaps, become a serious candidate in the life of her star daughter, Molly is instilled with new hope for the future. Her father's only comment is, "Maybe she'll get married and come home."

At Roundfire we publish great stories. We lean towards the spiritual and thought-provoking. But whether it's literary or popular, a gentle tale or a pulsating thriller, the connecting theme in all Roundfire fiction titles is that once you pick them up you won't want to put them down.